"If thou gaze lo[ng] [...]
will also gaze int[o] [...]

Abyss: The primeval chaos. The bottomless pit; hell. An unfathomable or immeasureable depth or void."

—*The American Heritage Dictionary*

You're holding in your hands one of the first in a new line of books of dark fiction, called Abyss. Abyss is horror unlike anything you've ever read before. It's not about haunted houses or evil children or ancient Indian burial grounds. We've all read those books, and we all know their plots by heart.

Abyss is for the seeker of truth, no matter how disturbing or twisted it may be. It's about people, and the darkness we all carry within us. Abyss is the new horror from the dark frontier. And in that place, where we come face-to-face with terror, what we find is ourselves. The darkness illuminates us, revealing our flaws, our secret fears, our desires and ambitions longing to break free. And we never see ourselves or our world in the same way again.

QUANTITY SALES

Most Dell books are available at special quantity discounts when purchased in bulk by corporations, organizations, and special-interest groups. Custom imprinting or excerpting can also be done to fit special needs. For details write: Dell Publishing, 666 Fifth Avenue, New York, NY 10103. Attn.: Special Sales Department.

INDIVIDUAL SALES

Are there any Dell books you want but cannot find in your local stores? If so, you can order them directly from us. You can get any Dell book in print. Simply include the book's title, author, and ISBN number if you have it, along with a check or money order (no cash can be accepted) for the full retail price plus $2.00 to cover shipping and handling. Mail to: Dell Readers Service, P.O. Box 5057, Des Plaines, IL 60017.

dusk

RON DEE

A DELL BOOK

Published by
Dell Publishing
a division of
Bantam Doubleday Dell Publishing Group, Inc.
666 Fifth Avenue
New York, New York 10103

ISBN: 0-440-20709-6

Printed in the United States of America

Published simultaneously in Canada

April 1991

10   9   8   7   6   5   4   3   2   1

OPM

This is for Jeanne, probably the most stimulating and gentlest editor the world has ever known, and for Perry, definitely the finest and most persevering agent, and, of course, for Davi, without question the world's longest-suffering and most forgiving wife.

These men are blemishes at your love feasts, eating with you without the slightest qualm—shepherds who feed only themselves. They are clouds without rain, blown along by the wind; autumn trees, without fruit and uprooted—twice dead. They are wild waves of the sea, foaming up their shame; wandering stars, for whom blackest darkness has been reserved forever.

—Jude 1:12–13 (New International Version)

PART I

WORKING GIRLS

1

Maxie waited, leaning against the deserted office building in a pink midriff T-shirt and micromini, trying to ignore her tight high-heeled shoes. A bead of sweat ran down her cheek, and she licked her lips with anticipation, trying to hold the glances of each man who stopped at the traffic light and stared. She saw their desire as they took in her sleek, tanned legs that glistened with oil and perspiration.

But the hours passed and the sun beat down on the tall buildings, and no one stopped.

A marked police car went by twice, and as they stopped at the light on the second pass, one of the officers gazed at her. He was young, and his mouth was half open in the vague grimace of a little boy who sees something he wants but knows he can't have. Grinning and licking her lips slyly, Maxie remembered the cop who'd arrested her last month: he'd wanted her first, and she had let him fill her with his taste before he dragged her to the station and booked her. She'd let him think he'd been using her, but it had been *her* victory . . . and long hours had passed before he faded from her tongue

That was the worst of it—that they faded. She knew the life essence of that cop was part of her now, but like that man Max who had come to her this morning, he was long gone with his brisk flavor, and his power faded. She had taken that businessman Max only hours ago . . . she *was* Maxie now. She was Maxie and Johnnie and Bobby and Ronnie and Charlie and Billy. But though she wore Max's name, the reality of him was already only a shadow, a memory. She was filled by such memories.

They called her a whore on the streets and a prostitute in the courtrooms, but she was far more.

She was citadel of life—*a vault of the forces of living*.

The cop continued to peer out his open window with wide eyes, wiping the beads of perspiration from his slick forehead. "Waiting for someone?" he asked in a crusty voice.

"Maybe. Maybe I'm waiting for *you.*"

The man's face went red. "Whore," he said. The light changed and his partner pulled ahead.

She watched the disappearing vehicle, waiting. Watching.

Maxie was hungry, but not for food. She lusted for every man she'd ever trapped between her lips and drained, swallowing life upon life until they coated her with the power that now defined her. They came to her like Max had, pleading for an interlude of excitement in an existence that had become boring and pointless. They offered themselves to her, and she took each one gladly, swallowing them whole.

Literally.

She swallowed and gladly received the cast-off wisdom and energy from the men who would waste the precious sperm between their clenched fingers or into the wives who didn't understand the mystery of what they were given; the millions of unborn intellects and essences, only half created without her or some other woman's partnership. Though that energy was locked into her for only brief moments, the lives were still one with her, and part of her, and could not die until she did.

And she swallowed it all, never gagging no matter how it might taste, wanting more each time.

They even paid her.

Still, Maxie was not ashamed. She did not take anything that wasn't offered, sometimes even begged from her, by men like that last one, Max. He himself had done just that with his twenty-dollar bill and wheedling, high voice. Some even believed they were stealing from *her*—that they were robbing her self-respect and wholesomeness.

But she had not possessed that supposed luxury since she was fourteen, when her stepfather, Tom, had taught her how to make him happy that month Momma was in the hospital. Behind the closed doors of her bedroom Tom taught Maxie how to touch him and hold him, and he enjoyed her growing mastery, continuing to find secret moments with her even after Momma came home. Sometimes he brought his friends home to enjoy her, too, splitting with her the money they gave him.

A long time ago. And then, Momma came home from her night job early to find him between her legs. Momma made him leave, and Maxie never saw him alive again: He was knifed three months later by a friend he cheated on a drug deal.

Yet in a way, he lived on inside of her. She took everything he let her have during those secretive two years they had together. He became a part of her, and she felt a growth in the power each time he gave to her. After he died, she could still feel his vibrancy, even when she approached his coffin and touched the still hand that rested on his chest. He was part of her, and she continued the ways he'd taught her, exchanging with so many others that he was only a small part of her expanding self now. He still lived on through her. People died, but she kept their life for them.

Like a bank.

The life kept her strong and beautiful, but she had to keep doing it because their energy faded away so fast.

A sleek gray Camaro stopped at the light. The driver wore white shorts that showed off his tanned muscular thighs. He leaned toward her, his eyes hidden behind dark glasses. When he grinned, she felt his urgings and crossed the sidewalk to the curb, rubbing her thumb over the copper-colored zipper of her jeans skirt.

He reached across the seat and rolled down his passenger window, bathing her with the breeze of an air-conditioned interior. "Hi," he said.

She ran her tongue along her lower lip. "Hi yourself."

"What's going on?" He mimicked her and licked his own full lips, displaying shiny teeth.

"I'm just working." She bent low to expose as much of her breasts as she could under the loose cotton top.

"Oh, yeah?" His glasses had slid down his nose, and

she could see in his eyes the familiar twinkle that made
her anticipation blossom like the blooming roses displayed at fast speed on TV science shows. "Looks like
a hot job," he went on. "Want to cool down in my
car?"

"I don't think it would cool me down," she flirted
back knowingly. "I might just *spread* my heat—"

The sudden blast of another car's horn made her
flinch and the tanned man jumped. A police car was
braking to a stop behind him. The officer who'd eyed
her a few minutes before waved the Camaro's driver
ahead. The man at her side looked up at the green
light and shook his head wistfully. "Gotta go," he
muttered, then pulled away.

Maxie's heart thumped hard in disappointment, but
as the police car cruised up to her and the young cop
stared at her once more, she made herself grin. "Want
to take me in now, big man?" she taunted him, ignoring his grizzled partner behind the wheel.

"You're not worth the trouble," he said. "But I
think we'll just stick around this area for a while.
You're taking chances, you know? A hooker like you
got killed just a few nights ago." He picked his big
nose and flicked a dark glob of snot at her feet on the
concrete. "So business won't be so good for a while, if
you know what I mean."

She sneered, but when the car didn't move, she began to edge away. She leaned against the brick wall
brazenly, daring him as she stroked her skirt. But he
just stared, and the car waited, and other cars with
men now passed without slowing.

2

Maxie was hungry. Even her stomach was growling now. When thirty more minutes passed and the patrol car was still there, she knew her time was wasting. The sun was down and she wanted a new name.

She turned away from the street corner's bright light and passed into an alley where overflowing trash cans marked a dark pathway of bottles and newspaper to her apartment.

She kicked a crushed Coors can. *"Fuck!"* she whined. The can crashed into a trash bin.

"You ain't alone out here, you know."

She jumped.

A tall, skinny man in a plaid shirt appeared in the shadows opposite her. He stepped from behind the trash bin and fixed her with a muddy glare. He wore scuffed, pointed-toe boots, ageless jeans. His bony face was expressionless under a cowboy hat.

Maxie inched back. She remembered the cop's news

of the woman who'd been killed last night. "What'cha want?" she began nervously, then bit her lip. *"Who* are you?"

He stretched up a long arm to tip his hat. "You really want to know?"

Maxie shrugged uneasily.

"It's long story, babe. Just now I'm another hungry cowboy trying to make my way in the big city."

"Uh . . . *rodeo?*" she blurted, studying the whiskery, gaunt face. He *did* look hungry. *Very* hungry. He looked the way she *felt.* She took another step back.

"Rodeo?" He shook his head. "You kidding? Hell, I'm a bartender. I used to make my way down at the border. Worked at a bar and I'd serve all the illegals skipping into this country drinks and food and tell them how to make a profitable stay here in America." He slipped the lump in his right cheek to his left, then spat a dirty brown liquid onto the pavement. "Me and my boys showed 'em how to make a brand-new start, but the Feds cracked down, and now we're just scraping by."

Less afraid now that she heard the longing in his voice, Maxie put a hand on her hip. "Oh, yeah? That's against the law, you know."

He snorted. "Hell, you should talk." He spit again. His eyes in the dimness were shiny and somehow compelling. "We were just showing the greaseballs a better plan to make their own way in this cold, cruel world. But there's not enough of them to go around anymore."

Uneasy, she took a step toward her apartment building. "So what do you expect to do *here?*"

The cowboy stared at her with interest, stopping her once more. Their eyes studied one another for a long moment, and he moved to stand in front of her. "It's a long story, babe. Years ago, a thieving preacher joined us. He said hunting was better than waiting and packed his bags like some asshole salesman. Maybe he was right. Sometimes you just gotta move on and go where the action is, so I left the Boss and the Mex at the border. Stuck in the past. Thought I'd try my hand here in south Dallas. I decided to try something I knew, so I opened a bar a few blocks over to see if I could make a real killing. Everyone wants to hit up a new bar, huh?"

"So what are you doing *here*?" She smiled. "Are you lonesome, cowboy?"

The cowboy shook his head. "I saw you on the corner and I liked what I saw." He grinned, showing gray teeth. One of the front ones was missing, and a lower one was black with disease.

Emptiness throbbed in her gut with its familiar longing. "Well, cowboy, if you're as bad off as you look, how about if I make you some dinner. Maybe you can trade me something for it."

"Maybe." The bony man chuckled.

Maxie batted her lashes. "Hey, I serve full-course meals, dude . . . if the price is right. Come on." She stepped closer, taking his hand in hers. His skin was cold. "Shit—your pickup must've had the air-conditioning kicked up high to make you so cold."

His brisk laughter made her cringe, but she didn't take her hand away.

"Come on," she whispered again.

"It stinks in here," the cowboy said, tossing his hat on the unmade bed.

Maxie sniffed the stale odor of past sex. "It's the smell of *life*," she replied.

"Life? You call *this* life?" He cackled, sitting beside his hat. "You call all this shit you live in *life*? That's the whole problem. No one knows life from death anymore."

The apartment had three rooms: bedroom, bath, and closet-sized kitchen. The bedroom was filled with scratched nineteen fifties motel cast-offs. The grubby carpet might once have been blue. The bathroom fixtures were stained, the toilet seat cracked. An assortment of makeups covered all available surfaces. In the kitchen, everything was coated with a yellow greasy sheen. The linoleum had long ago surrendered its pattern. The refrigerator gave off a constant buzz.

Maxie entered the dusky kitchen and flipped on its single bulb. "How about a sandwich?" she asked.

Long seconds passed before he answered, and she thought she heard the cockroaches scuttling between the walls. "Why not?" he said, appearing in the doorway.

She took out the makings for bologna sandwiches. "You really *do* look starved. Don't you know we have to eat to live?"

His features twisted humorlessly. "People live to eat, now, darlin'. No one in America eats to live, anymore."

"I do," she rebuked him. "I love living."

"More than the way you live?" His chuckle flowed into the silence, filling it with new despair.

"What the hell does that mean?"

"I know you, babe. We're both sick of just *existing*. I was so sick of my own life, I didn't even think it was real anymore. That was hell, too, because I used to think I wanted it so much."

"But you're tired of it now?" Maxie asked absently as she spread mayo on bread.

"I'm like you, whore. I want the green grass on the other side of the fence. I want the lives around me." He stared at her with depth. "Just like you. But you only drink the life they want you to have, life that they'll never miss." Slowly, he reached to clutch her. "I can show you something *better*."

This time she laughed. "Better?" He was like all the others, just a little farther gone; he didn't want the preciousness nestling inside him.

He wanted to be rid of it.

She dropped the butter knife on the counter and forgot it, laying her hands on his hips. "Do you want *me*?"

"What can you give me?"

For a moment she wanted to explain her self-appointed mission in life.

"What can you give me?" he murmured again. His shiny pupils held her.

Maxie hesitated. "You will live on inside me," she whispered. "Like my stepfather. He died, but I have so much of him, it's like he's still here with me."

The man cocked his head to the side. She unfastened his jeans and pushed them down to his boots. His skin was cold, as if he were a sculpture of ice. She knew he must be very sick. What little life he had remaining would not stay in him long, but maybe, just maybe, she could salvage that slightness.

He snickered gutturally. "But what do you do with this life you take, huh? What use do you have of life— what can *you* do with it?"

The foreign thought buzzed in her ears. "I keep it. I save it. It—it's not right to just throw it away."

"What right do you have to take it?"

The buzzing poured into her brain. She didn't know *why*. She realized that she didn't even care why. It was just her function and place in society, the way some people saved stamps and others saved coins . . . and . . . she was so *hungry*! "Because"—she ran her hands up and down his legs—"Because it's *good*. It makes me feel good to help people—to take away what they don't want and give them something they do."

"Give them some kind of eternal life inside *you*?" He shook his head. "Maybe you like to take only because it makes *you* feel good. It makes you feel good because it isn't yours, bitch, and you feed off it. If you'd face that, you could have so much more than you get."

Maxie sniffed at his crotch.

"The point is, babe, that what you're taking is not yours. It was never meant to be yours. So why not go all the way and take it *all*?"

She shrugged. "You're almost gone," she managed with pity. Then she stood and slipped off her clothes, sliding the skirt down her hips with long practice. She let him examine her taut, naked body, trembling under his intense gaze.

"Why don't you take your clothes off?" she suggested. She went toward the bed, stopping briefly at the window. The alley was filled with dented garbage cans, cardboard boxes, newspapers, and bottles. A dark figure dug through the discards.

One person's garbage is another's treasure.

Maxie sat on the bed and spread her thighs so he could see her triangle of curly hair.

"You won't be sorry," he said. He pulled his jeans back up to his waist and went to her, then let the jeans slip down his legs once more. Maxie slid her fingers around his clammy buttocks and pulled him into her face. She took him between her lips, feeling him slowly spring up and harden against the insides of her cheeks. She played her tongue around his sour taste as fragments of skin dropped off to float in her saliva. She had to swallow them, not daring to stop until she had him and saved him. She was helping him like she helped the others, bringing them pleasure as she savored their truths and kept them safe.

It made her feel even better to bring him, sick as he was, to life now. Gleefully, she wondered if this was her real purpose: to bring the life she stored to others for at least these short moments.

He was more than alive. She knew that when he moaned and laid his rough palms on her head, twisting his fingers through her silky hair, thrusting now. Thrusting back and forth.

In and out.

But never all the way out. She wouldn't release him, not until she had everything he was.

He exploded, filling her throat with a cool stickiness that tasted like raw, decayed pork left out in the sun for days. She wanted to puke more than she ever had, inhaling the stench that was almost as bad, but knew she could not. He needed her more than any of the others.

She swallowed hard, then just sat there with eyes shut, letting his essence whistle through her with a pounding excitement that was greater than anything she'd ever tasted—as if he was *full* of all the life she craved and tried to store. A great strength surged through her, and unlike the others, it did not begin to trickle away as soon as she devoured it. Startled, she looked up at him.

"Yeah." He sighed. "It *stays*—but you're still starving, aren't you? You suck the power from others and it withers away as soon as you taste it. You take the life that nobody wants, but think of the pleasure in taking the richness of what these lusting assholes *do* want. *Think of the power in that!*" He trembled, and she was suddenly a little bit afraid, recognizing the anticipation she so often felt . . . but in *him*. He let his cold fingers slide over her cheeks, forcing her jaws to open wide as he thrust in again. She shivered . . . and then he forced her teeth closer together until she was *biting* him—

"Mmmph." She struggled, pushing him back and coughing.

He laughed. "How does it taste, bitch?"

"Who—who are *you*?" She wiped her chin and looked at the gooey, thick blood that smeared her palms.

A brassy chuckle spread through the room. "I told you that I'm like you are. And I can give you what you're looking for."

All the past lives inside her shriveled as his moist words stuck in her ears. All the meanings that she had saved and accumulated. "What?"

He knelt in front of her and fixed her in those suddenly cold, shining eyes, then leaned his face down between her thighs, his tongue slithering out and mastering her until she shuddered and clawed at his shoulders.

He moved up over her body and she felt his mouth

sliding up and down over her breasts, nibbling her trembling nipples.

Sucking.

The room was suddenly full of shadows, and his mouth filled the shadows, unfocused, hissing. A long tongue darted into her view and paused, then moved on.

His mouth was so close . . . just inches away, yet almost undiscernible in the darkness.

Her heart beat relentlessly.

She couldn't help but gasp again.

Her legs were spread farther apart, and the mouth licked between them again.

Push, push, push.

Her thighs were quivering, and she felt moisture welling up between them.

"You like it, huh?" The mouth licked again, drowning her with a new shudder. "I knew you would. I'll make you just like I am. Think of how you'll like it when you're taking it *all* instead of just *tasting*. You'll suck a little life from everyone who comes to you, and plant the seeds that live on. They will be your harvest, and you'll have the strength of their lives. *Strength that will last.*"

She closed her eyes.

Her heart throbbed harder as he began to nibble with sharp teeth, then bit into her with a sharp stab that brought orgasm after orgasm. Stickiness covered the inside of her thighs, making her weak, but she knew she would have power.

And she would never be hungry again.

3

Samantha Borden whistled as she cleared the things from the top of her desk. When every pen and paper clip was filed carefully into her top drawer, she sorted a small stack of papers and dropped several into her outgoing basket. The incoming basket was clear.

All ready. She worked in Immigration, in the Surveillance Division, and unfortunately, what people said about government workers was true of most.

At five-ten the office had already emptied out. With its bland beige walls and department store paintings of squirrels and lake scenes, her eyes were drawn naturally to Walt's nearby desk. He'd left it covered with folders, dirty coffee cups, and mementos. Though she didn't plan on disappearing as he had, she didn't want to leave a sloppy desk behind, either.

Sam opened the one cardboard assignment folder remaining on her desk.

Something was going on, and after the furor over all

those bodies found in Matamoras far south of here a while back, everyone suspected it was something bad. Murders were occurring more and more frequently throughout South Texas. The meeting she'd attended yesterday afternoon had more than told her that. No one knew what was really going on, but the look on the others' perplexed faces was proof enough.

It could be just the opportunity she'd waited for.

She wanted to find a testimonial truth to back up one or the other of the conjectures she'd heard in that confidential meeting. One theory was that criminal illegals were being sent through here the way Castro had sent all those crooks and psychos out of Cuba. The man who ventured that notion hadn't been serious, but even if his guess was wild, she didn't find it any crazier than the others. Most said that a secret Hispanic religious group was responsible for the outbreak of murders sweeping Texas.

Helping to figure it out provided an opportunity to prove herself. And maybe the answer would halt the violent backlash against innocent Hispanics trying to live normal lives. She hoped to discover evidence that maybe the murders really *were* part of some bizarre plan to give criminally inclined illegals new identities.

Samantha blushed to herself. *Or something like that, anyway.*

So like a stupid ass, she had pushed and shoved to get the investigative assignment because it might earn her the promotion she had waited a year for . . . and maybe because of her past relationship with Walt too.

It made her almost glad he might be dead.

"You didn't get *fired,* did you?"

The voice behind her made Samantha jump, and she turned quickly to look at Tess. The dark-haired woman was dressed in one of her usual tight skirts that overemphasized the parts of her body it didn't expose.

"*Did* they fire you?" Tess approached like a vulture.

"God, no." Samantha forced her laugh. "I'm just going on a new assignment for a couple of days."

Tess stopped beside Walt's desk. "Too bad Walt didn't have your kind of efficiency. I hate to think of the things wasting here that should be getting done." She made her long face sparkle in a grin. "So tell me, Skinny, what's the poop you're going to scoop? Are you getting the brass to send you to help Walt?"

"Sort of."

Tess met her eyes knowingly. "I knew you guys would get back together. Is he leaving his wife?"

"That's up to *him*. Walt and I are finished." Samantha stood, picking up her assignment folder and purse. "This is business, Tess. Just business."

"Next you're going to be telling me that there's more to life than sex and money."

Sam sighed. "I hope there is."

"Not me. Fill my purse and pussy and I'll die with a smile." She bumped their asses together.

"You're really *sick*." Sam couldn't hold in her own giggle. "Damn, what an epitaph!"

"Hey, if Walt hadn't messed you up so bad, you'd agree with me all the way, Sam. You don't need to act so serious all the time about wanting to help other people. Selfishness is *in* these days. Forget those old morals and just be yourself, okay? You'll live longer."

"Hey—maybe I really *do* care," Sam said.

"Come on. Maybe ducks fly north for the winter, too, huh? It's human nature. People are all the same.

We all want what's coming to us. Want to go for a drink?"

Sam found herself thinking of Walt, and of what she might come up against down near the border. Suddenly she felt very frail and small to be going out into the desert plains virtually all alone.

"Just one drink?" Tess wheedled.

"One. But that's all, okay? I've got to leave early tomorrow."

"One," repeated Tess, raising a single finger. "Don't worry. I won't let you change your mind."

PART II

ghost town

1

It was hot as hell.

Samantha said it, wiping the film of sweat off her forehead that even the blasting air conditioner didn't stop: "It's hot as hell."

"Dunno," muttered the thick-skinned sheriff beside her between smacks of his chewing tobacco. He looked like a big, dumb bear in the midst of swallowing lunch. "I never been to hell. But some folks might say we're heading there now."

"Oh, yeah?" She smiled, glad to get more than a one-word reply from the man. Wet gray hair lay limply on his lined forehead. He wore dark sunglasses and a fine stubble covered his plump cheeks. He was a tall, bulky presence in a tan uniform ringed with sweat, and he smelled like he never met a deodorant he liked.

But then, in this pounding heat, she knew she stank too. Her mousy hair, pinned into a bun, had become welded to her head, and her T-shirt felt wet all over.

Sam wiped an already damp palm across her neck. She was self-conscious about her neck; she thought it too long and skinny. It made her look like a goose sometimes when she wore the wrong clothes.

He glanced at her. "Temperatures out here in Las Bocas are as hot as they get. I read something that said they're the highest in the nation, sometimes. Down here on this flatland and ringed by all these mountains, there's hardly any wind at all. Some say it used to be a volcano. If there's a Hell on earth, then *this* is probably it."

Even talking about the weather was better than his silence since they'd left Alpine some hundred miles back. "So you're taking me to Hell, huh?"

Sheriff Bill worked his mouth, then picked up the paper cup between his legs and spat into it, splashing dark brown liquid on his fingers. He grunted and replaced it. "I'd say you're taking me, Miss Sam. I sure wouldn't be going here if it weren't for you and that damn letter from the feds."

"Scared of the ghosts?" she asked. Behind them the Jeep was kicking up a huge cloud of dust, hiding the mountains. Ahead, flatness stretched out until the Rosillo mountain range reappeared like a protective fence. "Do you people really believe the ghosts of long-lost miners haunt this place?"

"Something does," he muttered, then shut his mouth and chewed again.

Sam pulled a long, displaced hair from her forehead and didn't even try to fit it back into her bun. "Like what?"

Sheriff Bill shook his head, becoming silent again.

Sam leaned forward into the blower, listening to rocks crack under the tires. Despite the sheriff's lack of conversational abilities she was glad he was with her. Walt Schector had been the last man to come out here. It was believed now that the body discovered across the border by Mexican authorities two weeks ago was his.

But it wasn't until Sheriff Bill discovered Walt's wallet last week that the evidence had pushed officials into trying to trace him, and it wasn't easy since this area was so large.

Sam felt very alone out here.

Still, she wasn't turning back. Not just because she'd once loved Walt either. She wanted to prove that she could handle herself as well as a man in this kind of a position. Better, in fact, because she had no intention of turning up missing like him.

Walt had been sent out here to check the area because illegal immigrants seemed to be passing through without challenge, and now she knew that much was probably true. The border patrolmen were like Sheriff Bill, and kept well away from Las Bocas after sunset. Bill said night patrolling was nonexistent.

"There it is, Missy Sam," said Bill.

She looked up and blinked even through the dark protection of sunglasses. The dusty glare reflected back from several old mud and stone buildings. "I don't see any ghosts. Think it's too hot for them?"

Bill picked up the canteen between them and offered it. "Maybe," he replied flatly. "But then, they only come out at night." He drove down the dirt road between roofless square rock structures, worn adobe buildings, and a three-story hotel. They all looked deserted.

Sam shivered in spite of the heat, staring at the remnants of the town with an unwanted identification.

Those walls were as empty as her life since Walt had pitched her that curveball.

Walt again. Walt had put her ambitions on hold for months.

Sam took the canteen, twisted off the black plastic top, and raised it to her lips.

Sheriff Bill spat into his cup and pulled the Jeep to a stop in front of the weathered hotel sign. "Bet you never thought water would taste that good."

"Pretty good," Sam agreed. "What happened to this place, anyway?"

"It was a company mining town." He found a bent tourist pamphlet on his dash. "Here's a souvenir. Las Bocas was a really booming place back before Pancho Villa wiped it out and looted it to support one of his revolutions."

"The Pancho Villa?" She looked at the retouched black-and-white photo of the bandit on the pamphlet.

"That's the official story. Back in the eighteen fifties, before the Civil War, a group of outcast settlers found silver and began mining. After the war a lot of ex-Confederates heard about this place and settled on the land to remake the fortunes they had lost. The population just kept growing, and in 1912 the fifteen wells that had been dug were all dry. The company that owned the town purchased huge barrels of water from the nearest city and had them brought in to keep the miners here. It's all in there." He touched the pamphlet.

Sam nodded. She didn't want to read—after the long, quiet drive she was glad he was finally talking to her. She took off her dark glasses and squinted at Bill in the sudden bright glare.

"One day in 1913 the barrels didn't come," he continued. "There's evidence that the shipment was attacked by one of Pancho Villa's bands. The people here were dying of thirst. Some went out in the cover of night to try and make it to the nearest river, fifty miles off." He tapped his thumb on the metal canteen. "Just imagine being out here under this sun for even one day with nothing to wet your tongue, swallowing your spit as it dried up like those wells."

"God," Sam said, picking up the canteen again. Just hearing about it made her throat sore already.

"They say three days passed, and no new shipment came. Looks like you can guess how they felt, missy. I guess that kind of desperation for life can do funny things to people." He waited until she'd taken another drink, shaking his head when she offered it to him. "You won't read it in that guidebook, but story was that the survivors began to kill the cattle and chickens and drink the blood, and when they were gone, the men began to kill each other for more, but no one ever proved it."

She made a crooked smile. "I can see why you don't advertise *that*." She stuffed the pamphlet into the green army-surplus ammo pack she had bought to replace her purse out here. "Why don't you tell me about it?"

"Not much to tell. When a new shipment of water finally arrived the next week, there were only two or three dozen of the miners left. Most of them left a day later when the Texas Rangers arrived, and the stories of what really happened conflicted with each other so much that the whole thing just kind of blew over. Almost all of the dead bodies had wounds like they were murdered, but the hotel owner said that Pancho Villa had attacked them to loot the camp after cutting off their water supply, and that his men had done all the killing. No one said he was lying, and even though there were no Mexican bodies found, that's the way the reports were finally written up." Bill shrugged. "It might even be true. Pancho Villa had destroyed a lot of other camps before this one to finance the revolution he started in Mexico a year later. But with the other stories kicking around, the company owning this place couldn't get many people to work here, especially when manpower dried up during the First World War. The company folded, and just about everybody left moved on except a few old geezers like the hotel owner." He stopped and took off his sunglasses, squinting back at her. "What's the matter?"

"I just didn't know you could put that many sentences together at once."

He laughed. "Hell, you ought to hear me after church on Sundays. . . . Come on, daylight's wasting."

"I hope so."

He turned off the motor, and as the overworked air conditioner died, the cab turned instantly into a stuffy coffin. They stepped out quickly into stifling dry heat. The silence there was huge. A slight wind made a high whistle from some small crumbling building to her left. No bird cries, no sound of distant traffic. It was almost as if she'd suddenly gone deaf.

She clicked her tongue for reassurance.

Bill reached into the backseat, where a dirty blanket covered several boxes. He came out with a Winchester, pointed the rifle at the earth, and cocked it.

"Worried that Pancho Villa's ghost might come back?"

Bill reached into the car once more and took out a

worn holster. "Not him." He handed it to her. "Buckle it on."

Sam sniffed its old leather smell, then timidly examined the gun.

"There's a shitload of rattlers out here," he warned her.

"I don't know how to shoot one of these things, you know."

"Just pull it out, aim, and squeeze the trigger," he replied.

Sam buckled the holster on the innermost hole. The pistol hung low on her hip. She laughed, the sound unblemished by outside noise. "Now all I need is a cowboy hat."

Bill pulled out two straw hats discolored with sweat. "Out here, you sure as hell do. The sun'll cut you down faster than Pancho gunned down those miners."

"Yeah?" She slung her army surplus purse over her neck so it balanced her, hanging against her other hip. Then she fit the oversized hat onto her head, feeling like the Woman with No Name in an unmade spaghetti western.

Sam pulled out the revolver and aimed it at various targets. The small dark buildings—it was hard to believe people had once lived in them. The hotel sign, chipped and beaten by constant windstorms. An old Chevy pickup.

Whistling lowly, Sam walked to it and touched the brittle white paint on its hood, feeling an incredible heat. "Wow," she breathed. "Twilight Zone. My brother used to own a truck like this."

"So did my son," Bill said quickly. "Come on. Around here, it's best not to touch things that don't belong to you. Let's do what you came to do and get back on the road. It's after four already."

Sam turned away from the truck. "Not close enough to sunset for me," she muttered. "Does this truck belong to the people you said still lived here?"

Bill took out his package of chewing tobacco and bit some off. "It does now." He nodded at the old, brown rock building.

Sam followed Bill up onto the shady porch. Their footsteps creaked loudly. A weathered white sign hung over the door: HOTELO LAS BOCAS. The painted letters were still vivid despite their wear, but someone had marked through the last two words with a brown-red paint and underneath scrawled *los vampiros.*

Sam touched the hot, discolored doorknob and cried out. "Damn it!" She put her fingers in her mouth.

"Should of brought you some gloves, too, Missy Sam." Sheriff Bill chuckled. He came up beside her, the boards creaking under his weight, then pulled an old pair of yellow gloves and a dirty handkerchief out of his back pocket. "Here." He handed her the hanky. "Sometimes you might try to grab your gun handle and even it's too hot."

"Thanks loads," Sam muttered, taking the filthy cloth, then standing back and waiting for him to try the door.

He didn't touch the knob.

"Aren't we going to go in?"

Bill spit a dark blob onto the floor planks, and it began to sizzle. "There's nothing to see," he whispered.

"We have to go inside to find out anything we can." She frowned, annoyed with his constantly changing attitudes—especially because they mirrored the nervousness inside herself. The man who'd come out here before her was missing and probably dead.

"Come on," Sam said decisively, wrapping the handkerchief around the doorknob and twisting it quickly. She knocked the door open with her knee and walked into a big room. A warm but welcome breeze slapped her face, and she glanced up at the ceiling fan first, then down to the stick-wood and plank tables and scattered chairs. The walls were a drab yellow-brown, and the curtainless windows were all glassed in. Despite that the tables were filmed with the red dust that seemed to cover everything. She looked back at the circling fan. "I can't believe this place has electricity," she said.

"I don't think it does." Bill crossed the gritty floor slowly, not touching anything. A long splintered bar stood at the far end and he stopped there. Liquor bottles lined the walls. Bill folded his glasses into a front pocket. "There's no one here. I told you, they come out only at *night*."

Sam took off the straw hat and ran a hand over her sopping hair, letting the fan blow down on her. *"Something's* running this fan," she said, wishing they had brought the canteen in with them. "And what do you mean by that: 'They come out only at night'?" She smiled with mild superiority. "I didn't come all the way out here just to see ghosts."

Bill picked up a half-filled glass on the bar's flat surface and stared at it. "There ain't no damn ghosts around here far as I know, missy. Come here."

Reluctantly, Sam walked away from the swish-swish of the ancient ceiling fan. She was leaving tracks in the dusty floor, she noticed, and the sight of several dozen other footprints all around hers made her stop for a moment. "Bill, look at all this—are these *old* footprints?"

He was shaking his head. "They're no older than the whiskey in this glass." He raised the half-filled tumbler up and stared through it at one of the windows. "There's a lot of strange stuff around these parts, missy. There may be ghosts and there may not be. I've never seen one, myself, so I don't give much thought to them. But there's no one to talk to here right now, is there?"

"Right. They only come out at night, huh?" Sam said, reaching for the glass, but he held it back. "What's wrong with you?"

"It's better not to touch things here," Bill muttered, and put the glass back on the bar. He wiped the gloves briskly on his khaki pants.

"You touched it."

"I got these damn gloves on," he snapped. "Some believe there's witches here like back in the old times. A Catholic priest was murdered two hundred years ago right here in this building. It was a church then. He said the Indians living here cursed him. They took articles of his clothing and things he had touched, and used those things to make the curse. Some kind of *voodoo* shit."

"*Voodoo?*"

He sniffed dryly. "That's what I call it."

Sam folded her arms across her chest, feeling superior again. "Is that the sort of thing you talk about on Sundays after church, Sheriff?"

Snorting, he looked at his gloves, then at the glass. "We *never* talk about it. There are some things you just don't talk about. But I've got ears. I've got eyes, too, and I've seen a lot of things you wouldn't believe, city girl." His tone was condescending. "If your eyes were as good, you'd know what doesn't come out except at night too. You saw the damn sign."

Looking behind her, Sam glanced at the open doorway. *"Vampiros?"* she murmured. "Hotel los Vampiros?"

"Hotel of vampires," Bill said.

Sam snorted, changing it to hard laughter that echoed in the stifling air. "I'm not some stupid tourist, Sheriff. I'm trying to find out about the illegal entry of Mexicans into this country, and whether it has something to do with this place, and maybe the disappearance of Walt Schector, whose wallet you found." She sniffed and walked back under the fan. "I don't give a shit about vampires."

Bill thumped his foot loudly against the floor. "There's a basement or something underneath us. I've never been down there, but if you want to go take a look, I promise I'll wait for you, missy."

"Look at what?"

"Look and see who left this glass half drunk . . . and made all these footprints. You don't think this whiskey's been waiting for us in the glass for fifty years, do you?"

"You said someone lived around here," she reminded him, swallowing spit.

"I said someone was staying here, not *living* here."

Sam kept her fists at her sides, trying to hold back her anger at his riddles. "I've got a job to do, Sheriff, and in case you've forgotten, so have you, and it doesn't involve standing out here in the middle of fucking hell and telling campfire stories. Does someone live here or not?"

He didn't say anything, and Sam stalked back behind the bar. Clean glasses stood in neat rows. An ornate door in the back wall interrupted the long shelves of bottles. She thought she heard something from behind it. A creak, and a shuffle.

The doorknob moved.

"Bill—" whispered Sam.

The door opened. "Please pardon me, señorita," rasped an old man's voice from the sudden dark rectangle the opening door made. "I was trying to sleep. Not an easy thing for an old-timer like me, but you kick the floor. You want drinks, maybe?"

A brown-skinned, wrinkled man with a sparse head of white hair came out into the bar. He was wearing a patched white shirt and loose slacks that reminded her of pajamas, and his feet were in sandles.

Sheriff Bill walked closer to the front door so that there was nothing between him and it. He stood grimly, touching the revolver's handle in his holster.

"You want drinks, gringos?" he asked again.

"Sure," Sam answered truthfully. He hobbled with elderly steps to the bottles. For a sudden silly second she thought of what Bill had said about vampires . . . but then, he'd said they only came out at *night.* "Why do you sleep in the day?" she asked.

He took the glass Bill had picked up and put it behind the bar, replacing it with two empty ones. "With this kind of heat you're a mule not to, huh? I sleep downstairs because it's cool there. Besides, my customers come at night. No one here in the sunlight."

They only come out at night.

"What kind of customers?" He was filling the

glasses with a bottle of tequila. Sam winced at the thought of drinking it, but the very thought of any liquid in her mouth was appealing. "Who comes all the way out here?"

The old man shrugged. "Some nights there is no one. But then sometimes people come out to look at the old mines and want to rest. Young gringos like you come from the cities to play . . . and sometimes a man and a woman like you two come to get away from their wives and husbands, huh?" He winked. "No one can find you here, huh?"

"That's not why we're here. *We* hardly know each other. We came out here looking for someone."

"No one can find you here." He winked again. "Lots of people come and go. No one stays but me and my workers."

Reaching for the glass, Sam remembered the sheriff's warning about touching things. "Who else comes here?"

"Like I said, señorita. Sometimes only a man and woman, young people, sometimes people who get lost . . ."

"People from across the border in Mexico?" she asked.

His dark eyes twinkled for a moment and he smiled, showing yellow-brown teeth that looked younger than he did. "Sometimes," he spoke softly, then: "People who are thirsty come here, señorita. Like you, huh?"

She picked up the tequila, feeling Sheriff Bill's eyes at her back. "It's not hard to get thirsty out here," she admitted.

He laughed. "That's why we stay. Hot is good for business."

The tangy taste burned down her throat. She started to put the glass down, but the memory of the mindless peace alcohol had once given her made her lift the glass once more. "I don't know how you stand it." Then she swallowed fast.

"You can get used to anything, señorita. Just like the tequila. You frown as you drink it now, but when it is all you have, you learn to love it, and then maybe water doesn't taste so good anymore, no?" He rubbed a finger over his dry chin and nodded at the sheriff. "He's not thirsty?"

"How about it, Bill?"

Bill shook his head. "It's four forty-five. I think we found out what we needed to, don't you?"

Sam frowned at him, then turned back to the bartender. "Hold my drink, okay? I'll be right back."

"*Sí.*"

She went to Bill. "You're not doing your job."

"Oh, yeah?" he asked, not lowering his voice as she did. "Well, for your information, young lady, regulations say I can't drink on duty, okay? If you want to touch things around here, that's your business."

Bill's voice was loud in the stillness, and she frowned again, glancing back at the old man, but he was staring at nothing. "Let's go outside."

Sam took Bill's arm and led him back onto the porch. The hot air seemed almost refreshing after the enclosed stuffiness of the bar. "I want to find out some more," she whispered, hoping he would catch her hint.

This time he did, and his voice grew soft. "You won't find anything more out until after dark. I told you, missy, I want to be well away from here by then."

He turned to the hotel sign. "We found out what we need to, didn't we? He admitted that illegals come through here. Just take that information back where you came from and let someone else handle this. You've done your job."

"I want *proof*," she breathed. "I need to bring back more than some old man's admission of guilt." Sam felt thirsty again and knew it was because of the tequila. "Damn it, this is important! I want to see if he knows what happened to Walt Schector!"

Bill walked to the edge of the porch and put his gloved hands on his hips. "That's my job," he said mildly, "not yours."

"Then why aren't you doing it?"

A long moment passed, empty in the quiet except for the whistle from down the street. It was so still, she almost thought she could hear the squish of the sheriff's saliva. Bill spit out his chaw of tobacco. "I know how to go about this, missy. I've been sheriff a long time, and I know how to get things done around here."

"Then why did they have to send me to show you what *needs* to be done?" Sam regarded him uncertainly. "I'm *not* going. Are you just going to leave me here?"

Bill crossed his arms in the way of a father unmoved by his child's pleas. "I could make you come back if I wanted to. I could arrest you."

The threat made the frown on her own face spread, and Sam fought to keep her voice level. "Then try it, because I *am* staying, and if you do arrest me, then I guarantee you that I'll have your job."

They stared at each other, then Bill's lips twisted

slowly. "You might, missy. But it might save you from ending up like your friend Mr. Schector."

Her hand dropped to touch the handle of the heavy pistol at her hip.

The breeze picked up and the whistle grew louder.

"I'm going," he told her. "You really want to stay here?"

Sam looked back over her shoulder at the empty bar. Her bluff was being called. "You'd actually leave me alone?" But by the look on his face she knew he would. "Will you come back to get me tomorrow?"

"You're serious? You'd stay here?"

"If you haven't got the balls to stay with me, *yes*." Sam said the words without even considering them. He was scared, and he was only trying to scare her.

But why was he scared?

Bill's frown dropped away to leave his face empty. For a moment she thought he might change his mind, but he marched down the steps to his Jeep and got in. After a moment Bill turned in his seat. "I'll drive back first thing in the morning," he told her grimly. "Keep the gun, okay? If I'm wrong, then it'll be good enough protection, but if I'm right, me staying with you wouldn't do either one of us any good." He tossed the canteen they'd been sharing onto the dirt by the steps. "Just in case you decide to leave on your own. And if you do, watch out where you put your feet down—there's deep holes all over this place where the mine shafts have caved in. A lot of people have disappeared down them. I got a load of dynamite in the back of the Jeep that I keep meaning to close all those tunnels down with, but—" He made a face and shook his heavy head. "If you ask me, though, the best thing for you now is to get a room here and stay in it . . . *with the door locked.*"

"Sheriff," Sam said, "I may be a woman, but I'm not stupid."

"Yeah?" He pulled off one glove, then the other, wiping his forehead with them. "I think you're a lot stupider than you look, missy."

2

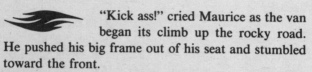 "Kick ass!" cried Maurice as the van began its climb up the rocky road. He pushed his big frame out of his seat and stumbled toward the front.

"Sit down, you asshole," Jerry barked. "Haven't you ever seen fucking mountains before?"

"Only in pictures and movies." Maurice pushed in front of the bench seat where Jerry and his girlfriend Tammy sat, and knelt in the tiny space before them, looking through the windshield. "That's why I wanted to come with you guys." He laughed.

"I thought you wanted to come to be with *me*," snapped a soprano voice from the bench seat behind Tammy.

Maurice glanced back at the redhead he'd been sitting with and rolled his eyes. "I saw you all winter long, MaryAnn. I told you, I've never been *anywhere*. I went to elementary school, junior high, and high school in Waco, and now Texas A&M in College Station, only a hundred miles away." He stared at the looming terrain with an open mouth. "I can't believe Mom let me go with you guys."

"Time to cut the old apron strings, Maury," Scott advised from the driver's seat. He stretched his arms and tossed his short blond hair with a shake of his head. He smiled in his familiar way, with the confidence of leadership. Though Maury was bigger than either Scott or Jerry, Scott was indisputably in charge. It hardly seemed fitting that Scott was majoring as a psychologist with a concentration in sex therapy, and not preparing for life as some big-time executive. Still, his newly learned psychological skills might be needed to deal with his girlfriend, Kathy, if they stayed together.

"Time to get out in the real world and have a real bash before we get out in the real real world," Scott said, letting his arm drift to lie on Kathy's bare leg in the captain's chair beside his. "If it wasn't so damn hot this place would be heaven, huh? First Mexico and a swim in the Rio Grande, then hot desert, and now we're in the mountains, heading for a *ghost town*."

Jerry leaned forward. "Yeah, maybe we can see a real *ghost*, too, right?

Kathy giggled. "I wonder if I can fuck a ghost?"

Tammy blushed and giggled too, but nervously.

"That proves it," Jerry said. "Scott, I told you that Kathy would fuck anything—"

"Can it, dweeb." Scott's voice dropped low. "Sexual fantasies are good for the libido. Don't screw with Kathy's brain."

"That's the only part of her she doesn't screw with!"

Half turning, the slender girl narrowed her eyes at Jerry. "For your information, asshole, I *wouldn't* fuck just *anything*. I wouldn't crawl in the sack with you even if you *were* a ghost."

Maury laughed, and he smiled as he heard Mary-Ann's echo from the back.

Jerry's face went red. He glowered at Tammy until she stopped laughing. "Come on, cool it, okay? This is shit, you bums. In three weeks we'll be back in class, and then before we know it the year will be over and it'll be graduation time and we *will* be in the real world! We'll go from the frat and sorority parties into being first-class yuppies with nothing ahead but nine to five, two-week vacations instead of all summer, and cutting grass and paying bills. I want to go back to Oz. I don't *ever* want to go home!"

Tammy laid her hand on his crotch, then clapped her feet noisily. "Uh, just click your heels together."

"I wish," Kathy agreed. She thumped Jerry on his knobby knee. "Why don't you keep your lip zipped, hose-nose? Just stop making fun of me and enjoy here and now. Don't turn this into bummer-summer. There's nothing we can do about it, so let's just enjoy ourselves while we can."

Scott dropped his hand from the wheel, then slipped his finger under Kathy's white skintight shorts, making her spread her legs and scoot to the end of her chair toward him. "Yeah, dude," he called back. "If we don't grow up, who will our kids have to hate and make fun of? I just want to see it all end with a bang."

"You should've pushed those niggers and greasers in the water back at the river, then," MaryAnn said from the rear. "They were just like the ones back at school, jigabooing around with their noses and asses stuck in the air. Like those freaks from Phi Gamma. If you'd have gone ahead and done it, I bet there would've been some real banging then!"

"We would've been the ones getting banged up too," Scott growled. "There were two dozen of those apes."

Kathy rubbed Scott's hand. "Maybe I could've gotten them to bang me instead."

He rolled his eyes.

MaryAnn shook her long red hair against her face. "Maybe the greasers, but not the niggers—*gross*!"

Watching the mountains close out the sky before them, Maury shook his head. "If anyone should be whining, it's *me*. This is my first and last summer to just be a kid," he muttered. "I'm making up for lost time."

MaryAnn climbed up beside him and laid her hand on Maury's arm. "Then come on back and let's make up for it, Bub. It's too hot to make out outside."

"You two are sex maniacs," snorted Tammy. "You're going to end up as Scott's first patients."

Maury blushed and followed MaryAnn back to their seat. "Hey, it's not my fault my mom made me live with my aunt's family instead of in the dorm. MaryAnn and I didn't exactly get the opportunity the rest of you had, you know." He nearly fell on top of her as the van bumped wildly.

"Don't crush me," she reproved, scooting over fast.

"Well," Scott called, "just you two remember not to get too carried away, okay? This old heap is bumping around enough without you adding to it."

MaryAnn waggled her tongue promiscuously and snickered. "You're just jealous, Scott." She pushed her lips into Maury's, opening her mouth to him as she tried to get comfortable. When he kissed her back, she closed her eyes, liking the careless freedom the movement of his tongue brought her.

But as Jerry had said, they were already almost at the end of that freedom. She remembered how she had once wished so hard that she were grown up, so she could embrace a world where she could do what she wanted.

It wasn't that way.

"I love you," Maury whispered in the high voice that was so out of place in his huge body.

She rubbed her fingers under the blue work shirt he wore. Everything about Maury was just as mislaid. With his sheltered youth he'd barely known how to talk to her, or any girl, for that matter. He was so ridiculous, it was funny. Then the date she'd made with him last semester for a joke made her humor warm. She felt that warmth again with the memory of his size between her legs. It was ridiculous that she had been his first woman, but she was glad for it, anyway. "I love you too." She moaned when he laid his soft hands on her stomach.

Jerry and Scott were talking about cars now, fending off comments from Tammy and Kathy with disdain. MaryAnn put them out of her mind. Maury represented them all, in a way: He was a child living in a grown-up body.

"I want to be a Toys-R-Us kid," she mumbled as her shirt fell open and Maury stroked her delicately, as she'd taught him. She shut her eyes and smiled, pretending he was someone she didn't know—*anyone.* She lapsed into her daydream that she was a hooker, taking man after man to her bed.

Maury's finger crawled under her shorts then, and the mirage blew away as she trembled. He was so much more attentive to her than her more experienced boyfriends had been. She liked the way the wet cold of the air vent caressed her like an extra hand, giving way to his warm, uncallused touch. Her nipples shivered, and then Maury bent down and covered one of them with his warm mouth and tongue, kneading her other with his fingertips.

They were doing what they wanted to now, but even that was not true. They were trying to cram a lifetime of pleasure into these short summer months before they had to go back for a last year of school. After that they would be trapped into the molds of their parents, becoming, like Scott suggested, the very things they hated now. It was a vicious circle, and they were all trapped, and one day she would have a daughter thinking these very same thoughts as the time ran out of *her* hourglass and the cycle began once more. "I don't want to grow up," she breathed.

Maury put his other hand between her legs, rubbing her gently through her pink shorts. She felt the promise of the evening that wasn't close enough.

She never wanted to grow up.

"Don't get too carried away back there," Jerry warned. "Remember, the eyes of Texas are upon you."

A bright light flashed and MaryAnn jerked, knocking her head into Maury's. Jerry and Tammy were leaning over the back of their seat, watching . . . and Jerry took another picture with his Polaroid.

"You *shit*! We didn't do that to you guys when you were back here."

The camera whirred as the front of the van screamed laughter, and Jerry took out the second photo, waving it and the first one through the air to hasten their development. "Confucius say, do in the private what you want to keep private . . . and do unto others *before* they do unto you." He cackled and peered at the pictures in his hand. "I just wish we had a video camera, huh, Tammy?"

MaryAnn met the girl's eyes in a squint.

"Leave 'em alone, Jerry," Tammy finally said, turning away. "Come on, turn around."

Maury closed MaryAnn's shirt and sat up. "Yeah, turn around." His face was red with a mixture of embarrassment and hostility, and he suddenly threw a fist at Jerry as though to strike him. Jerry flinched, and Maury snatched the pictures from his hand as he fell back against the driver's chair.

"Shit!" screamed Scott, knocked forward against the steering wheel. "You fucking *morons!*"

The sound of his panic made everyone freeze, and the van thudded into a boulder at high speed, hopping and spinning crazily. It shimmied and shook, hitting another rock with an explosive pop as the front right tire blew out.

"Shit—"

The van tottered, slowing, and then, like some kind of Achilles wounded in its heel, fell on its side with the clatter of breaking glass.

3

The sun dropped lower and lower, but the temperature seemed as high as ever. Sam sat at the bar like a lazy cowhand, sipping from her third glass of tequila and reading the old tourist pamphlet Sheriff Bill had given her. She knew she shouldn't be drinking this stuff, but she had already asked the bartender the same questions over and over, and none of his tight replies had led to a new trail of inquiry. It had been months since she had been really drunk—not since those weeks after Walt—and she was getting bored. The tequila made her feel better, as it had on those lonely nights. It made her feel less stranded, and less angry that the sheriff had left her like this. And besides, the heat made her *thirsty*!

The bartender was wiping the spigot on an old barrel with the care of a jeweler.

"You don't recall anyone coming here recently to ask questions?" Sam made herself ask again.

"People come all the time. Some ask questions.

Some come because they're lost and some because they *want* to be lost. I don't know where they go. I only know that they're thirsty, just like you."

"Okay. Maybe you can answer this, then: how come people are afraid of this place?"

He shrugged, facing away from her as he rubbed away the constant dust. "Old stories. *But it brings in the gringos.*" He put the darkened cloth in his pocket and stood up, pointing at the pamphlet. "Stories bring in the gringos who aren't thirsty for only a drink."

"Is that why you changed the name of this place to Hotel los Vampiros?"

"Maybe so," he answered. "But then, maybe it's *true,* huh?"

Sam giggled, licking at drops of moisture on the glass. "Maybe you're full of shit too. I'm not a tourist, you know."

"No?" He winked, his eye like a slippery worm writhing on a hook, then walked back through the door he'd come out of before. She slipped off the high stool, watching his back, and waltzed across the room to the table nearest the slowly swinging fan. Two hours had passed since Bill had left, and the bartender was even less talkative than that lawman. She was soaked all the way through now, too.

Maybe the sheriff had been right.

The notion annoyed her. It filled up her heat-weary body with the irritation she'd felt at his departure and made her all the more determined to prove him wrong: to prove to everyone that she not only had Walt's courage to come out here alone, but more than equaled his abilities. He took everything personally, and while his passion could be an asset, it could also distort his judgment. It was that attitude that had driven him to ask her out her third day on the job with him, beginning an idyllic relationship that she thought would never end.

Sam swallowed another drink. The soggy ideas spreading through her brain urged a weak smile as she imagined solving the murders all on her own, tying in her assignment with the snatches of speculation she'd heard, bringing an end to the low-key but wide-ranging investigation consuming local governments.

But she wanted to find out what had happened to Walt too.

She blinked back a salty tear.

His ambition had enthralled her, calling to her own, and unlike most Texas men, he'd treated her as an equal, listening to her hopes and dreams and taking them seriously. They'd joked about running for office in Texas and becoming senators, or at least working their way up the bureaucratic ladder until they achieved nonelective posts they could never be shaken from. But after a while she'd noticed the big difference in their goals. She wanted to go into politics because even though she knew better, she hoped that what everyone laughed at as her youthful, idealistic notions might make a difference if she pushed them hard enough.

She'd been through some tough times, and she thought she had something to offer. It had been difficult for her family when she was younger. Dad had received a good load of shrapnel to the skull in the Korean War, and through her childhood he scraped by from job to job. The veteran's check helped, but was hardly sufficient when the cost of living grew faster than his pension did. His frequent mental lapses made him unfit for all but the most menial jobs. Her older brother, Mark, had helped out when he'd gotten old enough to work, but then he was drafted for service in Vietnam. They shipped him home in a bag. Those traumas marred her childhood, but they'd given her a special empathy for the less fortunate, making her want to do something to change things.

Walt was just selfish and power hungry.

Putting down the glass hard, she remembered how stupid she had been, never suspecting the real reason for the unusual hours they met, or why they never went anywhere nice in public. Then it all made sense when she found out Walt was married. She saw him and *her* downtown at dinner one night with their child, and followed them to a home she hadn't known about. Walt didn't answer the phone number he'd given her even when she called into the early-morning hours, and so she came back to that house the next day, a Saturday. He was home alone, and when she confronted him, he told her he was trying to talk his wife into a divorce so he could remarry. She wanted so bad to believe him . . . she let him hold and kiss her, *and seduce her again.*

Then his wife and son came home from shopping early to find Walt between Sam's legs. Sam still had nightmares of that moment when she looked up and saw the woman's face in the crack of the bedroom doorway. Sam had screamed, her naked body trembling under Walt's while he ground into her with loud groans and licked her breasts. She could still smell the final mixture of their juices that covered the red-and-pink-flowered sheets.

She screamed and screamed until Walt jerked up and stared . . . seeing his wife raise her knuckles to her teeth.

"Oh, God," he had whined, shoving Sam away and dragging on his slacks.

"Walt—" Sam had cried.

He zipped up his pants, not looking at her. *"Get your clothes on and get out,"* he hissed, hurrying after his wife. *"I'll see you at work."*

But after he slammed the door shut, Sam left a note telling him it was over, then dressed and got out of that house, ignoring the shouts from the back rooms. She went home and unplugged her phone, then moved in with Mom and Dad for the rest of the weekend, as if she were still a teenager instead of twenty-seven years old. She even changed her phone number and left it unlisted.

She thought about quitting her hard-won government position in immigration surveillance so she could avoid him, and almost took a job of phone soliciting where she wouldn't have to face people at all. The way Walt had lied to her and used her hurt so bad she never wanted to trust anyone again—especially a man. The love he made with her a lie!

Sam wiped her forehead. The understanding that Walt had never loved her at all, and had probably not meant a single thing he'd whispered to her, made her hurt and angry, but the awareness that she had so enjoyed his attentions and sometimes even now wanted him back made her sick. She told herself over and over that she never wanted to see him again, but in the end she stayed at her job, even continuing to share an office with Walt; she wanted to use him back the way he'd used her. She had gone home to the bottle every night for weeks, filling her drunken thoughts with hate and revenge.

And now, almost six months later, he had disappeared, and she *was* using his death to move up in the world. She only regretted that he would never know it.

But how would she do it? Sam looked at the open door at the back. There was no sign of the old man. There was no sign of anything or anyone. Maybe the only thing living here—*staying* here, Bill had said—*were* ghosts.

Outside, the sky had turned red and the sun was setting at last. The bartender returned with oil lamps and began to place one on each table. They gave off a nasty, heavy odor.

Ghosts.

4

"So now what do we do?" asked Tammy from her seat on the jutting rock that had probably blown the front tire. The van lay overturned in the ditch beside the road, its quiet death-sigh in the dribble of water that still trickled from the cracked radiator.

Except for Tammy they were silent. Everything was silent except for the song of the wind and the sound of distant rattlers.

"If Jerry hadn't been such a hot-shit photographer, none of this would have happened," MaryAnn burst out. "We'd still be having *fun!*"

"You mean if Maury hadn't hit him!"

At the sound of the accusation Maury glanced up, his big body shivering as it always did when he got tense. "I didn't hit him."

"You tried to," Jerry shot back angrily, rubbing his limp arm. "If you weren't such a dick—"

"You're *all* dicks!" Scott shouted suddenly from behind them. His blond hair was discolored by blood and hung together in clumps. "If any of us had been seriously hurt, it'd just be tough shit out here. It may be tough shit anyway, because no one comes out here! Besides that, this crap is going to go on my insurance record 'cause I rented that damn thing!"

MaryAnn turned to Maury, rubbing a hand over his back. Maury had scraped his arm and face pretty badly when the window glass broke and he fell into it, and he had the shakes worse than any of them. Besides the gash in his scalp Scott was bruised, too, and it looked as if two of his fingers were broken. Kathy was only shaken up, with a couple of cuts on her nose, though her wrist might be sprained, and Tammy was shaken up almost as badly as Maury. She had cried for half an hour after the crash, making her plump body jiggle ridiculously. Jerry's pain was more serious. Though he had been down almost to the floor when the van crashed, the jolts had twisted his body unnaturally and now he couldn't move his arm. It was probably broken.

This was the real world.

"We can't just sit here and wait." MaryAnn shook her head. "We've got to get some help. It's getting dark."

"Why don't you and Maury just go behind some rocks and fuck in private, then?" Jerry spat bitterly.

MaryAnn stared up the road, which was covered by a thin layer of reddish dirt. They were near the top of a slope. Their belongings were dumped in a pile at the side of the road. MaryAnn dug out one of the tourist maps they had bought and held it up in the fading sunlight. "That ghost town you guys wanted to see is right over this hill," she said.

"I'm really in the mood to sightsee," shot back Jerry.

"There's a bar down there, this thing says, and a hotel. They at least might have a phone."

Scott hobbled to her slowly. His bruised left leg had turned a deep purple. "I don't see any phone lines," he said, looking over her shoulder. "Then again, it's going to be hot as hell here in the morning. It might be a good idea to get somewhere tonight. I haven't seen a car on this road except for that sheriff's Jeep we passed." He picked two canteens out of their pile of stuff. "Let's hoof it."

They walked. Jerry moaned with almost every step, while Scott hobbled silently in the lead, wiping away the blood that kept seeping into his eyes.

It was a lot farther to the top of the slope than it looked. They stopped once, the van a vague yellow-white blob that seemed miles away now, and shared the water from the canteens. When they finally reached the top and looked down in the final glow of the sun at the town that seemed even more endless miles away, the idea of reaching it didn't seem so good anymore.

Scott coughed in the growing chill of the night. "Do we want to keep going?"

"There's not a hell of a lot to turn back to," Maury's shivering voice replied. MaryAnn put her arm around him, surprised and a little proud that he was taking a stand. It wasn't like him, just like the way he'd jumped at Jerry in the van had been so out of character. But though what he'd done had caused the crash, she admired him for it, just because it wasn't like him at all and had showed everyone else he had the balls she fondled as often as possible. "If you guys want to wait here," Maury went on, "maybe Mary-Ann and I can keep on walking. Those guys down there might have a car and we can use it to come back for you. It was my fault, anyway."

"Damn right it was your fault," snarled Jerry. "And what are we supposed to do if they *don't* have a car?" His eyes shone in the darkness. "You want us to just sit up here and die?"

"What's all this talk about dying?" asked a low voice from behind them on the road.

A short man came out from the shadows. "Hey," MaryAnn said, "we need *help*!"

The man came nearer. "I see that." He grinned mildly.

"Have you got a car? We had a crash back down the road and we need to get out of here!"

The man stopped in front of Scott and looked at the ghost town below. "There's a truck down there. It's not really as far away as it looks. I was on my way in." He turned to them. "The bartender down there's not a doctor, but he might be able to help you out and fix your cuts up."

"How about a broken arm?"

"All you need for that is wood for a splint. Come on, but watch your step. That's an old mining town and there's underground shafts crisscrossed everywhere that have caved in. You fall into one of those and you won't need a doctor anymore. Come on," he said again, "I'll show you the way."

5

The town was empty. There wasn't even water in the hotel, and though Sam thought she remembered that Bill had left her a canteen, it had become so dark outside, and her eyesight was so fuzzy, that she knew she'd never find it now. There were no clues and no parade of illegals, only the sounds of the bartender as he wiped dust out of the clinking glasses, then began to sweep the floor with an old handmade witch's broom. He was like a thoughtful squirrel, murmuring under his breath and darting here and there, so precise that his slow movements seemed fast. Sam watched him wipe away her footprints from this afternoon, wondering if this man swept the floor so carefully every night.

It gave her a chill, wondering who'd made all those tracks.

"Do you always clean the place up like this?" Sam watched him through drooping eyelashes.

"The boss wants it ready for guests, señorita."

"What *guests*? What boss? Is he upstairs?" Sam glanced over at the hallway to the stairs. Earlier, she'd rented a room from the bartender. For five dollars she got the key to an upstairs room with undecorated adobe walls, a narrow bed, and a stick chair. There was no bathroom, only a big potter's urn in the corner.

It made her glad she had not lived her life back when the whole world was like that. She had opened her compact and stared at her dirt-streaked face in the mirror, feeling the uselessness of doing anything about her appearance, then left it beside her bag on the dusty bed.

She'd checked all the other doors upstairs, but they were locked. "Does he live upstairs?" Sam asked again.

"Too hot." The Spanish man chuckled. "Too bright. You can't sleep up there in the daytime." He eyed her empty glass. "Want a new drink, maybe?"

She nodded and folded up the pamphlet she'd read all the way through twice. With her fuzzy eyesight now, she wouldn't be able to read it again even if she wanted to.

But without a TV, getting stone-cold drunk was the only way of passing time and ignoring the heat's constant misery. She was not the first to be aware of this: The pamphlet explained at some length how Las Bocas was a town that had always lived only after dark. Booze was its fuel and a needed dessert after the day's temperature. During the sun's hours the miners worked deep in the earth; only an unlucky few braved the worst heat to bring the silver up into the light. It was just too hot for any other life-style. At dusk the workers gathered in the bar and drank and drank with the waiting whores until they were so foggy headed they forgot their miserable condition. She felt sympathy for them for having had nothing to look forward to but that drunken state she was fast approaching. She had no trouble believing it would be the day's high point at all. "So where is your boss man now?"

"He'll be up, señorita. He is old like me . . . even *older*. Sometimes he moves very slow—like you after these drinks, huh?" The bartender swept a pile of dirt into a corner and scooped it up with a metal tray. "But sometimes we old ones move fast too."

The boss wants it ready for guests, señorita.

What guests?

Bill had been right when he said there was nothing to stay here for. There weren't even any ghosts to liven things up, although Sam knew if she kept drinking she might see them yet.

But then, as miserable as she felt in this heat and with the constant thoughts of Walt, even liquor-induced ghosts would be a welcome change. Maybe she could imagine Walt's ghost and find out what happened to him. Maybe Walt hadn't even been murdered. He might have just gotten drunk here and staggered out to die innocently in the desert.

The alcohol made time pass slow, but took away her concern for that truth. She licked her lips, pretending in her clouding thoughts that she was a high-class whore the mining company had shipped in here like they shipped in the water.

Suddenly the porch was full of footsteps and creaking.

The bartender continued his sweeping. Sam pushed back her chair, wheeling around.

"Knock, knock," called a cheery voice from her past.

The door opened and she saw Walt.

"Hi, Sammy," he called. He smiled as if he wasn't surprised to see her at all. A group of young men and women followed him inside.

No way. She *was* drunk!

She tried to focus more clearly on the short figure in wrinkled blue jeans and khaki shirt. Something about him seemed elusive, strange. He was looking past her now at the bartender. "I brought you some company, Mex. These kids managed to practically kill themselves, they were so eager to come see you and this place."

"Gringos," the bartender muttered loudly. He carried the broom back behind the bar and, with an eye on the newcomers, pulled down a bottle of tequila and six glasses, pouring into each until they were half full.

"W-Walt," Sam said.

He was grinning and cheerful as usual. His face was the same: small, rounded chin under dark, oversized lips and a long nose that had once made her call him "the man with two dicks." As he poked his hands into his high pockets and slouched, her thoughts struggled crazily against each other.

It's a dream, thought Sam, closing her eyes and reopening them, remembering the ghosts.

But he was still there. He was *alive.*

No. She was hot, and drunk, and it *wasn't* real.

Walt laughed cheerfully again, coming toward Sam. He waved his hand at the six young people waiting at the door. "See if you can fix these dudes and damsels up, Mex. One of them's got a busted arm." He waved the group ahead to the bar and drinks. "A couple of sips of that stuff, chums, and you won't feel any pain at all."

One of them, a tall, lanky blond man, led the way to the bar, his shoes tracking red dirt across the carefully swept floor. Sam followed him with her gaze and worked her jaw sluggishly. As he tried to communicate with the bartender, his excited motions were reprised by the others. The bartender grinned as the kid with the limp arm rolled up his shirt and showed it to him.

The bartender nodded. "I get the boss."

She was just ripping drunk. She was so ripping drunk she was seeing things now, and *hearing* them.

"I didn't really expect to see you here this *soon,* Sam." Walt laid a heavy, cold hand on her shoulder. "I would have stopped in earlier."

Seconds passed, and the voices at the other end of the room slowed down and sped up ridiculously, slurring into nonsense in her ears. She felt very light-headed as she stared back into Walt's eyes. "I feel sick," she mumbled, letting her mouth slide open. A flood of words tripped over each other before reaching her numb tongue. He was blurry, and it wasn't all the fault of the booze. Sam raised her heavy hand, wiping at sudden tears. "Goddammit—*where have you been? Th-they sent a sheriff out here to find out what happened to you.*" She tried to stand up on trembling legs, reaching out to him—

But she was falling.

6

Floating. Up and down. Inside, upside, outside. Sam's stomach twisted, trying to dig its way through her skin to freedom like the creature in *Alien*.

Sour vomit swam up her throat.

The walls swirled in the shadows made by the flickering oil lamp beside the bed. With a start she realized someone was sitting beside her on the hard mattress, his face half hidden.

"I thought you might get them to send you out. I'm glad to see you, Sammy."

Tiny eyes and a gargantuan nose were visible above a soft mouth in the murkiness. Her mind was clearing, and she knew this was real. Walt was real, and he was *alive*. "Walt . . ." she whispered.

He touched her thigh.

"Where did those other people come from?" she asked him.

"Just some kids," Walt replied, his eyes on her unnaturally still. "They had an accident up the road. They're okay. Someone will come get them before long."

"Okay, but what . . . the hell . . . are you doing here, Walt? What's going on?"

Walt bent closer, his motions stiff. "I've found out a helluva lot more than I ever expected to, I'll tell you that. How many of those drinks did you have?"

Sam tried to shrug, annoyed when her shoulders wouldn't obey her. "Six or seven, I think."

Walt slid his cool fingers down her arm and bent closer. She started to pull away, but as he touched her hand, she felt the thrill of the old electricity she hadn't known for months. "How come . . . I didn't see your car and the bartender acted like he didn't know about you?"

"He doesn't understand English so good. Did you see those kids trying to talk to him?"

His hand slid over her cheek the way it used to. It made her swallow hard and remember all the times she'd wanted him.

She'd wanted him since the first time he touched her in the office. She wanted to sleep with him the first time he'd kissed her, and those desires had grown as she tried to see in him the man she wanted. Sam had made herself ignore the selfishness he displayed too often.

"You had way too much to drink," he told her softly. "That's what happened to me the first day I was here. I drank too much, and then I started thinking about you, Sam. I thought about us and how my wife wouldn't give me a nice quiet divorce."

The shadows on the ceiling swayed back and forth.

"You lied to me," she hissed, having trouble keeping her eyes open.

"You know, if I hadn't come when I did, Santa Anna down there would have probably left you lying on the floor."

He tilted her face up, so close to her that she felt drugged by his foul breath. "I *dreamed* about you, Sammy. I've thought a lot about you since I've been out here, and I know I did you wrong."

She tried to push him back. "You need to brush your teeth."

"So do you," he said, "but the only mouthwash out here is more of that damn tequila." He touched his clammy lips to her cheek. "I mean it, Sammy, I'm *sorry.* Sammy?"

"God damn you, Walt—you've got half of Texas looking for you. We all thought you were *dead*! Why the hell didn't you even send us a letter or something telling us you were okay? *What do you think you're doing?*"

Walt sighed. "It's not important anymore, Sammy, don't you understand that? I came out here, and now everyone thinks I'm dead. My wife, my creditors . . . *everyone.*" He ran a strangely icy finger over her lip.

"You're *cold.*"

"It's a cold, cruel world, Sammy. But that bartender told me how I could begin my life all over again and have that power and prestige we talked about all those nights. And now it's true. A new life, and you can have it too. We can both have everything we ever wanted."

"I don't need a new life. I worked hard to get where I am. You don't know me as well as you think, damn it. I'm *not* like you are—I don't think I want you, anymore, either, Walt. I *don't* want *you*."

"But you need someone, Sam. I understand need," he told her. "I'm not the same as I was before . . . and now, I need you."

"You *need* me?"

"I told you I did, didn't I?" His eyes brought back all the things she'd tried to forget fast and hard—him bringing her flowers every day, filling her desk with vases at work, him writing those long love letters. The small considerations blinded her to their bizarre relationship, and she fell in love. And she was still bitter about it because she'd never stopped loving him.

Her hand reached out, trembling when it brushed his, and he stroked it. Her heart flickered with that old desire.

"You can have it *all*." His eyes . . . showing her her past, but with a promise beyond; a promise *he* could give her. She saw herself in those black pupils she had once lost herself in as they made love, and those old cravings were formed in their blackness; of herself in bed with him as he loved her more passionately than he ever had before, the shadows of his past life and marriage forgotten. The union crescendoed with him becoming the selfless, loving partner she dreamed for. She moaned with pleasure and arched her hips. Then the strange vision faded from his eyes, but not from her mind.

"I was afraid to go through a messy divorce because that would screw up any political ambition I ever had. I just had no idea that the real power might be somewhere else. But now we can have *everything*."

"I don't want power." Sam squeezed her thighs together, still entranced by the offer in his shiny eyes.

"Yes, you do. Admit it, babe. You want to change the world, and only *power* can do that. Just keep looking at me, Sammy."

His pupils reflected her—that new and different her, freed from every loneliness and frustration, able to do things; *change the way things were*! She felt she was floating in his eyes now, floating away from the shackles. Nothing seemed real. In the fogginess surrounding her Sam suddenly hoped that the only reality that existed was the one she saw in his eyes.

Maybe all this *was* only an exhausted, drunken dream, and she really *had* passed out; was even now lying on the floor in the bar as the old Mexican swept around her. She caught a breath, feeling the heat expand between her legs.

He chuckled. "Tonight is all yours."

"Oh . . . yeah?"

"Yeah," he whispered.

He stood high above her. "You look beautiful tonight." He blew out the lamp, then let his fingers rest on her thigh. Bluish moonlight filtered into the room from the window behind her.

"Don't," she murmured, having to push the word. She closed her eyes and shivered.

"But you *want* it," said Walt.

His hands went to her gun belt, and she twisted restlessly. Then he left it alone to kneel on the mattress between her thighs. His jeans rubbed against hers as he pressed his cold mouth into hers. Strangely, it felt good. The way his tongue twisted against hers made her wet.

"You taste *sweet*," he murmured.

She laid her hands on his greasy hair and sighed.

But all at once it was like sticking her tongue into a package of cold, rotting bacon.

Sam tried to push away. *This was Walt, the man who had fucked up her mind and life!* He smelled, and his breath— She wanted to *scream,* but the sound from her mouth was a gasp. Her body was limp.

"Yeah," he murmured, his hand tugging her shirt up over her face. She suddenly felt so weak, she couldn't move. His hand reached behind her to unsnap her bra. He pulled it up and exposed a nipple, and a clammy tongue slid up her stomach to her breast. As his long nose pushed into her skin, he suddenly cringed, hissing out a long breath. He pulled her shirt back down.

Sam scooted breathlessly back over the sheets. His wet lips shone in the moonlight. "Take off your necklace," he growled.

"Wh-why?" A sudden glare caught her eye. Her compact's mirror reflected the moon's light. That tiny rectangle of glass lay beside them, reflecting her leg, but not his hand on her leg. Her eyes went back and forth between object and image.

A sensation of sickness stirred inside her.

She blinked, and suddenly knew that no matter how real all this seemed, it must only be a warped dream of masturbation. She knew when she woke up, she would be alone on that barroom floor, drenching her panties with an orgasm brought on by her own hallucination.

"Take it *off.*"

She shivered at the urgency in his tone, but it was only a dream, only an exhausted, alcoholic vision of a dead man she still loved and who had always given her the ends to the need deep inside her.

But now he was a man who smelled and tasted bad.

Her hand touched the thin chain circling her throat, sliding down to the small silver cross Mother had given her for her tenth birthday, just after her brother Mark got killed. If her mother could somehow see into this horrid, exciting vision, she would be disgusted. The cross seemed hot, burning her with shame. Reaching behind her, she found the clasp and tried to unfasten it.

"Can—" She breathed heavily, her desire still urgent for the feel of him. "Can you *help* me?" Her fingernail pinched the clasp handle.

"Just take it off," he whispered again. *"Take that shitting thing off and drop it in the dirt."*

She stopped, startled by his anger. But it *was* all just a dream, after all, wasn't it? Then the chain came loose, and she pulled it away and studied it.

"Throw it away," Walt grunted, taking a step toward her again. *"Just throw that thing the fuck away."*

But the cross tingled in her palm now, warm like the hands of her mother when she had first fastened it around her neck. The familiar heat surged through her, making her cheeks hot.

What was she doing?

"I can't," she said. She held it up and blinked back the tears that formed. "Can't I just put it down?"

"You bitch. It's a part of everything that has hurt you. *You have to throw it away and refuse it!"* He jerked back as her hand brushed him.

The cross dangled from her clenched fingers as she pushed it at him. *"You do it,"* she whined. She tried to make him take it, grabbing his fingers.

He screamed.

The cry echoed in the small room and she backed away, wanting to wake up. Where the cross had touched his wrist, his skin sizzled a glowing red. It burst suddenly with pus and luminescence.

"Damn you!" he screeched, falling to the floor.

She screamed, too, wanting to wake up.

"I'll kill you!" He rose fast and threw out a withered hand with long, knived nails.

Still screaming, Sam threw herself out of the bed and tried to run, nearly slipping on the dust. The door-knob was cold against her ass and she grabbed it with shaking fingers, bringing the necklace up between herself and the suddenly skeletal outline of oozing flesh that stepped into the moonlight. It seemed held together only by the clothes around it.

This is a dream!

—a *nightmare*—

His claws ripped into her hip—it hurt as if this were real even if it *wasn't*—and she thrust the cross into the hideous, inhuman face. Crowded, shining teeth filled his face as he lunged at her, and she threw open the door. *"No!"* she cried, backing out into the hall. She felt for the gun on her hip and pulled the door behind her as fast and hard as she could, slamming it into the nightmare creature's fingers so violently that she almost fell. All four of the reaching fingers broke off with a squishy crack and dropped at her feet. The freed digits danced their final quivers as furious new screams erupted inside the room.

"It—*this isn't real,*" Sam whined, staring down as one of the frenzied fingers flopped against her heel. She covered her mouth and backed toward the stairs, the necklace tight in her hand.

The doorknob rattled, and the door cracked open. Sam turned and ran, gathering breath to scream. Moonlight crisscrossed the floor from the now open doorways to other rooms, but they were empty. She glanced back only once when she reached the stairway and saw Walt crouched down, trying to catch his shivering, dismembered fingers.

"Don't play so hard to get, Sam!" called Walt. *"There's no place to go."*

Still half believing that this had to be only a nightmare from the heat and drink, she clopped down the steps loudly. "This can't be real," she muttered hoarsely, yanking the gun from its holster. She held it with both hands, the necklace dangling below it. Breathing hard, she started down the lower hall toward the dimly lit bar beyond.

"Get the fuck away from her!" a man yelled from the saloon.

Sam hesitated, then inched ahead. Scuffling sounds came through the doorway. The remaining edge of drunkenness made her feel part of some modern artist's surrealistic vision.

She cocked the revolver anyway, and forced her feet.

"Get the fuck back!" screamed out the voice.

There was a low chuckle.

Swallowing as silently as she could, Sam stopped just short of the doorway and looked back toward the stairs.

There was no Walt. No sound. She knew this had to be a vivid hallucination.

But she was scared. Her knees trembled.

"Help!" screamed a high-pitched woman's voice, breaking off too suddenly.

"God damn it," whispered Sam. She stepped into the doorway, bringing the revolver up and pointing it into the shadowy room. Three of the teenagers who had come in with Walt were spread-eagled on the tables nearest the bar. Bent over them were three strangers: a woman with long jet-black hair, a half-naked woman with blond hair, and an unnaturally pale man dressed in the bartender's pajama attire. Two of the teenagers were male and the last was female—there was no mistaking that. Their shorts had been pulled down to their ankles and the trio standing above them were nuzzling their pubic hair. Sam felt her eyes widen and blur while a wasp buzzed through her uneasy stomach and stabbed at her intestines, making her teeth clench. The blond woman bent over her female victim, sighed, and pulled back with a grimace of satisfaction, licking dribbling blood from her long, stained teeth.

"You bastards—you're *killing* them!" screamed a big teenaged boy.

He stood behind the bar with the other two teenagers. The old Mexican who had served her all those drinks giggled and poked him with a long, sharp knife, slashing the shiny steel into his upper arm. He brought the wet blade to his tongue. "We bring them new life and make them well, gringo. We bring you healing."

"You bastard!" The burly teenager punched the bartender in the mouth, forcing the knife into his cracked lips. Thick new blood spurted out and the old Mexican choked, spraying red saliva into the air. The young man wheeled and lifted a red-haired girl up onto the splintery bar-top, then swung around and lifted the plump girl too. Both of them slipped down onto the floor gracelessly and hesitated. The two women and the tall man straightened as if they were all parts of the same body.

"Run, MaryAnn! Run, Tammy!" the boy yelled frantically, lifting himself up to follow. "Run!"

The bartender licked his gory lips and dropped down behind the counter, then came back up fast with the knife clutched in both hands. Laughing berserkly, his hoarse voice rising and falling, he drove the glinting blade into the back of the boy's skull.

"Maury!" cried the red-haired girl he'd called MaryAnn.

Maury's mouth opened soundlessly, drooling blood like a flood onto his twitching fingers. The bartender jerked him back, dropping his dirty teeth into the flesh of the boy's throat and tearing a ragged hole there. "Run?" he gurgled, chewing the flesh that stuck between his incisors. "Yes, *run—there is no place to hide!*"

The girls backed away as the three pale creatures began to shuffle toward them. *"We offer you everlasting life,"* hissed the tall man as he wiped his jaw. *"You'll be young forever . . . just like you want."*

Sam's eyes went from one figure to another. Her grip on the gun was slippery with sweat. She could not believe it but could not forget that this was Hotel los Vampiros. She forced herself to pull the trigger and the revolver exploded, jumping in her grip. It seemed she could see the bullet shriek through the air and into the white pajamas of the tall man. A red geyser erupted on the man's back, squirting the women behind him.

But the man didn't fall. He didn't even cry out, or jerk with the impact. As the two teenaged girls looked desperately to Sam, he turned to them with a harsh laugh. *"There is no place to run,"* he wheezed. He reached a hand to his back and brought the blood there to his mouth. "Would you rather die and just be dead, or die and live *again*?"

Sam squeezed the trigger again and yelled at the girls, "Come on!"

The chubby girl began to run, diving low as the black-haired woman tried to cut her off. She ducked far enough so that the woman only grabbed a handful of hair. But when the hair went taut she fell back, and the woman dropped to her knees over the girl.

MaryAnn stood still at the bar as the tall creature stepped closer, holding out his arms. "You'll *never* grow up," he cooed. *"You'll never grow old."*

As she aimed again at the man, Sam saw the bartender move out of the corner of her eye. He was coming around the bar, but stopped and licked the blood staining his knife.

"H-help me!" cried out the heavy girl on the floor. The black-haired woman who had tripped her was already sinking her darkened nails into an ankle and drawing dark spurts. "Help me, please!"

Sam fixed the gun on that vampire woman's forehead and pulled the trigger again. The bullet slammed into its target and exploded, blasting pieces of skull, brain, and bloody tissue onto the squealing teenager. Sam forced herself to them, pushing away the woman's groping skeleton fingers and pulling the girl up as her attacker licked lustily at the gore running down her own forehead. Sam turned the pistol to the blond woman who had begun to run at them, her long nails slicing the thick air.

"Go!" shouted Sam, pushing the girl toward the doorway as she squeezed the trigger once more. She shoved the muzzle into the rushing blond vampire's

eye. With the wrenching bang, cold liquid splashed over her hands and up her arms.

The bartender was coming now. Sam's fingers burned with the hot metal and she backed up, finding him in her sights. The blond woman fell to the floor in front of her and clutched at Sam's legs with long, tearing nails. Fighting a scream, Sam kicked the hole running red in the woman's skull and reached behind her to push the girl again.

"Sammy, you *bitch*."

Walt stood in the front doorway, his fingernails digging into the girl's shoulder. His other stub of a hand reached toward *her*.

"No!" She let out the last air in her lungs, shooting him, too, right between his legs. The lead projectile ripped open his jeans and spurted more redness into the air separating them. But Walt just giggled absurdly. Then, remembering the shining silver necklace still draped through her fingers, Sam hit him with it and the gun. He bellowed as a new, flaming welt flared on his cheek. Sam belched her own frantic laugh and held the cross up to the barroom. The bartender and the two women stopped dead. The three teenagers on the tables just lay still, dribbling their remaining life into mud on the dusty floorplanks. MaryAnn was in the tall man's arms now, helping him remove her shirt as he bent his lips to her naked breasts.

"MaryAnn!" shouted the teenager beside Sam, her mouth wide.

The women and the bartender started toward them. Sam grabbed the girl's wrist and shoved her out onto the porch. The night's mugginess was cut by a needling, chill wind.

"Go!" she cried breathlessly. *"Go!"* She ran down the dirt street, propelling the girl ahead of her.

A cloud covered the moon. The ground was black and the sky was black, and Sam could not tell where one began and the other ended. She and the girl charged together, gasping, though the girl was starting to sob now too. Sam beat at her back hard with the gun butt to keep her moving, then darted ahead and began to drag the girl faster. Sam remembered the white pickup and forced her eyes over her shoulder until she saw it far behind them, on the other side of the hotel's open door. The white-suited old man stood on the porch, his knife gleaming in the light from inside. His hand dropped fast, and she saw that glinting streak chasing her.

Sam shoved the girl violently to the side to escape the attacking blade. It whispered past them. They continued forward toward the barely visible black shapes of the hills. The sheriff had said there were mine shafts all over, and she wanted to find one and hide until the sun she'd hated all day broke into the sky, driving this nightmare from her soul. Her feet stung as they pounded the ground as fast as they could, harder and harder as the sound of Walt's taunts bit into her ears:

"There's nowhere to go, Sammy-bitch! Nowhere to run and . . . you'll get real thirsty like I did—and then, welcome to Hell!"

Sam had once told Walt she would see him in Hell. A fiery stitch welded itself into her side.

"I . . . can't . . . go . . . on," puffed the girl. Her feet moved more and more slowly. "I . . . *can't!*"

"We've got to!" She led them down the road farther from the scattered buildings and tried to recognize a

constellation that could guide them. They ran between
a cluster of boulders into the shadows.

"I've . . . got . . . to . . . *rest!*" gasped the girl.
She staggered to the side and waved her arms suddenly above her while her wide mouth stretched in an
unheard scream. She disappeared into the ground.

As the loose ground shifted beneath her feet, Sam
threw herself to the side, slamming into a boulder. She
dropped face first to the ground, gritty dirt spilling
down the sudden slope. A rising, cold breeze slapped
her forehead.

Then a loud, sticky thump sounded below her and
she knew the girl had landed on the mine tunnel's
floor.

7

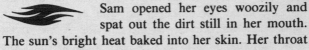 Sam opened her eyes woozily and spat out the dirt still in her mouth. The sun's bright heat baked into her skin. Her throat was sore and dry, almost as sore as her muscles.

But not nearly as painful as her splitting head. At that moment she had no idea what had driven her to drink so much.

Squinting at the heat-marred landscape of red rocks and dirt, Sam pushed herself up to her knees. Her arms and stomach were covered with scrapes. She rested her hand on her hip and felt the empty holster, then clawed the sand beside her until she found the gun and her necklace.

Sweat coated her like the dirt and she felt its tracks. Her mind wandered over last night's impossible horrors.

Were they real?

Though she wanted to pretend it was only a drunken dream, she could not. Sam forced herself shakily to her feet, inching away from the black pit in the earth. "Hey," Sam croaked. "Hey!"

She put her necklace into her pocket and reached down for a small stone. She dropped it into the hole.

A long moment later Sam heard a soft clunk, and the hiss of a thousand busy rattles. Aiming her gun at the hole, she backed away. "God . . . damn," her cracked lips mouthed, but the sound of her voice was so low, she almost couldn't hear it. She backed into a boulder and rested her back against the hot rock, squinting at the yellow-white haze of the sky. No birds. Only the sounds of the angry rattlers.

Her throat and lungs were on fire, and she craved a drink, even the tequila. Sam studied the unfamiliar terrain and crept sideways, peering back the way she thought she'd come. The road was visible between more boulders. She moved closer under their cover, then flattened herself into the dirt and scanned the road for a sign of the sheriff's Jeep.

Nothing. A hundred yards down the road the crumbled stone buildings waited, looking exactly as they had when she'd first seen them: empty of life.

Vampires?

"I had to be fucking drunk," she grunted, wiping greasy hair off her dust-caked face.

Vampires? No way.

But she'd shot them. She'd shot that tall man more than once, and he'd only bled . . .

And bled.

Sam checked her gun, releasing the cylinder. Spent cartridges fell onto the ground.

She had shot all six bullets.

"Shit." She reloaded the gun with bullets from her holster belt.

She had shot six bullets, one of them point-blank into that woman's eye, but none of her targets had died. "Shit," she whined again, wanting something besides spit to moisten her lips. She was so damn thirsty! The door to the hotel was closed; it looked quiet. She pushed herself up, wanting to go in and get a mouthful of something wet—even that hellish tequila—before she did *anything.*

There's nowhere to go, Sammy-bitch! Nowhere to run and . . . you'll get real thirsty like I did—and then, welcome to Hell!

Already she understood too well the desperate thirst that had driven those long-ago miners to kill each other and drink blood.

You can get used to anything, señorita. Just like the tequila. You frown as you drink it now, but when it is all you have, you learn to love it, then maybe water doesn't taste so good anymore, no?

Sam shivered as she shuffled between the rocks toward the road.

Drink.

Sheriff Bill had tossed a canteen out on the ground beside the hotel's porch. Breathing heavily in the dry, stifling air, she kept on, holding the gun in front of her. Finally she saw the metal canister, dropped to her knees and reached out to it.

"Shit!" Sam shoved her burned fingers into her mouth. The water had to be near boiling now. The only refreshing drink was in that bar.

Welcome to Hell.

"Goddamn it." Sam crawled onto the porch and lay under its welcome shade. She wanted to keep going into the bar and sit and drink the bitter tequila, letting its moisture refresh her as the alcohol took away the agony filling her body.

But she was too tired. It would be easier to just die.

Sam closed her eyes.

"Missy?"

The voice was loud, but millions of miles away.

"Missy?" Two strong hands clamped her under her arms and hauled her up, but she barely felt them or even cared. There was no spit left in her mouth and her eyes felt bone dry. She knew that even her blood must have evaporated through her leathery skin pores and up into the sky.

"I gotcha," drawled the voice as it strained. The hands pushed her up over a meaty shoulder as if she were a sack of dried potatoes, and she felt her face flop against a broad, damp back. She recognized the voice as Sheriff Bill's but didn't want to open her eyes to the brillant glare of her solar assassin. She opened her mouth, but only a scratchy cough came out.

He pushed her into the car as she tried to lick her lips with a sandpaper tongue. The door slammed shut and then the sheriff got in next to her. After another endless minute she heard the grinding engine catch and flinched in the sudden hot blast from the vents. After a moment the blowing stream became bearable . . . even cool.

"I got my damn air conditioner fixed, Missy Sam." The sheriff sighed, and she felt his body heat and smelled a strong gym-room odor as he leaned over to her. "It's not a helluva lot better, but at least it'll dry your sweat faster than it pours out now. Can you open your eyes, missy?"

She fluttered her eyelids briefly and caught sight of

the brightness, then clamped them tight once more. "Thirsty," she managed.

Styrofoam pressed into her lips and she swallowed the cool water eagerly. Her arms shook as she tried to push her hands up to meet his, to force him to tilt the water down into her screaming throat faster.

"Slow," Bill warned. "Go real slow or you'll faint and throw it up, okay? Easy does it." He tipped the cup a little more, and she guzzled the drops that streamed from it until the glass was empty.

"Just a second," Bill said, and she heard the pouring water and felt a new strength as he emptied the second cup into her, and then a third. After the fourth she opened her eyes and kept them open in a squint, holding the cup herself as he poured a fifth. "You okay, now?" he asked, swigging from the open canteen.

Sam nodded, her senses now focused on her raw, burned skin. She sipped from the cup slower, savoring the liquid. When it was half empty, she poured the rest over her seared forehead. She wiped at her eyes and glanced at her scarred watch face, unable to make out its tiny hands and the numerals. "What time?"

He put the car in gear and started back the way they'd come. "It's just after nine, missy. I got an early start, but to tell you the truth, I expected to find your dead body on the floor of that bar. I never figured to find you *unmarked*."

"I look pretty marked up to me," she said, finding her voice with an effort.

"Huh-uh," he replied, twisting the wheel. "Marked is what those teenage kids I found in a van up the way is. You're damn lucky they happened along or every one of the fucking bloodsuckers here would've been stompin' out for you."

Sam remembered those kids last night lying on the tables as that man and the women pressed their faces into their groins, making loud slurps and sucking noises. "They were in the *bar*," she whispered.

"Then they moved 'em out. Wrecked their van too. Real convenient, 'cause no one'll figure what really happened to 'em." He stuck a plug of chewing tobacco between his teeth and bit some off. "No one ever finds a dead body in that fucking place. They move 'em *all*."

"Th-there's a girl," Sam muttered, "that got out with me. But she fell into a hole."

Sheriff Bill grunted, chewing lazily. "Rattlers'll pick her clean and only a pile of bones will be left. One of these days I gotta come out here and blow those damn things closed, blow this whole damn place off the earth."

Sam stared at him dully.

"But, hell, not even the preacher's got a nerve for that. They'd come for us *all*." He paused, the lines in his face deep. "I guess there's just not enough goodness left in the world to stop this kind of evil anymore. You just thank the good Lord you're still breathing and whole and forget the whole damn thing, missy."

Sam gave her head a sudden, violent shake. "But you *know,* damn it. We should tell someone. We should do *something*. You're the sheriff!"

"I *can't*!" He lowered his head. "Hell, just forget it. I know you were stone drunk as soon as I left yesterday, missy. You turn in a report of what *really* happened out here and they'll laugh you clear out of your uptown Dallas office. Sometimes it's better to just close your eyes and let things go. Hell, you're going back to Dallas and you'll be far away from this crap, and I sure as hell ain't coming back. Just forget it, missy. It ain't your problem. Me and my people gotta live here, not you. We've lived like this a long stretch now, and none but us whose families been here for years even guess at what might be out here anymore—so just leave us be to handle things in our own ways. Live and let live, huh?" He snorted. "Or like that old rock 'n' roll song my boy used to listen to, *live and let die.* Just go back to the big city and forget what you saw, 'cause no one's gonna believe it, and even if they did, I wouldn't put my money on the feds against the vampires. They're both fucking bloodsuckers, anyhow. If we can live with one, I guess we can live with the other. . . ."

PART III

dallas goes to hell

1

Sighing with an empty bitterness, Mike Hossiason backed his six-year-old Chevy junker out of the parking space, then headed through the parking lot to a street full of evening traffic. He steered carelessly and aimlessly, as he had navigating through the mall from shop to shop, thinking about the job he wasn't going to get and the money he didn't have to pay last month's rent on his one-room apartment. His unemployment had run out, and the drug test they'd given him at the mall janitorial service had shown traces of that reefer he'd saved and smoked yesterday.

And Lynette had thrown him out of her life, once and for all.

On the sidewalk beside him people headed toward the mall, relaxing in the twilight hours. The men carried their suit coats and rolled up their sleeves; the women pulled their long hair off bare shoulders.

They walked with purpose because they had jobs

that paid for their meals and beers and shopping. They had husbands and wives or boyfriends and girlfriends, and sometimes both. They knew where they would be in the morning, and every day. They had purpose.

He drove on without purpose, letting the miles and buildings pass aimlessly as the gas needle steadily drooped, just like his life.

Then, two blocks from his apartment building, he went by the old plumbing warehouse. A woman stood under the streetlight, hiking her pink miniskirt for someone's attention. Even she had a job . . . and undoubtedly a man to sleep with every night. She could take her pick.

Mike sniffed with self-pity. Her legs were pale and well formed, her body top heavy and crowned with blond hair. The smile she gave burned him with a vague memory. She licked her ruby lips, her tight half T-shirt seeming ready to slip up over ample breasts with every movement. Those twin globes jiggled a friendly greeting, their nipples pushing against the constricting material.

She was *very* familiar looking, even to the way she was standing.

He pulled over to the curb and rolled down the passenger window. The woman watched him, her lips pouty but inviting.

It couldn't be her.

"Who—who are you?" Warm air floated into the car.

Her eyebrows arched as though she could see into his confused thoughts with some kind of mystical X-ray vision. She smirked. "Does it make a difference?"

It seemed like he knew her—that he remembered

her. He remembered her on another corner not far from here when he had stopped just like now. But it had been a long time ago, when money was plentiful, before his two-year stint with Lynette. "Can I . . . talk to you?"

A vague new interest formed on her face, and the woman made a slow smile. "Pull over there." She gestured at a side street between the warehouse and the flickering sign of a pizza joint.

With a tingle that ran up from his spine to his scalp, Mike pulled the car up the two-lane street to wait for her. She walked slowly after him, swinging her hips with a tired flatness from too many hours spent on her back, enduring joys that had become so everyday and constant they were monotonous. *Just like the other woman she reminded him of.*

It *couldn't* be her.

She bent beside his open window, exposing the breasts beneath her open, button-down shirt. "What'cha want?"

"Don't I know you?"

She shrugged, and her lips curled smugly. "What'cha want?"

"Didn't you used to live a couple of apartments down from me?"

She raised her thin left eyebrow high. "Maybe I did and maybe I didn't."

He shook his head. "You couldn't be, though."

She shrugged and threw her blond hair back over her shoulders. "Have it your way." She returned to the corner without another word.

He was remembering the night two and a half years ago when he heard the screams from the hall outside his apartment. He got up from his snug blankets, finding the switchblade on the nightstand. Pulling on his jeans as fast as he could, he flipped the blade up, and stumbled through the dark to his door.

A woman was screaming, but the other tenants waited inside their rooms, lights burning beneath their doors.

He followed the noise down the hall and heard the new crash of glass inside one of the apartments. He threw open the door and a big sweating man charged past him, knocking him down. A half-dressed woman cowered beside the bed.

This woman, or someone who looked just like her.

"Hey!" He leaned across the seat and stuck his head through the car's open window. "Hey—come back!"

For a moment she kept on walking, though he knew she'd heard him. Then she stopped and turned around slow. "You got a problem?"

She walked back toward his Chevy. She couldn't be the same woman. He was making an ass of himself on top of everything else today. Why the hell should he care who this whore was?

She stopped five feet away, on the curb.

"Hey, sorry. I know I'm bugging you. Forget it, okay?"

She winked, smiling warmly.

"Sorry," he repeated.

"Are you that hard up, sugar?" the blond woman asked.

Mike tried to wipe away his blush with his hands, not able to meet her eyes now. "Yeah . . . I'm that hard up. You just reminded me of someone I knew."

She bent beside the car once more, resting her chin on the open window. "Old girlfriend?"

He pushed out a hollow laugh. "I guess she was, in

a way. A woman living down the hall from me was a hoo—a working girl like you. I helped her out when some guy was beating the shit out of her one time. She used to let me stay with her the nights she didn't have customers." He took a cigarette from his shirt pocket and stuck it lazily in his mouth, lit it, sucked smoke in deep. "Then I started dating this girl, Lynette, and we got pretty serious. I started thinking about the chances I was taking. We were going to get married." He took another deep drag of smoke. "With all this AIDS shit nowadays I can't believe you girls still got the guts to walk the streets."

The whore shrugged. "At least I get paid for it. You're playing the same damn game with that smoke, asshole, and you gotta pay someone else for the danger."

"Ooooh—touché," he grunted, taking another drag.

"Besides"—she batted her eyelashes with a grin that made her familiar to him all over again—"I'm real careful, babe. I can guarantee you I don't have AIDS."

"At this point in my life," Mike sighed, "I don't think I give much of a shit. How about a nice freebie for a poor asshole down on his luck, huh?"

"A *freebie*?" She shifted on her heels, licking her lips with the air of long practice. "Then this Lynette dumped you and you're out of a job too?"

Her words brought his desperation home to him harder than when Lynette had left the sacks filled with his clothes packed up outside her locked door, harder than when the man at the janitorial service shook his head grimly and apologetically. "I'm a lonely guy right now," he admitted.

She touched her cool finger to his cheek. "Hey, if

you're that desperate, hon, why didn't you just say so? Maybe we can work out a trade. Maybe I can show you something *new* that will change things for you, huh?"

Mike shrugged.

"How about your place?"

"I really *don't* have any money," he said, liking the feel of her hand on his face. "I haven't got anything to give you in return."

"Yeah?" She smiled and opened the door.

He lay on the damp, white sheets, his sweat sticky against her cool flesh. She rubbed lazily against his hot skin. He had not spoken since those loud, wrenching moans when his body shook and he spilled his precious contents down her throat. She'd drunk him thirstily.

He smiled with the moment's respite. She had bounced him all over this bed until he was so weak he could hardly think, and now the day's misery was far from his mind. He could still feel her urgent mouth, draining him again and again.

At last he sat up and retrieved his frayed blue jeans from the end of the mattress. "I've never been fucked like *that* before."

She got up and went to the dresser to rub perfume on her neck and breasts.

He remembered the strange decayed scent he'd smelled through that perfume previously, when she'd been underneath him and grunting with his hard, staccato strokes, and he hadn't had time to care. Mike shifted to the side of the bed and began sniffing for it again, searching the corners for a dead rat. Then the movement pinched and he groaned, looking down at himself and seeing indentions through his curly pubic hair. "Shit, you even left teeth marks."

She giggled, buttoning her shirt. "That's just my fee. Want a Band-Aid, sugar?"

He stood up, suddenly dizzy, and hobbled to her weakly. "It's just been so damn long since I had a workout like that. Shit, I thought you were sucking me dry!"

"Don't tempt me."

He leaned on the dresser and met his tired brown eyes in the mirror. "Tempt *you*? Shit—you're the best lay I ever had. What—what's your name?" he asked.

She snorted. "What's yours?"

"Mike."

"What a coincidence." She smirked. "I'm *Mikie*."

"Yeah?"

She walked across the tiny room. Though the mirror reflected the entire room, he was alone in the reflection. He heard the twist of the doorknob and the door opened.

"See ya' around," she ventured brightly.

His gaze jumped nervously back to her smile.

He forced himself to smile back. Then she stepped into the dark hallway and closed the door. He shivered with a sudden spasm as her steps died away.

He barely managed to stagger back to the bed.

2

"I just got back from picking him up," Sherry whispered softly. Her reflection in the mirror reminded her how much time she'd spent getting ready. Her kinky dark hair was perfectly arranged; her silky yellow dress highlighted the strong points of her figure and flattered the rest. Around her, the apartment looked aged and dull. The TV cabinet had been discolored by a leaky ceiling, and the yellow carpet lay like cracking, dried mud. The walls she'd wiped down yesterday only looked more worn, and the wood on the newly polished furniture already seemed dull, like her hopes that everything would go back to the way it was before.

Sherry shut her eyes tight, wishing it all to magically transform into Cinderella's ballroom. "He got home and hardly even said hello. He just changed clothes and went out to that damn bar."

Kirsten nodded sympathetically. "Take it easy on him. He's probably embarrassed. After being in prison two whole years, he probably wanted to get out of any confinement at all. I mean, look at it from his point of view."

Wiping her eyes, Sherry forced a nod.

"I mean," Kirsten went on, "he's been stuck between four concrete walls without getting to do anything he wanted to for all this time. I know it's hard on you, but I can't blame him for wanting to go out into the world and just get good and stinking drunk."

Rick had hardly looked at her when she came to get him this afternoon; he'd barely spoken during their long drive back into the city. She didn't know him now. His daily letters from the penitentiary had become weekly and finally monthly, with contents that could have been copies from a single repetitious letter except that each was handwritten. She had read and reread each one, waiting for him, for the day she could finally be with him again.

Today.

And he had changed clothes and gone off to that new western bar down the street.

"He shouldn't have ever gone to prison, anyway," Kirsten went on. She lifted her chocolate legs onto the orange sofa she'd helped vacuum. "God, I should have said something during the trial. Something to keep him out of there." She rubbed her tousled black mop furiously. "I should have just told them I did it."

"Then *you* would have gone to prison." Sherry looked down at her own legs, which she'd carefully shaved and perfumed for Rick's homecoming. They weren't nearly as dark as Kirsten's. The bleached tone of Sherry's skin sometimes made her wonder if maybe her real father had been white. She brushed that thought away, though, remembering how she'd fluffed the pillows on the bed, wanting it to be perfect for the reunion she had planned so long.

Kirsten shrugged. "At least I wouldn't have had anyone waiting for me." She smiled. "I'm glad you stuck it out for him."

Feeling the heat of a blush, Sherry didn't look at her.

"Most people couldn't have stayed true to *anyone* that long," Kirsten went on, "especially when they're not around. Hell—just look at the way my ex balled around!" Then she stopped suddenly.

A long minute passed. Sherry buried her face in her hands.

"What's wrong?"

She couldn't stop the sob that bloomed in her throat. She'd tried so hard to wait for Rick, but sometimes it had just became impossible, like that time she'd been in the grocery store and the cute white sack-boy had carried her packages out for her, watching her so closely. He had watched her every time he carried things for her, and that time, as she bent to help, he looked down her open shirt and told her she was beautiful. She looked at his young, muscular body and thought of Rick and the long fourteen months she still had to wait.

She'd told the teenager her address in a voice so low, she could barely hear it herself. She told him that she would be alone that night. Then she'd driven away, taking her purchases home and waiting until the white boy knocked on the door nervously three hours later and she let him in wearing only her robe.

"What's wrong, Sherry?"

The boy had only been the first. He had come back as often as she'd let him until last fall when he'd gone away to school, and even then he returned to her on Christmas break. She remembered how she taught him to do the things that Rick had done, remembered well the sight and feel of his stiff, pale flesh entering her darker color. Then there was that plumber she called out to fix the sink, and even the older Indian man from the telephone company. They had helped fill the emptiness she felt in her life, but in a way, they'd made her hurt to be with Rick even more.

Now it made her sick with guilt. Each infidelity had been heavy in her thoughts as she cleaned the apartment so carefully and primped and perfumed to make herself appealing. She had to make it up to Rick, even though he would never know.

Kirsten's hand touched Sherry's neck gently, and she scooted until they were so close together that they touched. Sherry wiped her wet cheeks and shuddered in her sister-in-law's curiosity. Kirsten was a part of it all, too close to be denied. Rick had gone to Kirsten's apartment to borrow her camera, and he'd found her ex-husband raping her. It seemed so long ago now.

Rick had *killed* him. He'd taken a knife from the kitchen drawer and stabbed Kirsten's ex-husband through the heart.

Kirsten took a hand away from Sherry's face. "You weren't completely true to Rick, were you?"

The ball in her throat spread out, larger and larger, and Sherry sobbed, unable to hold back the torrent of unhappy emotion. "I—I *wasn't*."

A short burst of sympathetic laughter stung her ears. Kirsten rubbed her palm slowly. "You tried, though," she whispered. "It's okay. You did wait for him. At least you didn't run off with someone else. You're still *here*."

"I . . . tried so hard at first." Sherry shuddered, reliving every guilty pleasure in that instant. She clenched her fingers. "I really did. Then that white boy—" Her voice was shaking. "After him I wanted every man I saw." She faced Kirsten, pleading forgiveness. "I started to fuck everyone—*anyone*!"

The clock ticked loud above the TV and Kirsten's fingers stroked her palm calmly. "I kinda thought that, sometimes," she said sadly. "I know how bad it was for you. When I got sick last week, I called you up for two days straight, late into the night, and no one answered the phone. I've called late before, but that time I *knew* you had to be with someone else."

"You—you didn't tell Rick, did you? That's not why—"

"I didn't tell him. I told you that I understand how hard it was for you."

"Thank God."

Kirsten stood up. "It's nearly ten o'clock, girl. He'll be coming home soon. Come on and get a shower to wipe away those tears. Then you'll be ready to welcome him the way he should be welcomed. I'll clean up the place a little more before I go, okay? I want Rick to have a happy night tonight. I want everything to be perfect for him."

Sherry forced herself to her feet. "You've been so much help already."

"Rick helped me. I owe it to him."

"But . . . he shouldn't have *killed* him." She shook her head. Rick had never shown such a temper. Ever.

But he'd come home that night, shaking and barely able to speak, and told Sherry what he'd done. He cried and then called the police, admitting everything.

"Do you know why I divorced Dan?" Kirsten suddenly asked.

Sherry shrugged. "I thought he divorced you."

"I made him do it." Kirsten pursed her dark lips together. "I told him *I'd* kill him if he didn't. I told him I'd kill him if he ever touched me again."

Sherry's mouth dropped open. "You never said that in court."

"Rick told me not to. Dan was so cruel to me, Sherry. He used to get stoned and beat the shit out of me. He always said he was sorry, but goddammit, I knew better. When he sobered up and tried to talk to me, I told him how it had to be. I *made* him leave." Her lips turned up. "He kept trying to come back to me, even after we were divorced. He swore he'd never hit me again, but I hated him." Kirsten took their glasses into the kitchen. Rick told me not to tell anyone about it, though. Rick wanted to protect me . . . he cares for me so much!"

Turning, Sherry went down the hallway, an odd tingling spreading over her scalp. She closed herself inside the bathroom, locked the door, and turned on the shower.

She waited until the water was hot, trying not to think about what Kirsten had said. Then she closed herself behind the purple curtain. The soap dissolved into a lather between her palms.

The door creaked.

"Kirsten?" The lock wasn't working again. Sherry rinsed the lather from her hands and pulled the curtain to the side. The room had gone steamy, the mirror covered with condensation. The door was open. "Kirsten, are you in here?"

Beneath the sound of the water, Sherry heard a faint whirring hum. "Kirsten, close the door, okay?"

The door creaked again and closed. Sherry sighed, pushing her face into the water's spray and closing her eyes.

That hum became louder.

"Kirsten?"

The hum became slower . . . then faster.

"Kirsten—*what the hell are you doing?*"

An ominous shadow passed across the curtain. Sherry jumped back. A hand jerked the curtain open and she saw a figure dressed in a black coat, holding a long, pointed object high above its head—

Like Norman Bates in *Psycho.*

"No!" Sherry slipped and fell to the bottom of the tub. *"Goddammit—no!"*

But through the water pelting her, she knew it was Rick and that he knew about her. He'd kill her like he'd killed Kirsten's husband.

Laughter. Shrill and pitched.

After an eternal moment Sherry moved out of the water's spray and wiped her eyes.

"I've always wanted to do that!" Kirsten giggled wildly, holding her stomach with one hand and a long, rounded gray tube in her other. She bent down into the shower's rain, and brought the tube down to Sherry's sprawled body, touching her right leg gently so Sherry could feel its rapid quiver.

Her vibrator.

Kirsten slid it down through her pubic hair.

"Wh-what the hell are you doing!" Sherry screamed, dazed and shaking in fear.

Kirsten fixed her with deep eyes. "Making you *horny.*" She grinned. "You said you were horny for

that white boy, right? But he couldn't satisfy you like I
can, Sherry. What you need is a woman—a real
woman like *me*." Pulling back, Kirsten slipped out of
the old coat she'd taken from the closet, revealing her
nakedness. She giggled again, climbed into the tub,
and crouched before her sister-in-law. "I got so sick
after going to that new bar last week, I thought I was
going to die. But I went back there anyway—I called
you to get you to take me, but you weren't home and I
had to go by myself."

Sherry was trembling all over, almost as furiously as
the high-speed vibrator Kirsten brought back between
her thighs and drove slowly into the pinkness of her
body.

"Does it feel good?" Kirsten whispered.

Sherry couldn't take her eyes from Kirsten's. Her
rigid arms pushed against the slick sides of the tub.

Kirsten smiled. "While I walked to the bar, my legs
felt like they were just crumbling under me, and then I
danced with this big guy that looked like Eddie Mur-
phy until I fell on my face. I mean, I really did—*I fell
on my fucking face.*" Dropping her head, Kirsten
drove it down after the ribbed vibrator, licking with
fast and knowing strokes, making Sherry squirm unwillingly. Kirsten's voice was slow and muffled: "The
bouncer and Eddie wrapped me up in a plastic bag and
buried me in the vacant lot next door. They put me in
a big wooden box before I even stopped *breathing* but
I didn't scream because they said I could do anything
I wanted to when I woke up, *and I've always wanted to
scare the shit out of someone just like I just scared
you!*"

Kirsten stung Sherry's pink flesh with the sharp
pricks of her teeth.

"Ow," grunted Sherry.

Kirsten's teeth stabbed deeper, and her tongue lapped the warm ooze spilling through Sherry's bush of hair. "Just wait till Bubba Rick's home," she mumbled. "We'll have a *real* party!"

3

Except from the initial questioning of Mike Hossiason on July seventeenth by Patrolman Jay Adwon:

Adwon: What do you mean, she was dead?

Hossiason: Goddammit, I knew her. She used to live down the street from me before I moved. *(Pause.)* I read about it in the paper. It was only a month ago. She—she was sort of a friend. Sometimes she used to give me freebies.

Adwon: Freebies?

Hossiason: Goddammit, she was a hooker, okay?

Adwon: A dead hooker, right? Then she came back as a ghost to haunt you?

Hossiason: You son of a bitch. I'm serious. I read that she died. I saw her picture on the evening news three weeks ago.

Adwon: Maybe she came back to haunt you for all those times you didn't pay her, huh?

Hossiason: I'm not making this up. I asked her her name then and she asked me mine. Both times when I told her I was Mike, she called herself Mikie—

Adwon: Yeah. And she lived close, and you were her friend, and you never even knew her real name. Now you say she came back from the grave and *bit* you?

Hossiason: She—she's a vampire.

Adwon: *(Long pause.)* What makes you say that?

Hossiason: Goddammit, I told you. What else can she be? I—she sucked my blood. She sucked a lot of my blood.

Adwon: You let her bite you?

Hossiason: Yes.

Adwon: *(Long pause.)* On the neck?

Hossiason: *(Laughter.)* No way, man. You want to see? Here, take a look.

Adwon: *(Long pause.)* She made that mark by biting you?

Hossiason: I sure as hell didn't do it trying to suck myself.

Adwon: Maybe you just cut your meat when you zipped up your pants.

Hossiason: Yeah, right. I cut myself so bad that it made me faint, and then I woke up in the hospital. Look, I was sick, man. I was *weak*. If my sister hadn't come over and found me, I might've died. She called the ambulance and they had to give me a transfusion. Just read that fucking hospital report.

Adwon: Really, maybe you just somehow cut yourself and bled a lot. You were stoned, right? You said you couldn't remember anything when you first woke up.

Hossiason: I don't think I was stoned, and I sure as

shit know I'm not now. Test me, man, 'cause I'm sure as shit not stoned *now*. There was no fucking blood anywhere on me. No blood on the floor of my—

Adwon: Maybe your sister cleaned it up.

Hossiason: No way. Why would she lie about that? She was scared shitless and they had to hospitalize her too! Look, I don't know why I didn't remember before, but I sure as hell do now.

Adwon: Maybe you cut yourself when the whore was with you, and she cleaned—

Hossiason: I remember seeing her bend down and drink my blood, damn it! I felt it. I remember how she looked up with it dripping from her lips.

Adwon: *(Very long pause.)* Maybe she was stoned and licked some of it up, then got scared and ran off?

Hossiason: *(Shouting.)* Bullshit, man! I remember! She *sucked* it. She was sucking me hard and even though I could feel my life drain out and knew she was taking it away, *damn it, I didn't care then, 'cause it felt so fucking good!* She just kept sucking, and then I couldn't even see her in the *mirror*! Shit, just find the report on her when she died! The TV said *she* died of a massive blood loss.

Adwon: So you think another vampire bit her?

Hossiason: Shit if I know—but I told you, man, she's *dead*. I saw her on that corner again tonight and everything came back just like that. And I think she saw me, too. *(Long pause.)* A dead whore sucked my dick. A dead whore sucked my blood.

4

Sam filed her report, leaving no detail out, then was put on a forced sick leave after a psychiatric evaluation finally showed her the wisdom of Sheriff Bill's words. She kept quiet about the experience back in Las Bocas now, just letting herself recuperate and oiling down her peeling skin three times a day. She felt very alone. Her continued insistence that the "impossible" things had really *happened* would only end by getting her locked up. Holding the gnawing experiences inside seemed to snap her out of her insanity, and after three careful days of new psych tests and study, she was told she could return to her job in another week. She came back to the welcome home celebration the other workers were holding for her in the lobby only to find her stories had already made the rounds. Her friends and co-workers looked at her with mild sympathy, making bad vampire jokes and asking her how Dracula was these days. After an hour of it she managed to slip away under the pretense of going to the bathroom, but went to her desk instead.

The first thing she saw was the newspaper. Her eyes scanned it curiously until she found a one-column story circled in green marker near the bottom on page four.

SUICIDAL ADDICT VICTIM OF VAMPIRE? read the tiny headline.

Sam fought the hot flash that rode up inside her. She buried her face in her hands and let out the pent-up tears that she had to hide now, even from Mom and Dad. She stayed there for a half hour before she felt well enough to face the others. She kept her gaze off Walt's messy desk. Remembering him and the consuming hunger he'd inspired in her right before he attacked was just about the worst of it.

She had wanted him so bad!

But the *most* awful part was that now, even in her nightmares, she sometimes wished she hadn't pulled away from him . . . that he *had* fucked her.

It was scary. Walt wasn't the first man she had gone to bed with, but he had been the one who'd filled her with the insatiable cravings for sexual ecstasy that still taunted her. The ideals of love and marriage had disintegrated into dreamy unreality after the way he'd used her.

Sam stuffed the newspaper into her handbag and went to the bathroom to reapply her makeup. Sam stared at the streaks of sun-darkened skin visible under the light-colored powder, then went down to rejoin her co-workers, enduring their now careful words and a geeky new employee's invitation to take her on a date. Tess encouraged the outing by offering herself and her fiancé's company to "double." "Of course,"

Tess whispered in the bathroom later, trying to hand Sam a drink, "if you guys hit it off we'll conveniently disappear. After Walt and everything else that's happened, what you need now is a little romance to take your mind off things. Nothing straightens my head out better than a good lay . . . huh?"

"Maybe," Sam replied, but inside she only wanted someone to believe her. She wanted to tell some caring man her story and for him to take her seriously. *Then* she might want to fall into his arms. After the desire Walt had reawakened inside her, she was afraid she might even *want* to spread her legs for that geek, if only she could talk to him about the horrors warping her thoughts.

She didn't drink any alcohol . . . especially not the margaritas. The very scent of tequila made her ill now. She stayed there until nine-thirty, then excused herself due to the pain of her sunburn. In her Grand Am a few minutes later she cried at how out of place she felt among her friends. They didn't guess that she believed the tales dismissed as heatstroke. Wiping angrily at her face, Sam started the car and headed toward the precinct station on the city's south side.

Sam stood across the desk from a chubby, uniformed police officer now, and read over the police transcript taken when Mike Hossiason had come in to file his complaint.

"The guy had to be stoned out of his gourd." Adwon chuckled, tapping the sheet of paper with his thumb. "I had to work hard to keep from laughing. Are you guys in immigration working this overtime 'cause you think he's an illegal?"

Sam picked up the paper. "Maybe."

Adwon frowned. "I wish I could tell you that he is,

but we've busted that asshole too many times and I know better. He's just a dealer and a thief—used to be, anyhow. A couple of years ago we used to lock him up almost every other day, but he always came up with bond cash and was back on the streets in three hours. The only time we ever managed to make something stick—possession of coke—his lawyer got it thrown out because one of our guys had gone through his apartment without a warrant." Adwon stuck his thumbs under his gun belt. "They suspended Dave for three days without pay for doing it too. Is that justice?"

Sam shook her head. "Mind if I make a copy of this?"

Adwon shrugged. "Why not? You're not supposed to, but half the division did. Hell"—he wrinkled his lips—"I got a copy hanging on my living-room wall. It gets a helluva laugh."

"I can imagine." Sam went across the lobby to the copy machine and made a photocopy, then returned the original to Adwon. "Do you have Mr. Hossiason's address?" she asked.

Adwon looked over the transcript. "Funny thing," he said without his previous smile. "I did check up on that hooker who died, you know? We're supposed to do that even when the report is this nutty, and she *did* die when that dopehead said she did . . . and it *was* from a massive loss of blood."

Sam raised her eyebrows, pretending surprise. "Oh, yeah?"

"Weird," Adwon muttered. "Two or three other hookers have died in the same way this past month. Some of the guys here think maybe this is connected with that other string of killings that's been going on, but I think it's something else, you know? I think half of the murders are copycat shit. . . . Or maybe Jack the Ripper's back, huh?" He grinned again, but without his previous humor. "We've been keeping an eye on this guy, you know, 'cause you never can tell." He scribbled Hossiason's address onto a sheet of paper.

"No, you never can." Sam took the paper. "Hey, thanks."

He winked, watching her to the door.

Back in her car Sam read the address three times, knowing it was in one of the worst and most dangerous areas of Dallas. She wished she had Sheriff Bill's revolver back. Or as quiet as he'd been, even Sheriff Bill himself. After her ordeal, he'd driven her back to his home in the country and carried her into that house. His wrinkled wife, Dorothy, looking the pioneer grandma straight out of that old TV show *The Waltons*, clucked over Sam and fussed over her wounds, then dressed her in one of her old splotchy-design gowns that hung on Sam like she was a gawky scarecrow. Grandma Walton put her to bed in a quiet room and watched her, keeping a cool wet washcloth on her forehead.

When Sam's fever broke the next morning, Sheriff Bill drove her into Alpine to her motel room. Neither of them spoke, and when he let her out he only waved and drove away.

It left her more alone than she'd ever been.

In the motel Sam bought a newspaper with a headline story of the wrecked van found on a deserted road with five dead Texas A & M students inside. A sixth was missing, and it was assumed she had wandered into the hills to fall down one of the old crumbling mines there. A search party had turned up no sign of her and, due to the heat, was already being called off.

Case closed. The dead bodies of the teenagers were being returned to family members, who all lived in the Dallas–Fort Worth area, except for one named Maurice—the boy she had seen that bartender kill. He lived in Waco.

Case closed.

Sam locked her car door with a shiver. The sheriff had told her that she was going back to the big city, far away from the infestation of the ghost town, but he had lied. The hellish nightmare was pursuing her. Vampires' victims died, and then they came back.

Like Walt.

Sam revved her engine and pulled out onto the street. She wanted to meet Mike Hossiason.

5

Rick emptied the brown bottle and pushed it away. Country music blasted through the barroom. Bull's horns and branding irons decorated the walls.

It was almost ten-thirty. He had waited so long for today, and then, instead of responding to Sherry's eager love, he'd come here to drink away the humiliation of the past two years.

After his first few months in jail, he'd actually begun to enjoy those sudden, brutal encounters. He would close his eyes in those brief minutes, with another inmate in some toilet stall or in his cell, and pretend they were Sherry or some other babe from the freedom of his past.

One night he even pretended one was Kirsten, his sister.

Now it made him sick. The system had fucked him up the ass and driven him to homosexuality.

Faggot.

And now he could only think of those sweaty moments when he looked at Sherry.

"How about another beer?"

The short white waitress's tits were bulging out of her low-cut top.

"This is enough for tonight," he said, and belched, tasting the bottles he'd guzzled. "Got a woman waiting for me, you know?"

The waitress cocked her head. "So do I, honey." She let out a short cackle and waltzed on.

She stopped halfway to the next table, her dark eyes fixing on him. "You wanna join us? I'm off at ten-thirty. You can watch, or you can join us and be our big black stud, huh?" Sparkling teeth seemed to fill her mouth.

He forced himself to shake his head. "Maybe another night, okay? I already kept this woman waiting too damn long."

"Maybe another night," she repeated, moving fluidly away.

Sherry was waiting.

Rick stood with groggy determination, wishing he'd stopped at bottle number three. He scuffed across the hard plank floor passing a table of laughing men. Rick staggered onto the littered sidewalk. Above him glowed the red neon sign, CORRAL.

Sherry was waiting. Sherry had waited for two years.

She loved him.

Anger stifled his thoughts at what he'd put her through. He'd fucked up their lives for the sake of his sister when he killed that asshole ex of hers. He loved his sister, too, even though she was a bitch, but he never would have done it if he'd known the hell he'd go through—and the loneliness he'd put Sherry through. Considering his own infidelity, Rick actually hoped she'd been unfaithful and gotten herself some relaxing pleasure from time to time. *As long as it wasn't with anyone he knew.*

Rick's gait became quicker, his heart flying in the alcoholic surges of affection. He tried to skip down the block to the brownstone apartment building, staggered, and switched back to a walk.

The lobby of his building had the same peeling green wallpaper from two years before. He passed a dozen shut doors before coming to his own. "Sherry baby!" he called.

"Back here," declared a muffled voice from the darkness. "I got a surprise for you, Ricky."

Pushing the door shut behind him, Rick wiped his lips, trying to remember how soft her skin felt.

His cock sprang up through the wash of beer. "I got a surprise for you, too, honey"—he grinned, unbuckling his belt and jeans while he walked toward the dim yellowish light from their bedroom—"a *big* one!"

Giggling sounds made him move faster, and he ignored the jolt as his knee hit the divan. He stopped in the bedroom doorway and kicked out of his pants. The dim light came from the half-open closet door. The shadow of the door fell over the bed, and he could just make out a form in a yellow dress.

"I hope you're naked under that thing, Sherry doll, or I'm gonna split those panties right in *two*!"

Her arms surrounded him as he pushed up between her legs, dragging him inside her fast, and he panted at her moist, smooth tightness, spent almost as soon as he entered. "Shit," he whimpered, but pushed deeper anyway. She poked a buzzing tube of plastic under his hairy balls, and he sighed, taking the vibrator from her and stroking their meeting point. He bent down to meet her open mouth with his.

She tasted like *shit*—like she'd been eating shit for a month and hadn't brushed her teeth once since she started that new diet!

"Motherfucker!" He pulled back with surprise. "Is that the way to greet me after the shit I been through? Why didn't you brush your fucking teeth? *What the hell you been eating?"*

She giggled louder, pulling away the rumpled blankets beside her.

Rick swallowed, his eyes growing more accustomed to the dimness. He saw the shape of another woman . . . a sagging, naked tit . . . a shoulder . . . a *face*—

Sherry's face.

He recognized Kirsten's giggles now, and her deep eyes held him tight. Her thighs clamped him powerfully as she rubbed against him.

"No—"

"Your bitch tasted fine, Bubba," she whispered, imitating his low, tough talk. *"Real fine."* Kirsten opened her mouth to show red-stained teeth. She twisted the tongue he'd wrestled with moments before. "Let's see how you compare."

Frozen by her eyes, he watched her kneel on the bed, watched her bend down.

Dad's stories of coon-town vampires raced through his head in dizzy, pulsing confusion. Kirsten lowered her face to his thighs and razors sank into him. He aimed the vibrator down at Kirsten and, screaming, drove it down into Kirsten's spine. The plastic cracked in a damp explosion and the broken edges sank into shredding flesh. Her teeth clamped into him. Cold blood jetted from the ragged hole he made, covering his eyes and face.

Rick shrieked hysterically.

Her voice came calmly between slurps. "Plastic don't work, Bro. Sometimes you just *can't* replace the real thing."

But when she loosened the grip of her incisors and just sucked . . . it felt *great*.

6

The garlic he'd draped over the windows and door made Mike sick to his stomach. Despite the feeling of safety it gave him, at last he'd pulled each bulb away from the nails and put them back in the refrigerator, hoping the stench they left would be enough to drive away any vampire.

It was sure as hell enough to make *him* want to leave. More than that, it made him long for the nonchalance and attitude of the drugs. Lynette had forced him off them, promising herself as the prize for his success. But Mike had gotten more out of dealing drugs than just money. More than any of it, he loved the power of life and death; of giving his followers satisfaction and watching them beg him for more. He enjoyed the way the schoolboys looked up to him and dreamed of being in his shoes, and the way the girls offered themselves to him, promising anything he wanted.

But after he had failed to drag Lynette into his

world, he had seduced her into helping him kick his habits, even seducing himself into that belief.

But then it had blown up in his face.

He had reformed just for her. She'd helped him plan to invest the riches he'd compiled. He even gave that money to Lynette to hold in her bank account until they could figure out the best way to invest it. Though he'd avoided being caught thus far, Lynette had convinced him it was only a matter of time. She convinced him that the money was a dead giveaway and that he had to get out of it all *now.* He only agreed because she was a woman who excited and satisfied him even more than his life-style and the dope. But after showing up to work drunk just once, he'd lost his new job, and she'd given him the boot. There was no hope of ever seeing his ill-gotten gains again, and all his drug contacts were gone now.

"Drugs include booze," she shouted through the door. "It even includes your damn cigarettes, and you've never even tried to quit them!"

He didn't understand how she knew he'd been fired before he even told her—until the next day, when he went back to try and talk to her. His former boss opened her door, wearing only his undershorts under a stretched potbelly. Mike turned away without a word, suddenly knowing where his boss had been spending the long lunches, and why Lynette could never be found during her own lunch hours.

And now, to top it off, he'd found out that Ma hadn't been kidding when she said prayers over their doorstep every night and put up crosses in every room. He'd laughed at her warnings of the vampires who lurked in the graveyards and dark alleys. Like most of his friends whose folks gave the same warnings, Mike figured her speeches were an old Mexican woman's scare tactics to keep him from a life in the underworld. He blew off her eyewitness accounts by telling her she ought to write scripts for bad horror movies.

But then, Ma had never even learned to read.

He could hardly believe it even now, as he nailed boards together in the shape of crosses. When his sister, Nancy, visited him with the stupid newspaper story that came out yesterday, she told him that Ma didn't want to see him again until his mark was gone, that the only way to remove it was to kill the whore who gave it to him. Nancy crossed herself in Ma's old Catholic ritual, teary eyed, and handed him a sack full of garlic and a bottle of water.

"It's from the church," she said. *"It's holy. Pour it on the bite every night, Mama said. Pour it on the bite and pray for deliverance. Mama said you have to find the one who did this to you and destroy her by hammering a wooden stake into her heart and sealing the wound in her with this water."*

Mike wanted to laugh, but she crossed herself once more. *"I don't want to see you until you're clean, either, Mikey."* She pulled the door closed behind her.

Listening to his sister's feet on the stairway, Mike called Ma. Their short conversation was like every conversation he'd had with her lately. She criticized his life-style and told him he needed to come back to church. Then she asked him if he'd used the holy water and when he said no, she hung up on him.

The dial tone still throbbing in his mind, Mike opened the bottle slowly, sniffed the contents, and unbuckled his pants. The red, throbbing welt above his penis had been growing hotter all the time. He closed his eyes and splashed some of the water on the flesh.

Sudden agony flashed through him, and he bit his lip until it bled. But then the fire disappeared, and a soothing relief overcame the wound's itching. It even eased the persistent hunger that wouldn't leave no matter how much he ate. The wounds were still there, but the skin around them was nearly its normal color once more.

There *were* vampires. He had been fucked and sucked by one.

The best fuck of his life.

Would it be so bad to be one of them? Would it be that much different from his life as a pusher, spreading this new addiction?

But first he would have to succumb to it himself and make himself into a crazed addict.

It stopped him, because Mike remembered too well how uncontrollable his lust for drugs had been before he met Lynette. When they'd watched *Scarface,* that movie starring Al Pacino, Mike had seen *himself* as Pacino, ingesting the drugs he sold until he went crazy. Instead of exciting him as that film once had, Mike just felt sick.

Don't get high on your own supply was the drug lord's rule in that flick. Pacino had ignored it, and it made him fuck up bad.

Mike shivered, trying to imagine himself high on someone else's blood—stoned and crazy, lurching from bedroom to bedroom to sample the life from different women's bodies, driven on by a lust he couldn't control.

The idea was riveting with promised excitement, and the bite tingled, making his dick hard as he imagined dropping his face between hundreds of sexy women's thighs and sucking them until they dropped dead in the final, screaming orgasm he brought them. He could get his revenge on Lynette like that.

The images in his brain made him smile, and he felt his penis strain against his jeans as he gazed at the makeshift crosses that would imprison him.

When the knock came from the door, Mike was still staring at the crosses from his rumpled bed, reliving the ecstasy of his evening with the hooker who'd listed herself with his own name.

But he'd been on the receiving end then; was it as good and thrilling to *give* as it was to *receive*? The temptations faded with the question, because if it wasn't, it would be too late to undo it then.

He would be dead. But for now, he was filled with unending hunger that no amount of food would take away. That craving would only leave when he gorged himself with blood.

The brisk knock came again from the door.

"Mike Hossiason?" called a woman's voice.

The desire bit into his heart anew, and he dropped the bottle of holy water onto the bed beside him. It would cool his increasing hunger.

But he didn't want to cool that fire, did he?

Did he?

The door thundered. "Is anyone home?"

Mike scratched his groin until it stung, then opened the container and unzipped his jeans, dripping a few drops until the itching went away, taking his excitement with it. The fire only smoldered now, and he glanced at himself wistfully, thinking of all the women he could make his. "Just a minute," he grumbled, replacing the bottle cap, zipping his pants, and sliding from the mattress to his feet. "Who's there?"

"Mr. Hossiason, *please*, I really need to talk to you."

Mike counted the crosses nailed in the room—five —and wondered whom the strained voice belonged to.

It wasn't the whore, but . . .

His heart beat with indecision, and then he grinned. Let fate make his decision! He grimaced at the brown water-stained ceiling. "It's your decision, Big St. Daddy in the Sky." He almost hoped it was a vampire, one who was as pretty and as capable with her body as Mikie.

He opened the door hopefully, grinning when he saw the long-necked brunette in her blue chiffon skirt and aqua blouse. He laughed crazily, backing to his bed, anxious for her to follow and strip off his trousers.

"What's wrong with *you?*" Her eyes studied him, then flipped up to the cross nailed over his bed. Her hand rose to her throat, and she drew a necklace out of her shirt, holding it up in the light. *A cross.*

She had not come to suck and excite him.

"Who are *you*?" His throat was dry and crusty in the glimmer from the silvery object.

She sniffed the air with a wrinkle of her nose. "I'm Samantha Borden." She sighed, then made an uneasy smirk. "Uh . . . love your interior decorating. If you'll tell me who did it, I think I might want to use him to fix up my own place."

7

The preacher freak was back again, the silent black-haired woman he claimed as a wife at his side. Adwon pretended to be reading one of the desk reports as the tall man put two big hands in the middle of the precinct desk.

"Ahem."

Adwon didn't look up, wishing he could ignore these weirdos until the end of his shift half an hour on.

"Officer?"

The preacher had been in last night too. He and the wiry woman had started saying some off-the-wall shit about the inexplicable rash of murders, and as Adwon had listened and watched, he hadn't been able to stop the possible scenarios that began forming in his brain. The whiskery, hard-faced man looked more like a disguised combat soldier than the minister he claimed to be. He wore Rambo's face, and Jay had found himself guessing that his unpressed suit coat hid a closetful of psychopathic weapons.

"Sir?" The man spoke louder, his voice tight.

Both the man and the woman were thin and pale—
tired looking. As though they were carrying a burden
far too large for them, even together.

A burden of guilt?

"Listen, Officer, I really think you should listen to
what we—"

"We appreciate the concern, Reverend," Adwon
said gruffly. "But I told you last night that we can deal
with this situation without your help."

"But you're *not* dealing with it," the woman said.
"You don't know how to."

"Emily." The man raised a hand. "You don't even
understand what you're up against," the man said to
Adwon. "You're *not* dealing with a normal murderer
here. There may be more than one of these things, and
if you people don't start keeping watch over every
graveyard in town, you're going to have a bloodbath
that would make Charlie Manson blush in shame. I
don't know if I can find you proof of what I know, but
I'm planning to go down to Woodlawn right now, and
if you're smarter than you look, you'll get on the radio
and call some cars out to meet us. Otherwise, you may
be reading about more than one murder in the morning papers."

Adwon felt the threat in that man's voice. "Well, sir,
I think the best thing for you and your wife is to go
back home. We're doing everything we can, and I
think that our experience counts a little further than
your theories." He felt his chubby face stretch midway
between uneasy laughter and hostility. "Just go back
home and let us do our job, okay?"

The woman dragged the man back angrily. "Come
on, Warren. You were right. They won't even *listen.*"

"Right," Adwon agreed more mildly. "Just go on home and get some—"

"We're going to the cemetery," the man whispered.

"Come on," urged the woman. She tugged him again, and they walked together to the front door.

For five long minutes Adwon couldn't think of anything but the man's thinly veiled threat. Though his gaze had been gentle at first, it had grown hard. Adwon found himself guessing that the freak had killed before, and might easily do so again. He looked up at the wall clock with clenched teeth.

Explanations would take too long, and as he thought of his hope to be promoted to the detective division, he made his decision. His shift was over in another half hour, anyhow, and if he was wrong, his promotion would be no farther away than it was now, and he would go home to drink a cold beer.

But if he was right . . .

8

 The strange stink of the room irritated Sam, but she kept herself from mentioning it as she sat on the chair across from the handsome, equally peculiar man on the bed. Mike Hossiason avoided her eyes, his fingers straying constantly to his crotch, scratching incessantly. But politely, she said nothing about that either. His skin was a warm brown, the coarse hair too long for his skinny face, and his nose was prominent between his muted brown eyes. His forehead shone with sweat. The room was warm, the heat moderated only by a small 110 window-unit without its plastic air direction front. The meager furnishings were only the chair she sat in, an old, noisy refrigerator and range, the bed, and a tall, unpainted chest with two of its six drawers unaccounted for. Stray underwear, socks, and other clothing carpeted the filthy, otherwise bare floor. A rat trap baited with moldy cheese waited in a corner.

The walls were bare except for the crosses made of floor molding.

"You told the police you saw a vampire," Sam said, after introducing herself as an immigration officer. She was still edgy from the way Mike Hossiason had first looked at her. She'd left the door to the hall open slightly for that reason, disliking the warmth that came in but reassured by the ready escape.

Mike shook his head. "I told them I was *bitten* by one." He touched the copper button at his waist with a sudden, crooked grin. "Wanna see it?"

"I believe you," she replied.

"Okay, so you guys in immigration believe me even if the cops don't. You going to try to get that hooker deported or something?"

Sam sighed. "I said *I* believe you. I didn't say a thing about anyone else. I've seen vampires myself, and I knew they were coming here. I just didn't think anything would happen this fast."

He leaned forward and looked at her with seriousness. "What do you mean, coming here? They've been here all along. My ma—*everyone's* folks—told us they were here. I just didn't believe 'cause I never saw one." He dug a pack of Camels from under the pillow. "Want one?"

"I don't smoke."

He lit up anyway. "Ya gotta die from something. So what gives? What do *you* want?"

"I don't know. I just feel so alone because I can't talk to anyone about what happened to me. I saw a vampire too. I saw more than one, and I knew they would turn up here. I just wanted—needed—to talk to someone who wouldn't laugh or tell me I was crazy."

A minute passed in the blast of the air conditioner,

then Mike stood up and walked to the refrigerator.
"How about something to drink? The Health Department turned off my water 'cause of the rusty pipes, but
I got Coors and Michelob." He pulled out a can of
each.

"Okay," she answered finally, thirsty in spite of her
reluctance for anything more potent than soda pop.
"Either one."

He put a cold can in her palm and sat opposite her.
"What happened to you, then?"

She took a slow sip of beer, making a face. "I think
I found out where these things are coming from.
There've been a lot of murders recently throughout
Texas, but the police have been keeping most of the
details under wraps—like the fact that almost every
one of the victims died of enormous blood loss. Sometimes the killers do things to disguise it, like cremating
the corpses, but careful examinations can show
whether or not even a burned body had blood in it. I
went down to the border to check out some ideas, and
I found a ghost town full of *real* vampires." Sam
paused, then slurped an unladylike mouthful of beer,
steeling herself for his laughter.

Mike didn't speak for a long moment, but his eyes
remained narrowed on hers. He gulped as though he
were trying to get down a big mouthful of food. "I—I
guess I'm not surprised. I was driving down a street
not far from here the other day." Mike whispered,
bending toward her. "My girlfriend had kicked me out
of her place, see, and I didn't have a dime. I was feeling really shitty. . . ." He took the cigarette out of his
mouth and flipped the ashes onto the floor.

Sam listened.

* * *

"At least you didn't get bitten," Mike said when they'd both finished an hour later. She had told him everything in wild relief. She even told him about Walt, and what he'd done to her.

The flood of emotion that passed between them was something Sam had experienced only once before. The other time was a year after her brother was killed in the war, when a buddy from his platoon came to their home and sat and talked to Mom and Dad about Mark for hours, sharing Mark's life with them. Though everyone thought Sam in bed, she had crawled into the hallway behind the clothes hamper and listened. She cried hard that night, dreaming of her brother and his friend watching everyone around them in those far-off jungles dying. The next morning, Mother showed her Mark's drawings the man had brought and her eyes filled with tears again.

Sam drank from her third beer. Mike had shared his story, too, telling her how he'd given everything up for that woman who'd discarded him like a sack of trash, and the lonely despair that had driven him into the arms of the prostitute. Time became meaningless once they began, and she felt almost comfortable with this kindred spirit.

At least you didn't get bitten.

"What," she whispered, "what was it really like?"

Mike dropped back down onto the sheets. "Really . . . it was great. It felt better than anything I've ever felt. I never wanted it to stop. But after she left, and I was so damn weak I couldn't do anything but just breathe, it started to hurt. It made me sting and it makes me hungry. I can eat two Big Macs and I'm still hungry. And I dream about sucking blood. I even tried it. I cut my thumb with a knife and tasted my own blood, and I can guarantee it was fine. I thought about cutting my wrists and guzzling myself until I got weak and just died, but . . . I'm too scared to do *that*."

Sam touched the cross dangling at her throat. The explicit sexual feelings the vampire had created in him recalled those desires Walt had reawakened in her, and Mike's detailed description had made her body as hot as her blushing face. He was attractive, though street educated and brusque, and the way he grinned at her told her without question that he found her as attractive.

"I thought, what if"—Mike shuddered—"what if it doesn't taste so good and feel so good after you're *dead*, huh? I mean, I used to down so many drugs that I didn't even enjoy them. I just kept doing it because I got the jitters when I didn't. Cold turkey is hell, but after it's over, and you see how you were before, you know that was hell too. I mean, imagine just eating the same damn thing for breakfast, lunch, and dinner every day, forever and ever—*not even eating, 'cause it's a liquid diet!*

Sam nodded. "And they stink too. Walt had really shitty breath."

"It's too damn scary. I want it really bad, but then, I think about it, and it just freaks me out." He touched his fingers together. "It's getting worse."

"What do you mean?"

"My stomach growls all the time, and all I can think of are all the babes like you out there, Samantha. All you babes with long legs and tight pussies just waiting for my teeth—"

"Mike!" Sam glanced at the open door.

Mike sat up, picking up a clear bottle from the bed. Without warning he unzipped his jeans and pulled them wide, exposing himself. Sam didn't turn away, not believing he was really doing this right in front of her. He opened the bottle and poured out a thin stream. She started to stand. The water touched him and turned to steam.

"It's *holy* water." Mike snickered with a red-faced grimace, closing the bottle cap and his pants. "Almost enough to turn you into a believer, isn't it?"

Slowly, Sam became conscious of her grip on her necklace and released it, sitting back down. "What does it do?"

"It makes it better for a couple of hours. It hurts like shit, and then all those thoughts go away for a while—the pain and hunger go away. But it doesn't last long. My sister told me I had to go find the bitch that did it to me, kill her with a piece of plywood, and then pour this stuff on her to be free. Sounds like a crock, doesn't it?"

"Not to me." She continued to gaze at the bottle he'd dropped on the mattress. "Uh . . . are you going to do it?"

"Maybe," Mike finally replied. "Maybe if I get drunk enough, I'll try. The problem is, right now, I know that if I do see her, I *won't*. I'll just want her to suck me again like before, and I think that this time, she won't stop. *And I know I won't want her to stop.*" He snapped his fingers. "And that'll be that. I haven't exactly had a helluva lot to look forward to since my girl dumped me and I lost my job. Nothing but bills and sober, lonely nights."

"I . . ." Sam gripped her knees. "I could help you."

"Why?"

She touched the hanging cross again, finding its reproductions on his walls. "Because I don't want them *here.* I don't want people to turn into those things. It's hard enough to sleep at night knowing that they're anywhere at all—"

"Oh, yeah?" Mike stood. "So you really *are* a first-class world-saver, huh?"

She scooted back on the seat as he approached, passed her, and shut the front door, then walked behind her. Her hand did not leave the silver cross. "Maybe." She jerked when his hand touched her shoulder. He squeezed. Then she relaxed, because it felt good and reassuring, and she felt the sympathy for which she'd been so desperate. A tear seeped from her eye and she wrapped her hand around his, holding him tight.

"Well, why don't you start with me, then, babe, and give me something to live for, huh? Maybe if I got you to think about it'll help me stop thinking about this other shit . . . and wanting to give in to it." His hand dropped down to her upper arm and he pulled her to her feet, then pulled her closer until they were facing each other. He cocked his head to the side and brushed a length of her hair from her forehead. "Give me a purpose, huh? 'Cause I don't really care if the whole world turns into vampires right now or not. I can't see a helluva big difference. They *want* me, and no one I care about seems to feel that way. Maybe if I cared about someone and had someone who cared about me back, it would give me something to live for. Want another beer?"

She looked his husky body up and down more carelessly, liking the way he accepted her despite the nervous turn in this conversation. She tossed her head at his offer of another drink, knowing she was already drunk, and already horny. She'd been horny since the day Walt's wife had found them. "I didn't come all the way to this side of town just to get laid," she said stiffly. "I wanted to find out what happened to you."

"Oh, yeah? Well, I went to that blond hooker just to get *laid*, and instead I found out about vampires. Now even my family won't come near me."

Sam felt his impelling eyes stroking her, and she felt the strange companionship they'd begun urging her to release all of the tensions she'd been forced to hold back. She tried to convince herself that she was thinking like this only because she wanted to help him. She couldn't believe that she was even considering giving in to him. "How . . . do I know you haven't got AIDS or something?" she whispered.

Mike giggled, his eyes smiling for the first time since she'd seen him. "You're worried about that? Hey, the only thing I'm infected with you already know about," he said. "And I promise not to bite you very hard. I won't even suck your blood." He took her hand and walked her to the bed, picked up the holy water and gave it to her, then began unbuttoning his shirt. "If I try, just pour that stuff on me, right?"

Sam sat and watched him strip. "I don't believe this. Shit, I *am* drunk!"

He held out his hands and she touched them, feeling an electric surge. His palms slid over hers, flooding her thighs with sudden warmth. When Mike leaned down and fastened his lips to hers, she opened her mouth, tasting the bitter flavor of beer and tobacco, but not the decayed, sour pork flavor of meat gone bad. His hand lifted her skirt and rubbed through her panties.

She started to push him away but stopped because she would only be denying *herself* too. When his warm touch made her sigh, she replied by relaxing, then circled her hand around him, feeling her power in the way she made him shiver . . . wanting him, and admitting it to herself without apology.

"I want to fuck you, Samantha. Just *fuck* you. That's all. I get off just fine on that."

Smiling with her own anxiousness, she eased herself back on the stale sheets, gazing at the wood crosses he'd made as his fingers found her skirt's zipper and loosened it, then pulled the material down her legs. "I . . . think I . . . want to fuck you, too, Mike," she whispered, savoring the confused, mounting excitement as he slipped down her hose and panties, then pushed his bare legs between hers until their sexes barely connected, teasing each other. "I *do* want you. I get off just fine that way too."

His hands worked with her blouse buttons, taking them apart, dragging out the anticipation of their impending union. Lifting her up, he helped her take it off and then unhooked the front clasp on her bra, letting it fall on either side of her as he ducked down and ran his smooth tongue around her nipples with an excited pant . . . drooling.

But then he was in, and they both tried to slow down, their tongues furious in another struggle. He pushed her into the middle of the bed, and her legs locked around him, pulling him inside.

There was no love involved because they were *fucking,* purely and simply, and not trying to impress each other with ability. Sam only wanted to quench the burning fire Walt had begun so long ago and never put out.

And that fire was burning hot and bright now as this man, Mike, fanned it into a blazing inferno. She tried to dismiss any emotional association with what they were doing.

They fucked.

9

MaryAnn laughed. She scanned the half-moon tombstones surrounding her with an eager awe. She stood before one in particular. MARYANN GIMBLE, it said, with her date of birth and date of death neatly beneath her name.

But she wasn't exactly dead.

And now, she would never have to grow up!

Feeling her smooth, naked flesh, MaryAnn giggled louder, then pumped her feet up and down on the grass beside her grave, feeling the endless power of her muscles. Her red hair bounced like she'd always wanted it to; when she looked down at her beautifully formed body, she knew she could even change the way she appeared, becoming exactly as she thought of herself. She felt the new rules of this life-style, liking them immensely. She could make her body toned and voluptuous without ever exerting herself physically—without having to work through Jane Fonda's tedious exercises.

It was all in her mind . . . and in the minds of her beholders.

It was *great*!

"You really fucked up, Maury. We *all* could have been Toys-R-Us kids." She licked her lips, feeling the sharp new teeth. Her other life was obscure behind a thick fog, but she could still remember what had happened. Maury had tried to protect her and Tammy, and he'd died. She wanted to feel sad that he was gone and she'd never feel his massive length again, but she didn't. After all, there were a million men just like him, and now she could have any of them without the irritation of love's little games. She didn't need to give anymore.

Only take.

MaryAnn was hungry.

Hungry?

She walked across the manicured, gently sloping lawn, gazing at the headstones and ground plaques with a leisurely interest. She wondered if any of the others were buried here. Without Maury she'd be the odd kid out, of course, but she was sure she could find a replacement for him. That tall, strange man back in the ghost town had promised her so much, showing her the beauty and excitement that lay beyond death.

She *had* died.

But she wasn't dead. Not hardly.

But she *was* naked.

One of the nicest things about her new existence was that she felt everything acutely, like the soft grass under her heels. But those sensations were only distractions, neither hurting nor bringing pleasure. Her real feelings were deep inside her.

Hungry.

That man had put his freezing lips around her and sucked blood, making her come so many times, she'd lost track of everything else. Her stomach had tightened in the unexpected ecstasy that was everything she ever wanted, bringing her more orgasms in those short minutes than she'd known in her entire life.

And he never even *entered* her.

MaryAnn tittered, stretching her thoughts to her new powers. She thought of who she might share her new secrets with—all the boys who had wanted her and begged her to go out with them. When she went to them now, they would welcome her with open arms.

But first she needed some clothing so she could find them without attracting attention. She knew from what that man had whispered to her as he sucked her that it was very important that she *not* do that.

Clothes. She imagined herself in high heels and a long pink opaque gown with nothing underneath. A low-cut gown to show off her bulging breasts, slit candidly up the side so that it would flash an onlooker if she took a long enough stride.

"All right!" she squealed as the dainty fabric suddenly formed around her, shaping like her body had inside her imagination. She walked nimbly in the heels like never before.

Who first?

MaryAnn thought carefully of all those boys who'd called her on the phone, lusting for her body and begging her to give them a chance for just one evening. It made her giggle, trying to pick out the one she might enjoy surprising most.

"Kind of late for a walk, isn't it, miss?" asked a deep voice from the clump of trees beside her.

She stopped, startled when she realized she was not

afraid. A face was visible in the shadows. A lanky, unshaven man stepped forward and brushed a leaf off his dark suit-coat. The hunger grew stronger inside her, and she smelled something strange, something that made her lick her lips and caused her sharp new teeth to ache. She wanted to sink them into something, as a baby instinctively gnaws a teething ring.

The man stepped closer and the tantalizing odor became stronger. It was *him.* She shivered with excitement and tried to keep her steps toward him slow.

"Did you hear me?" he asked sharply.

She tried to reply, but her tongue was darting too frantically in her mouth to obey. She started to run toward him, not even taking a second to be amazed as her high heels didn't make her slip.

"Hold it!" shouted another distant voice from the raised slope to her back.

But she was hungry, and *nothing* could stop her!

The man in front of her stood tautly, bringing up something from under his coat. Another something flashed brightly in his hand.

"This is the police!" hollered that distant call again. "Both of you, *hold it*!"

MaryAnn did try to stop then, but not because of the command. The wild senses in her mind lost the scent of blood as the man held up a strangely frightening metal cross. He pointed a sharp stake at her onrushing body.

She screamed.

A loud crack exploded from behind her, and MaryAnn squealed, throwing herself into a headstone. She felt no pain, but it jarred her. The man with the cross and stake crumpled soundlessly to the ground. Blood spurted from a hole in his forehead, tingling her nostrils again with the smell she craved, and in an instant she dived toward him.

"Oh my God! *Warren*!" shrieked a new voice—a woman's—from a distant scatter of trees on the right. MaryAnn's eyes darted back and forth. The woman came toward her, holding up another fearsome cross. The blood scent was so strong. But at last MaryAnn lurched to her feet, zigzagging mindlessly through the slapping bushes.

"You bastard!" the woman screamed, but Mary-Ann didn't look back. Instead, she enjoyed the roller-coaster speed of her pace and slammed into a shoulder-high stone wall. She caught its rough top with her fingers, pulled herself over with ease, and dropped down onto a sidewalk facing a lonely street. In the distance MaryAnn heard traffic and saw the blazing city lights. She recognized the Dallas skyline.

Forgetting the meal she'd been driven from, Mary-Ann licked her lips again, getting her bearings and remembering the boys she knew who lived here, boys from high school. "Girls just wanna have f-un," she sang, "Girls just wanna have *fun*!"

10

"Where the hell are we?" asked Sam, turning the wheel of her car. Mike was humming the theme song from the old TV show *Combat*. She wished they hadn't done what they'd done. The moment they'd become still, she felt embarrassed, as if they'd only engaged in mutual masturbation, using each other the way Walt had once used her. She dressed quickly because she'd known that fear was true. On top of the self-serving guilt, their mutual therapy had wasted her in exhaustion, and her sunburn stung like hell.

Mike stopped his attempt to imitate a dozen trumpets and lifted the long piece of jagged wood he'd pulled up in the apartment. "We're deep in the evil heart of the real Dallas, Texas. If JFK had been shot here, no one would have been surprised." He peered out the window at the congregations of teenagers and dopeheads, the parking lots that resembled dumps, the short-skirted women that clustered on street corners.

"Lots of juicy snatch out here, but not ours. Keep driving, though. This is her area. She may have a customer right now."

Sam flinched at his vulgar term *snatch* and wondered if that was how he saw her. But then, after his ease at getting her into his bed, maybe she deserved that. He had been just as easy, though, and she guessed that earned him the title *cock*. That made her feel a little better. "Lots of juicy cock too."

"Oh, yeah?"

"The problem with men is that we girls have no idea of what we're in for until it's too late. You keep the merchandise too covered up."

Mike turned back to her. "Is that an expression of dissatisfaction?"

"No," she answered honestly, feeling a little strange to be talking about their sudden coupling. "No," she said again.

"Good. Because I loved it, Samantha. I was hoping we might even do it again, sometime."

"Maybe," she said, trying to get her mind off the guilty pleasure. "But let's take care of this, first, okay?"

"Slow down," he told her three blocks later. He pointed at a lone woman leaning against the front of a parked station wagon. She wore tight jeans cutoffs and a button-down top open high above her navel. Mike gulped. She trailed a finger down her bare tummy.

Her teeth almost glittered.

Sam tightened her knuckles on the steering wheel and looked at the woman's icy blue eyes as the car rolled near.

"That's *her*." Mike's voice shook. "Get over to the curb, okay?"

Sam pulled up at the curb, and Mike rolled down the window. "Hey," he called out. "Don't I know you?"

The slender woman pushed away from the wagon and crossed her arms. "Whatcha' want?"

"Some *fun.* Me and my babe are bored shitless. Been checking out the other girls back the way but they ain't going for a threesome. Seems like I remember a real good time with you way back—can you get into it? We don't have a lot of money, but hell, it's late and there's not a bunch of people out tonight."

Bending, the blond woman met Sam's stare and then shrugged. "You guys got a place to go?"

"Just the place." Mike unlocked the back door, and she got in. He put the sharp stake between his legs.

"Hey, Mike," Sam breathed.

"Let's go," the whore said.

"Let's go," repeated Mike, touching Sam's thigh as though to reassure her. It didn't. In the rearview mirror she saw no one. Sam made a U-turn and started back to Mike's place.

"What are you guys into?" the voice from the backseat asked. "Do both of you like to suck twat or what?"

Sam glanced at Mike uneasily, saw him staring behind them and rubbing the splintery wood. Her heart thudded. Suddenly she felt unsure of him. She wondered if he *had* been overcome by that bloodlust and was using her to meet his desires—*planned on making her his first conquest with this sleazy hooker's help!*

Her necklace had helped her before. But what were the rules here? Would it hurt him if he was an atheist?

"I'll suck any babe's twat," Mike said. "And this

babe, Samantha, will suck anything that moves. She's my Kirby, but she don't clean floors worth shit."

The hooker's clothing rustled. "Yeah? Well, why don't you take the wheel, Ace, and let me give her a test drive. I promise I'll save some for you too."

Dead silence. Sam stared into the mirror that showed nothing but her backseat, feeling her uneasy fear grow.

"Uh . . . I don't know if I could handle that." Mike forced his words. "Shit, I might have a fucking wreck."

"Stop the car."

Sam's jittery leg moved and her foot touched the brake pedal unwillingly. "Mike." She gasped.

"Stop the car, Samantha." Mike sighed.

"You—"

He shot her a nervous wink.

The car stopped in the middle of a quiet street, between a dark concrete-block warehouse and a vacant lot filled with discarded tires, pipes, and old lumber. Sam turned her neck and met the blond woman's vivid eyes. She saw herself lying beneath the woman, gnawing her sex feverishly as the woman dropped her face down to Sam's crotch.

She shut her eyes. The very thought made her sick and want to retch.

"It's all *real*," the soft voice taunted her. "What you see is what you'll get, and so much more. I have a thousand lives locked up inside me, and they can be yours too. *Both of yours.* Your boyfriend knows because he's already part of it, honey, and now you can be *in* me with him. I have hundreds of souls locked in my heart. When I know your secrets, I can make them real. And he's told me *yours*."

Sam turned angrily to Mike, and saw that he had brought the piece of wood up to the edge of the seat back.

"Get back there." He chuckled. "I'll watch you two for a minute, and then I'll bring us home where we can do some real bed-bouncing."

"Come on," the woman whispered, unbuttoning her cutoffs and pushing them down her legs.

Sam's throat was tight. She pulled up on the door's creaking handle. She wanted to run.

"Come on, Samantha, just like we talked about before, huh? I won't be jealous, 'cause pretty quick, I'm gonna stick her real hard, myself."

The edge in his voice was the only thing that kept her from running. She only hoped that the wood he stroked faster and faster was what he would stick the woman with. Sam climbed out of the car and opened the back door.

"Shut that damn door!" Mike shrieked. He brought the wood up over the seat and rammed it hard into the blond's shoulder. "Don't let her get away!" Sam screamed with surprise and jumped back at the cold, wet spray of blood, stumbling back as the whore dived toward the car's open door and howled.

"Shit!" Mike was shouting. *"Shit! Shit!"*

The back of Sam's skull hit the street with a loud crack, splitting her brain with a thousand red flashes. The gleaming teeth above her separated and the dark mouth grew.

"Get up! *Get up! I can't hold—*"

In the center of the shining pulses that marred her vision, she saw the vampire's taut face, spit dripping from her mouth. Mike still had a hold of the wood protruding from between her shoulder blades. Blood shot out from the wound.

"I *can't*—"

The woman's eyes flared bright and she drove herself backward, grabbing Mike's fingers with her teeth and biting down with a snap.

He screamed.

"*No*—" Sam wheezed, pushing up from the street. She got to her knees and grabbed for her necklace. The streetlights shone off it, sending a wild reflection through the car interior. She flashed it onto the monster's cheek.

The vampire forced the wood out of her body and lunged out the door straight into Sam, knocking her back onto the pavement. As the figure towered above her, Sam fumbled inside her shirt for the cross. The woman sank to her knees over Sam's face, pushing her bare ass against Sam's nose. Sam's stomach flopped at the stench of death. She couldn't breathe. The woman clutched Sam's knees and drove her head down under Sam's skirt. Sharp canines stabbed through her damp cotton panties and grazed her skin. "*N-no!*" Sam wailed. She bit into the cold skin smothering her.

The vampire laughed wildly. "Suck my life, little bitch—*suck me hard!*"

Sour blood spurted onto Sam's face. She spat, forcing her knees up into the attacking head, and rolled away. The blond's head cracked the cement now, and Sam rolled again until she was under the car. A siren howled in the distance.

"You will both live inside me!" growled the suddenly hideous voice. "*You will both die inside me!*"

"Mike!" Sam yelled, her eyes darting over the hot undercarriage. "Mike—*kill her!*"

A minute passed as the siren grew louder.

"S-Samantha?"

She clutched her necklace, the muffler's heat searing her forehead. The siren lowered in tone and stopped almost on top of her.

"What the hell's going on here!" shouted a deep voice. Feet stopped beside the car. "Shit, call an ambulance. *Look at this poor bastard!*"

Sam scooted to the edge of the car body. "Mike?"

"Someone's under there."

Seconds later Sam was looking at a gun muzzle and the stern face behind it. *"Help me."* She stretched out a hand.

"Who is it?"

A bright light blinded her. "It's a *lady*. Whoever jumped these two must've pulled her out of the car." The light shifted down her body. "You okay?"

He pulled her out from beneath the car. Two other policemen stood nearby.

"Don't move, miss," one of them drawled. "We got an ambulance on the way. Just lie steady and take deep breaths."

Sam didn't see a sign of the woman who had attacked her. "Did . . . you get her?"

"We got two more cars circling the area—just breathe slow and deep, okay?"

"What—what about . . . Mike?"

The tallest cop looked up, and she followed his gaze to the open driver's door.

"Mike?" She pushed herself up on an elbow, gasping at the dizzy pounding in her skull.

"He's alive. Just be still, ma'am. Okay? Make our jobs easy. Things are crazy enough already, tonight.

This place is going nuts. We found two dead niggers. . . ."

Sam lay back and shut her eyes as the voice evaporated in the noise of another siren. Her fingers rubbed the cross like a good-luck charm.

11

 Jay Adwon sat in the plastic chair and tried not to move, because every time he did, the chair squeaked and made him blush.

"We'll have to suspend you, Adwon," the shiny-headed sergeant said dismally. "You know that every time you pull your gun you're up against it, and you not only pulled it, you *used* it!"

Adwon cringed and blushed as the chair creaked loud again. "I told you, that guy was trying to hurt the girl with that pole he was carrying." He pointed at the sharpened stick on the sergeant's desk. "He was going to *kill* her!"

"I think you're exactly right," the sergeant said, "and I know that's the reason you cut out of here early after they left. I overheard you talking to them before. You thought maybe he and that girl were the psychos killing people and draining out their blood, right?"

"He was *weird*," Adwon muttered, looking up at his

award certificates on the wall. "He and that woman came in here asking about those hookers, and it just stuck in my craw. He asked us what we were doing to prevent any more deaths, and he laughed when I told him. It pissed me off."

"And you figured he had something to do with it?"

"I fucking know he did. Look at that shit he was carrying, would you? And then that damn woman with him beat the shit out of me when I tried to calm her down. I had to cuff her to that tree just to keep myself from being killed. She kept yelling about *vampires*!"

The sergeant nodded. "We had to send her on to the hospital after we tranquilized her. But the point is, Adwon, you killed a man, whether he's nutty or not, and that girl you said he attacked is nowhere to be found. It's not like you happened on a rape being committed by some wiped-out freak in these slums. You followed those people to Woodlawn Cemetery, and you didn't even tell anyone what you were doing. Shit," he grumbled, "in my book that makes you as crazy as him."

The chair squeaked again, and Adwon hung his head. "Goddammit, how the hell was I to know he really *was* a fucking preacher? What the hell kind of preacher goes into boneyards in the middle of the night to hunt down vampires, huh?"

"I don't know. But the woman that you handcuffed really is his wife, and he was here as a guest of one of the local churches. If that other girl you say he was attacking doesn't show up, I think you're in for a shitload of trouble, my man . . . not to mention the whole department. Reporters are going to come down on us like flies on shit, and if your mysterious victim doesn't turn up quick, I'm going to save the department's ass, not *yours*."

First it had been Mike Hossiason. Then that sunburned woman from immigration. Only two hours after she'd left, the preacher had started going on about vampires. He still felt the threat in that tall minister's voice.

"What are you waiting for?" the sergeant barked. "If you've filled out your report, you're dismissed without pay until further notice."

"I f-filled it out," Adwon stuttered, "but he was saying *crazy* things. If I hadn't of left and gone after those two, there would have been another murder . . . *and that's just what he said.*"

"That's what he said, huh?" The sergeant grabbed Adwon's arm. "Go home, and you better pray like hell we find that girl."

Adwon shook his head. "He said he was after *vampires.*"

A long moment passed, then the sergeant pushed him at the door.

12

The fuzziness of her memory was annoying MaryAnn now. The treetops shivered and she studied the block of two-level houses carefully, trying to remember which one belonged to that computer nerd, Steve Gutski. Out of everyone she knew, he would be the most awestruck to see her.

It would be hilarious, and when she sucked the life out of him and left him motionless for his mother to find, it would be even funnier.

Don't be a glutton. The deep words seemed to form in her mind. *Just sip a little here and a little there. Keep a low profile. Calling attention to yourself will call attention to us all. The preacher told us that years ago. Restrain your hunger for now and feast lightly. It will spread our power much faster. If even one or two guess what they're dealing with, they can do us much damage. Out here, no one cares or even knows when a wetback turns up missing or dies, but in the cities . . .*

In the city. The vampire man was cautious and had

stayed in the desert, taking only the refuse of mankind. The vampire *geezer* warned against filling the world with Undead, because it would create a blood shortage.

MaryAnn snorted, not giving a damn about the future. She was hungry now, and she wanted a taste of blood *now*.

More than a taste.

This was her first time, just like that shitty fuck in the back of Mr. Keener's truck ten years ago, when he'd brought her home from baby-sitting his dirty-diapered son. That had been before she'd known all the wonderful things a man could do for her. She'd obeyed his every command and brought him far more pleasure than he'd given her, and had almost sworn off sex for the rest of her life because of it.

Restrain your hunger.

"Why should I?" MaryAnn whined from behind the bushes. "Especially not my first time."

Thinking of the way Mr. Keener had introduced her to sex, teaching her how to please him and only returning pleasure when it could bring him more, made her wonder if the vampire man who'd changed her was the same. Perhaps the joys he'd given her were only the tip of the iceberg. Like Mr. Keener he had fucked her through his bite. Since she hadn't been able to bite him back, she had no idea of the pleasure he obviously felt in the act.

But now she would. Giggling, she imagined Steve's surprise when she stripped him and gave him the thrill she knew he had wet dreams over. She would take him in her mouth like those women in the ghost town had done to Jerry and Scott, and drive her teeth into his hardness as he spasmed and soaked her throat with his juices. She hoped he was still completely a virgin, so she could give him the first and last fuck of his life.

In front of the corner house she recognized the beat-up VW Steve had souped up in his high school efforts to be "cool."

She marched from the bushes to the house. A ham radio antenna was attached to one window, so she knew it was his. She pulled a few roses from the bush under the window. She could sense him inside, and mashed them into a bouquet. Their thorns didn't even sting.

Her teeth were tingling again, and urgently. She ran her long fingernails over the window screen with a metallic scrape, then stood back and posed with a hand on her hip.

His acne-scarred face appeared as he pulled back the curtain. His eyes were wide and disbelieving, and the window frame creaked as he strained to pull it up. He pressed his nose into the wire mesh speechlessly.

She held out the roses. "Hi, Steve," she purred. "Wanna fuck?"

He pushed out the screen until it dropped at her feet and held out his hands. He grunted as he hauled her in. By the time her feet touched his floor, he was shoving down his pajama bottoms and kicking them aside. He trembled as she knelt before his tiny offering.

But MaryAnn didn't laugh. For the first time in her existence she found herself agreeing with the old axiom that the importance of a man was what was inside him.

Steve's blood tasted good.

13

Detective Lieutenant Golan picked through the stack of paper on his desk. He had gone to sleep cheerfully last night, with only the unexplained murders of three prostitutes—maybe or maybe not related to the recent rash of unsolved murders—hanging over his head. He'd awakened to a loud, ringing phone at five this morning. In one grisly night his job had become almost as violent a nightmare as the days back in 'Nam. His only consolation was the rest that he'd gotten.

Not to forget the cherished act of intense intercourse with Tonia. After twenty years of faithful marriage—at least on *his* part, and he was pretty certain it was the same with her—it was difficult to get excited about sex when he knew he had to face a stacked desk in the morning. But last night he had been nearly as carefree as a horny teenager, and after their three youngsters went to bed, she sat down beside him and took his hand, pushing it under the folds of her robe until there was no doubt she was naked underneath it.

They made love right there on the living room floor, and it had been good, and they even whispered those stale, sweet nothings to each other, the words meaningful once more in the memory of their origin. They loved each other tenderly. It was very good, and the strength of their revitalization made Golan once again understand why he chose to remain monogamous even in a world where infidelity was encouraged. Nearly everyone he worked with responded with sad peculiar looks when he told them he wasn't interested in whores or *Playboy* magazines, but he had enough battles in life without taking on the sexual obsessions the world seemed possessed by.

Quite simply, he was satisfied in *that* way at least. He loved his wife and she loved him. They *shared* each other, and that shared strength drove away the stress and horror that was a part of his job and past.

After they climaxed together, he wondered if any of the kids had gotten up and peeked in, but it only worried him for a moment. At least it would prove to them that their parents weren't so old as they might think, and that there was room for sex in a faithful marriage too. He and Tonia left the living room, their hands clasped, and they slept naked together.

And then the damn phone rang.

Last night a woman from U.S. Immigration and a suspected drug dealer had been attacked by a maniac the dopehead claimed was a vampire. He told them he'd tried to kill her with a stake, and though the bloodstained weapon was found, there was no trace of a body. He told them the vampire—supposedly one of the three hookers who were killed—had forced him to suck *her* blood.

Golan glanced at that report and the one taken from the woman, Samantha Borden. Although she hadn't used the term *vampire,* her testimony corroborated Mike Hossiason's. The sergeant had done some digging and located a recent psychiatric evaluation on her. She'd used that term freely only a week before.

Putting those sheets down, Golan studied the report of Patrolman Jay Adwon's unauthorized activities. He'd shot a minister in Woodlawn Cemetery when that man had tried to put a stake into an unidentified woman.

It was more than enough, but not all. Back in the slums a black ex-con released from the pen only yesterday and his wife had been found in their apartment, both bodies drained of blood. And in the nicer neighborhoods on the north side a young man named Steve Gutski had been found naked on his bed the same way. A few blocks away Rhonda Black, from Gutski's high school graduating class, was discovered unconscious, her veins nearly empty. And *that* underlined the peculiarity of the disappearances of whores, winos, and druggies these past weeks. There were those in the department who connected these occurrences with other statewide killings and disappearances.

Golan snorted. He didn't miss the bums or the paperwork he had to do as they were locked up and released.

But with everything happening now, it made him wonder.

Despite the wide range of the slaughter, Golan himself guessed that somehow they were all tied together, maybe even linked to all the disappearances, and he cringed at the favors the department had used up to clamp down and keep it all quiet. It wouldn't stay that way for long, though, because ever since Watergate the press had been feeling its oats and were hard to keep cooperative.

Not to mention the victims' families. Golan stood up and stuck the sheaf of papers under his arm. There was too much to do, but the only way to get it done was to tear into it. He loaded the stack of reports into his briefcase and headed out to his car, glad that Mike Hossiason, the immigration agent, and the minister's wife had been taken to the same hospital.

A half hour later Golan knew his luck wasn't that good. Hossiason and the woman from immigration had been released, and the other woman, Emily Mac-Donald, had calmed down and reversed every accusation and statement she'd made the night before. Golan scratched his cheek as he studied her slender, emotionless face. They were sitting in an administrator's office he'd commandeered for convenience, but he didn't care for its prim, tight-assed atmosphere at all. It wasn't making the situation any better.

Emily pushed hair back from her forehead. Her eyes were bloodshot, her eyelids bright red. "We were just visiting a grave," she whispered.

"At ten P.M.?"

Emily shrugged.

"The gates were locked," Golan prodded, "and your husband was carrying a very sharp stake that Officer Adwon said he was using in a threatening manner. He said he spoke with you two earlier at the precinct station and that your husband threatened that there would be another murder in that graveyard if we didn't send out some men."

Seconds ticked by silently in the small room, and Golan leaned forward on the tidy desk. There wasn't even an ashtray.

"There *was* a murder," she replied, "because one of *your* men shot Warren."

"Adwon said your husband was trying to use that stake on a woman. What the hell was he doing with something like that if he wasn't trying to hurt someone? Adwon said you two were after . . . *vampires*."

"He's full of shit."

Golan raised an eyebrow, remembering that this woman was supposed to be a minister's wife. But then, what kind of a minister had he been? "What were you two doing out there with crosses and stakes, then? I've seen as many of those damn horror flicks as anyone. It sure looked like you *thought* you were after vampires."

"There's no such thing."

"That's not what you were saying last night."

Emily twisted her lips in a sickly smile, her words a raspy whisper. "What would you say if you saw a woman just buried rise out of the ground in a mist and take solid form, Detective? What would you say if you saw sharp teeth sparkling in her mouth, and if your own parents had been killed by teeth just like that six months before?"

There was bitterness in her face, and earnest malice in her eyes. He watched her carefully, calculating how near she was to a total breakdown. She was damn close.

"What would you say if the only man who ever treated you like a person and who really loved you got shot and murdered trying to save the world when he could have stayed home and minded his own business, and maybe have lived to a ripe old age?" She stood, shaking uncontrollably. *"How would you feel if the cop you begged help from followed you while you tried to do his fucking job and shot you in the fucking face! And goddammit—it was my fault, because Warren wanted us to take care of it ourselves, and I made him tell you bastards! I honest to God thought you would listen and help! But you dicks fucking killed him."* She pounded the desk with doubled fists.

Golan didn't let himself examine her words. He didn't want to. Instead, he pressed the intercom buzzer that would summon help, grabbed her wrist, and walked around the desk to force the trembling woman back into her chair. As she sobbed, he couldn't help but feel sorry for her. He tried not to look at her young features that were worn by hate, frustration, and a burden no one her age should be bearing.

But she was insane. Golan told himself that over and over as he kept her there. Her burdens were in her own mind. She was tormenting herself—trailing the fictions of her warped intellect.

Maybe Warren MacDonald had been insane too.

Or maybe, as in Vietnam, the world was the psychopath. He remembered all the mind-bending terrors he'd seen in his horrid, unwanted army career. Nothing had surprised him in those days. Anything had been possible then.

Anything at all.

14

 "I thought they were going to lock me up this time," Mike Hossiason muttered as he got out of the car.

Sam turned off the engine, glad that one of the policemen had driven her car to the hospital. Working for the government had its advantages. She climbed out of the car, squinting in the sun. "They *would* have if I hadn't been there, too, you know. You don't exactly have the world's finest reputation."

"I come by it dishonestly."

"I've heard." Sam smiled unwillingly.

Cars drove quickly past on the two-lane street. Even so, Sam noticed that the sidewalks were close to deserted. When two black-and-whites passed in close succession, she understood why. Though Mike's apartment was several blocks from where they'd been attacked, the murdered black couple she'd heard the police discussing had lived only two or three apartment houses away.

The passing patrol cars ignored the hookers on the corner, but the second car honked at three small Hispanic boys playing tag in front of a bar. The frontier-styled pub was housed at the near end of the long concrete building directly across the street. Its sign, CORRAL, was unlit over an old wood wagon wheel, waiting for the night. For some reason it made her think of the saloon in the ghost town.

"You want to come in?" asked Mike.

"Yeah." Sam fingered the silver cross around her neck. She was exhausted despite all the drug-induced sleep she'd gotten in the hospital. Even with that drug her mind had filled with nightmares. "Yeah . . . I want to talk to you, Mike."

Their hands came together as they walked into the apartment house. Mike entered the apartment first, then closed the door securely behind Sam, twisting the dead bolt and sighing. Sam sighed, too. Crosses surrounded them on the walls, and the smell of garlic lingered in the air.

"What do you want to talk about?" he asked. He picked up the beer she hadn't finished last night and lifted it to his lips.

Sam shivered, eyeing the rumpled bed where they'd made love. No: where they'd *fucked.* Her only emotions had been fear and the need to unleash the frustrations of these recent weeks. His emotions were no more, only aggravated by the peculiar lust of his disease.

Yes. Because he was diseased, wasn't he?

But in the routine tests the hospital had made on them both, they'd found no trace of his bizarre infection. They'd only given him a tetanus shot.

Mike lay back on the bed and dropped the can. The air conditioner was still whining tirelessly.

"What really happened to you last night, Mike?" She settled herself into the chair. As they'd loaded him into the ambulance, he'd regained consciousness and shrieked to the flat-faced cops that a vampire had attacked them. Sam calmly contradicted him, convincing them he was hysterical because a hooker had tried to rob them. The medics sedated him. He had no wounds except on his knuckles where the whore had bitten him, but blood was spattered all over his face. "How did you get all that blood on your face?"

Mike slid off the bed and opened the tattered curtain. He dropped back onto the square of light on the bed.

"Why'd you do *that*?"

"I think it helps. The light makes me feel sluggish. It has ever since that night when she bit me. I feel more in control when I'm in it."

"She bit you again last night, didn't she?"

"She—she bit my hand, but she didn't suck my blood. Not much, anyhow."

Suddenly, Sam didn't want to continue. She didn't want an answer to *any* of it! She wanted to crawl into a closet and hide, as she'd tried to hide from her childhood nightmares. Always, someone was pursuing her. In those horrible visions she had no thought of defense at all, only to get away and hide. She would sleepwalk and curl up under her bed or in the closet. She would close her eyes tight, listening to the heavy steps and breaths approaching, praying hard she wouldn't be found.

Then she would wake up.

"Did her blood get on you when you stabbed her, Mike?"

Wake up!

"No."

Wake up!

"But it was *hers*—or somebody else's she'd sucked inside her."

She closed her eyes and opened them to the sun-drenched walls. She was already awake.

Mike lifted himself on an elbow and finally looked at her. His brown face was dark. "She made me suck her blood," he whispered brokenly. "She made me suck it until I had to swallow, and she wouldn't let me puke it up. She bit herself and filled her mouth with that shit and then she kissed me and spit it inside me. I —I was choking. *I had to swallow it!* It tasted worse than anything you can ever imagine."

She remembered how she had bitten that bare flesh suffocating her. "Maybe . . . I can."

"Then I felt her inside my *own* blood," Mike contin-ued. "She was trying to swallow me from the inside. I can still feel her now, especially when I'm out of the light. The sunlight seems to deaden the effect, like when you puke after some good drinks until you're sober enough to drive home."

"You have to find her again, Mike, and *kill* her. Do you still have that holy water?"

His voice was sleepy. "I think it's in your car, Sam, but the problem is, I don't know that I really want to kill her anymore, and even if I do, I don't know if I *can*."

"Why not?"

"You never took drugs, did you?"

"I smoked grass, Mike. Everybody does that at least

once in their life . . . and I did it three or four times."

"I'm talking the *real* shit," he murmured. "Grass is bullcrap. You can get hung up on it, but not like the real thing. Think of craving a drug like food or water."

"Okay."

"Now pretend you're really hungry and thirsty, and how it would make you feel if you had to kill your own pusher."

Sam swallowed, the dryness of her throat in the ghost town coming in clear. "Yeah?"

"That's how it makes me feel when I think about killing that bitch," Mike growled. "She's got her hooks in me deep, and I know that if I don't stop her, I'm going to end up worse—a lot worse. But that's a lot farther down the road than the pain I'll have if I drop her, and goddammit, cold turkey is *hell*!" He covered his face.

Sam stood hesitantly, torn between her desire to run and her desire to help.

But if she ran, she wouldn't wake up this time, would she? No matter where she went, she would always be running, and it wouldn't end.

He groaned, raising his knees to his chest.

Sam sat beside him. When he looked up, she gave him the best smile she could and undid the top button of her blouse.

His slitted pupils hung on her movements. As she took his hand, he giggled throatily, his smile mean and thirsty and not like last night. He licked his lips.

She darted back, and held her cross out between them. Mike's face went pale and he jerked, gritting his teeth savagely.

Sam scrambled off the mattress and backed away. "Mike—"

He held his head. "I *lied* to you last night, Samantha," he panted. "I lied about how fucking you would *help* me. I just—just *wanted*. It was just too good of a line to pass up. I just wanted to *fuck* you, Sam, and I want to fuck you now, too, but this time, when I do I want to bite you and taste your blood."

Words wouldn't come. She just stared at him.

"But thank God or Whoever is running this dump" —his voice cracked—"I can't bring myself to do that yet. I can't because you cared enough about me last night to fall for my line. Goddammit, I'm not one of them yet—*I'm still a man!*"

She wanted to call him a bastard just like she'd wanted to call Walt a bastard. But as Mike began to sob, she convinced herself that it *wasn't* the same. She'd been selfish too. She laid a hand on his shoulder. "I'm going to get that bottle of water. I'll be right back."

The way his lips twisted then was horrible, but not like before. "I don't think I'm going anywhere," he said.

15

MaryAnn was hiding in the bushes across from Steve Gutski's house in the heat of the day. The man who'd made her what she was had told her the sunlight wouldn't harm her. Though the sun made her nervous, she wanted so badly to see the chaos of her handiwork that she decided to believe him. After all, he'd been around for a long time. He said he'd been a part of the Inquisition in Spain.

The problem was that at dawn's first light, every one of her special abilities became muffled. And though the clothes she'd imagined for herself still looked as good as if she'd bought them at a department store, she couldn't change them into something less conspicuous, could not glimpse the thoughts of Steve's mother and father as they'd found him and screamed. She only knew the little she could hear from this vantage point. She was very vulnerable now, just as though she were really alive.

It was like waking up Christmas morning and finding that all those presents under the tree weren't really there after all.

The failure of her new senses frustrated MaryAnn, and she watched the sun closely, praying it would drop over the horizon before she went crazy.

The last police car finally drove away from Steve's house. She'd heard them say earlier that Rhonda Black, that cunt from two grades below her in high school, had been found several blocks away, partially drained of blood.

But who had done that?

MaryAnn muffled a giggle, wondering if it had been her friends, Scott or Jerry . . . or maybe even Kathy. They had all gone to high school together, and once upon a time there had been that ugly rumor that Kathy was a dyke. Before Scott started taking her out in college, MaryAnn had been sure it was true.

Or maybe Scott had taunted Rhonda the way Mary-Ann had taunted Steve. Jerry was almost out of the running, because she was pretty certain he would go after someone who had rejected him. Rhonda wasn't attractive, and she'd probably have gone to bed with Jerry if he'd ever had the nerve to ask her.

The thoughts gave her a longing to see her friends from the past. Perhaps they could plan further and more outrageous excursions together. And she could brag about the turmoil she'd already created on her own. Death had given her a lot of things by taking away a lot of others—mostly things she didn't care about or want. But she was glad that it had left her with her pride.

Time passed, and only her anticipation eased the boredom as she waited for the sun to set.

* * *

It was dark.

Yawning out of habit though she wasn't in the least tired, MaryAnn pushed out of the bushes and imagined herself anew, in the clothing of one of the streetwise ladies of the night she'd seen on TV. A silk blouse and tight black skirt slit up her thigh showed off her figure. Gleefully, she did a little dance in her high heels, wishing she had a mirror.

But that was one of the liabilities of being *undead*. Even if she had one, she wouldn't have been able to use it. It was another old habit that would die a lot harder than she had. She had to be satisfied that she could see herself perfectly in her mind. The knowledge of her appearance tickled her then, making her wish that she had come to Steve like *this*.

The brief annoyance that she hadn't thought of this look before passed as she contemplated all the other guys out there like him. She glided into the street. Passing a dozen blocks of houses in the gray darkness, MaryAnn steered for the south side of Dallas. She smiled at the cars that slowed beside her. Men called out to her. They built the hunger inside her. Though she wanted to wait until she'd found someone she could really surprise, she knew it wouldn't be long before she gave in to one of them.

She passed through a district of new concrete office buildings and then a Skaggs store. More men whistled and called out, and she gave one of them the finger, hoping that he might stop to argue. When he didn't, she crossed the street and went on, passing frame houses that grew progressively shabbier until they disappeared.

Half a mile on, she passed the sagging movie screen

for a deserted drive-in theater. She could remember a good time in the backseat of a car there. Next door was a Dairy Queen. She tried to remember the taste, the texture, of ice cream. Slowing, she tried to recall those memories of her life more fully, but except for the knowledge that they had once been part of her, that past was gone.

MaryAnn shrugged and imagined a new kind of Dairy Queen, offering special creamy servings of frigid blood topped by whipped cream and a cherry!

Giggling to herself, she began to dance past warehouses and industrial buildings. The cars passed less frequently now. Then the frame houses sprang up again, became old stores and apartment houses. This was that raunchy, bad part of town Mother had always warned her away from. MaryAnn harbored the fantasy of turning the tables on a would-be rapist or robber that might lay his hands on her.

A police car cruised by, and as its taillights faded in the distance, she heard a trash-can crash behind her, then slow steps. She smiled, kept walking. She wanted whoever was behind her to keep coming.

He did. *They* did. MaryAnn heard the whispers come nearer, planning her surprise.

"Hey, *bitch*," a loud voice called, "one of you cunts gave me the crabs back when I was only fifteen—"

"Scott?" MaryAnn spun around, recognizing his voice. She stared into his surprised face. Jerry was beside him, his broken arm as healthy as if it had been healed by a TV evangelist. "Hi, guys." She posed in her disguise. "I was looking for you. Where's Kathy?"

Jerry sniffed, brushing back his brown hair that was perfectly combed for the first time ever. They were both dressed ruggedly in cowboy hats and jeans, western shirts bulging over thick muscles that told her they had learned as many secrets as she had. "Do I look cool or what?" Jerry thrust out his chest.

"You look like a gay John Wayne. You both look like real *Texassholes*."

Scott took a cigarette out of his shirt pocket and lit it, blowing smoke in her face. "You look like the Happy Hooker Goes to Hell."

MaryAnn raised her nose snobbishly into the air. "Smoking causes cancer, dick-breath." But she stopped herself, and began to snort and laugh, their grating, malicious glee so much heartier than their old laughter. "Which one of you guys visited Rhonda Black last night?"

Scott tapped one of his new oversized teeth. "She ain't much for looks," he drawled, "but she sure knows how to scream when she comes. I got so excited I almost couldn't stop. What have you been up to?"

"Steve Gutski," she told him.

"He's a nerd," Jerry said.

"A dead nerd." MaryAnn walked with them down the sidewalk, one on either side of her. "I sucked him real good."

"Great," muttered Jerry. Scott passed him the cigarette. "And now he's one of us, whether we want him or not."

MaryAnn shrugged. "It was worth it. He'll probably try to bite a computer. Just think of him walking around with that damn pencil saver and his pocket calculator. People will die laughing before he can ever *bite* them."

"Where's Tammy and Maury?"

"I think they're dead."

Jerry snorted. "We're *all* dead, dumbass."

She stopped and regarded them seriously, barely feeling anything for Tammy and Maury. "Really *dead,* I mean. I know Maury is." She took Scott's chilly hand and pushed it under her skirt so he could feel that she was wearing nothing underneath it. "Where's Kathy, Scott?"

He squeezed her thigh and shrugged. "She went home to Momma and Poppa. She was really weirded out. Me and Jer decided to hit the streets and the bars just like we used to talk about. Thought we'd screw around with the rednecks' heads and try out their women. Besides, Jerry hasn't had any dinner yet. He's pretty desperate."

A car cruised slowly down the block toward them. It was a police car, and the jowly cop riding shotgun aimed a spotlight on them. MaryAnn was a little surprised to see she no longer cast a shadow on the cracked sidewalk, and neither did Scott or Jerry.

"How desperate *are* you, Jerry?" murmured Mary-Ann, dropping her hands to her hem and raising the material to expose her nakedness. With that special sense that had returned with the darkness, she felt approval stir from them both.

Scott dropped his hand to hers and helped her show off. "Great idea, bitch."

Jerry trembled, dropping the cigarette, but none of them moved as the two policemen got out of the car and walked toward them, their hands on the guns.

Then all three of them moved at once.

16

Gunshots and broken yells blasted the silence of the evening, and five minutes later sirens screamed. Sam looked at Mike's dull pupils from the chair where she had dozed off. Mike crouched at the window. The air conditioner rippled his loose shirt. Sam stretched with a vague feeling of normality. She'd dozed off twice in the chair. She clasped her fingers around the bottle on her lap. It was still half full, even though she'd poured a lot of it on Mike earlier.

"What's going on?" Sam asked thickly.

"There's a lot of cops out there. Like some kind of a bust. They're all up the street."

Sam's heart leapt with hope. "Do you think—"

Mike bit his lip, his grimace frightening in the brightness spilling through the window. "I think someone else got killed."

"God," she whimpered, her heart thudding, "it's

happening so damn *fast*! They're going to be everywhere!"

Mike squinted as a spotlight flashed him through the glass, then ducked down. His fists were clenched. "What makes you think they're not everywhere already? Don't you remember what I told you about my mother? Do you think that any of this would be happening if they weren't?"

Sam went to the window and tried to make out the commotion on the street fifteen feet below. "Shit," she whispered. "We've got to find that woman who bit you and kill her, Mike, and then I want to just get the fuck *out* of here." Sam wrapped her arms around her stomach. *Yes, because staying here frightened her more than the running of her dreams.*

"I thought you were a world saver."

The running in her dreams never ended until she woke up. She reached out to take his hand. "I didn't say I wouldn't come back, Mike. But . . . I'm *scared.* We have to convince other people to help us. Then maybe we could find a way to deal with these things. Someone else might even figure it out and maybe *they'd* stop them. But I need to think. I have to call my folks and tell them to get out of here for a couple of months."

"They'll come after you if you try to leave," he whispered. "Running from these things won't do a damn bit of good."

"I know." Red and white police lights blazed through the room. The air conditioner's whine muffled the noise below.

"Samantha, I drank that slut's blood and I can feel her in me. She wants us both. She's *pissed.*"

Sam held up the holy water in the flashing light.

"Then kill her, Mike. If you know where she is, go fucking *kill* her."

He shook his head. "I think she's coming to do that to *us*."

"What?"

"I feel her really close, now, Sam. And I think—it's hard to tell—but I think I feel others all around us too."

"Others?"

Mike took a long, deep breath. "God damn. It's just like when I stopped the drugs, but worse." He took a stumbling step forward, and she backed away. "Goddammit, Sam—*help me!*"

"So you can trick me again?"

His hands shook. "No! Open the bottle so I can have a drink. I don't know if it will help, but I know if it doesn't, you're going to have to kill me, too, because I think that whore is right outside my door."

She thought of running again, and then knew she couldn't even if Mike was wrong about them following her. In those faraway nightmares, the scary unknown monster was only after *her*, but in real life they were after everyone. If she ran, she would be running from the ones who would be like sheep waiting to be slaughtered too. She twisted off the metal lid and pressed the bottleneck to his cracked lips.

Mike flinched as the water steamed on his tongue. He swallowed with a groan. It hurt him now. His hands clasped hers and he raised the bottle higher as he took another deep swallow.

"Shit!" he howled.

He collapsed, and she fought to keep hold of the container. She pulled the bottle out of his spasming fingers, keeping it upright so the precious fluid wouldn't spill. Setting it down, Sam bent cautiously to him.

Something scratched at the door.

That whore is right outside the door. They're going to come after you.

Sam stood and went toward the light switch beside the door. She slowed as she neared the door, straining to hear. Biting the inside of her cheek, she made herself stretch out and flip the overhead light on, then blinked. One of the two bulbs popped and went black. Crosses still protected the walls, and she remembered the garlic smell. She checked the refrigerator. The sliced garlic bulbs sat alone on the top shelf. She pressed the garlic into the crook of her arm and clutched the bottle in her hand, then marched back to the door like a trooper headed into cannon fire, or like the little pig in his house made of straw as the big bad wolf huffed and puffed until he blew the house down.

Her fingers touched the dead bolt.

17

Mikie passed the patrolmen gathered around the limp bodies of two of their own. The street was barricaded with sawhorses. She walked alone, stung by the humiliation that that john and his stupid girlfriend had tried to destroy her. The man was already part of her, but like a cancer, he'd betrayed her and trapped her, spilling the blood she so carefully collected from others before it had completely combined with her. The souls were still *hers,* but the vitality they had brought was diminished.

But now that betraying bastard and that bitch would replenish her with their own lives. The man was wasted and barely worth having, but that girl—

". . . both dead, just like those niggers we found down the street last night. The medic says every bit of blood was removed from their veins . . ."

Mikie frowned wistfully, knowing the lives of the dead patrolmen had been stolen from her by someone else.

Someone had eaten well.

The thought made Mikie hungrier. She wasn't even Mikie any longer, but it was too hard to remember the names of all the souls she had devoured; at least one a night, sometimes two. She'd let the first few live, as the cowboy had taught her, but not anymore. There were too many like her now, and what she didn't consume, others would steal.

Like they stole those two dead cops.

Bitterly, Mikie continued down the sidewalk, ignoring the raggedly dressed bystanders and policemen and their flashing lights. The grumble and murmur of the crowd faded with the knowledge that others like her were among them and that inside the crumbling building before her, the man and the woman who'd hurt her were hiding.

Those two didn't understand that she only wanted to bring them the new life within her, as she did to *everyone.* She gave them the freedoms they craved; the freedoms they denied themselves but that Mikie kept securely inside her. She hated the taste of the blood as much as she'd detested the gummy moisture of sperm all those past years, but it was her sacrifice to gain the lives that kept her going, gave her meaning, and kept her young and attractive.

A meaty hand closed over her wrist, jolting her out of the thoughts, and she snarled at the big policeman in front of her.

"Better get inside, miss," he said, barely glancing at her long legs.

"You wanna arrest me?"

He shook his head. "Just get inside—" His eyes studied her more closely. His jaw trembled. Her stare teased him with possibilities. His longing sprung up in his trousers. "Stick around." She smirked. "If you're here when I come back, I'll give you something to remember." Then she turned and slipped into the building past a crowd of junkies and dwellers, leaving the lawman on the sidewalk dazed.

Mikie felt life inside. The life she had been cheated of. The lives she *wanted*.

She wanted them now, and she wanted them fast, because that cop was waiting on the street. She raised her pale, long fingers to the door and trailed her sharp nails across it, harder and harder, stretching her will through the door.

Seconds passed endlessly, and the dead bolt clicked.

You want me, her thoughts spoke, and she felt him squirming.

The doorknob twisted slowly, and the door crept open an inch, then stopped. The light inside went out. But she felt the invitation, unwilling though it was. *What'cha want?*

She pushed the door open and shifted inside. Though it was dark, she had no trouble seeing.

The man shuddered on the floor, waiting for her and overcome by her, and she knelt beside him, entranced by his ragged, stuttering breaths and the unsteady rattle of his heart.

"Momma's here," she cooed, wiping the black tangle of hair from his warm cheek. "You are so afraid . . . but there's nothing to be afraid of. I'm here to tuck you deep inside me and keep you safe. I won't leave you alone again."

The door closed with a slam.

"That bitch!" Mikie spun around on her knees, steeling herself to leave him even though she craved

him more than ever. *Because she wanted them both— and even the policeman below!*

"Get away from him!" Sam stammered, standing between Mikie and the door. She turned the dead bolt. *"Get away!"* She slapped on the light, and Mikie cringed as the single light bulb sprang to life, illuminating the crosses surrounding her. But they were stationary and weak with uncertainty. She kept herself from looking at them, fastening on the bitch instead.

They locked eyes, and Mikie showed her the temptations.

"No!" Sam forced herself closer.

The garlic made Mikie cough, but she laughed too. *"Freedom,"* Mikie taunted. She shrank back from the threat she sensed in the bottle. The garlic was bad, but not bad enough to stop her from the feast these two bodies offered. *But she felt a danger inside that glass container.* She jumped at Sam, raising her long nails high. Sam stumbled back and banged into the chair. She threw out her arms to catch herself and let go of the bottle as she went down. It shattered on the floor. A splash licked Mikie's arm and legs and stung her deep, but she laughed now, sidestepping the puddle. *"Freedom,"* she gurgled once more, bending over the trembling, fleshy pile of Sam. "I will give freedom to you. But now you must wait while I give it to your man first. Watch me close."

Mikie squirmed in anticipation of the woman but floated back and bent back over her appetizer, wanting to save the best for last. She might even let the cop go his own way tonight and find him later. She licked her hard teeth as they tingled; pushed Mike's shirt up to his chest and sank those teeth into his soft belly . . . deep, wanting to savor this.

Salty blood and stomach juices drenched her tongue, invigorating her.

"No!" Mikie shrieked. Agony scalded the roof of her mouth as his liquids squirted into her, ripping like a stream of molten lava into her throat. Steam erupted from her lips.

"NO!"

Flames billowed inside her, and Mikie lurched up to unsteady feet, waving her hands frantically. The inferno was *inside* her. She ground her finger claws into her cheeks, her stomach tumbling berserkly. Her next scream was strangled as the fluid blasted back up her burning throat.

Screeching, her powerful senses overwhelmed by the pain, she clawed herself blindly, stumbling over the soft body before her and throwing herself onto the air conditioner, then through the window with the crash of exploding glass. The shards ripped deep into her skin and the air conditioner toppled, dropping after her through the muggy night air that pulsed with siren lights.

Her bones cracked against the sidewalk, the glass smashing deeper into her dead flesh. The air conditioner crashed beside her, splattering her with shrapnel and hissing freon.

"God damn," said a hushed voice.

Mikie lay still in confusion and disbelief, hurting and starving for life—*any* life! She smelled it all around her, and her teeth tingled harder than ever before, almost leaping out of her mouth as the cop knelt at her side and laid a warm hand on her wrist.

"She's dead," the cop said, dropping her hand.

Mikie blinked, thrust up her arm and pulled him to her teeth. She dove into his flesh thirstily, guzzling his life so quickly that he barely flinched. As she licked the last drops off her chin, the others were running away. But another policeman across the street had started toward her.

She waited.

18

 "You better stay inside," the cop
said.

The bony-faced bartender nodded from the Corral's
doorway as the policeman passed. He tipped back his
straw cowboy hat and watched the spectacle: para-
medics huddled around the two fallen officers across
the street. Others surrounded them with drawn revolvers, and the muggy air squealed with the sound of
another ambulance. The bartender slammed the front
door against the sirens and walked to the table where
three young converts sat: two young men and a
woman.

These three newborns had run in here right before
the chaos began. And now they were singing some of
that stinking rock that passed for music in this bizarre
world. His face twisted. "Don't you fucking kids have
your own bar to go to?"

The blond one grinned widely, showing red-stained
teeth, then strummed an air guitar. His dark-haired

buddy beat the first two fingers of each hand wildly against the table. They were both dressed like some kind of Hollywood cowboys, but he could tell they didn't have a drop of cowboy blood in them. A red-haired hooker sat with them. "Did you hear me?"

"You play shitty music in here, so we have to make our own."

"Motherfucker," groaned the bartender. "This whole place is going to *hell*." He walked back to the bar, avoiding the other tables filled with winos and wildly dressed addicts and whores. They were easy catches, and not his either. Their uncaring hungers worried him. "With all you assholes in here, I don't have room for any *real* customers!" He grabbed a wizened, foggy-eyed rummy by his hair, making a sour face. The untempered lusts and cravings of this bunch made them like some nightmare nursery, and he had not come here to baby-sit. *"It wasn't supposed to happen like this!"* the barman bellowed, and everyone got quiet. One of the immigrant greasers who'd come from the border with him turned off the jukebox, making the big room silent except for the sirens outside. The bartender stuck his thumbs in his jeans and passed his eyes over the nursery.

"What do you mean?" the dark-haired young drummer yelled.

The barman chewed on his plug of tobacco. He'd dipped it in a woman's wound last night, and now tasted her anew. "None of you got the fucking brains you died with. Your shenanigans have brought the law right here to my door, and you keep coming back here like a flock of dumb-butt sheep. We gave you freedom, but you come back *here*." He lifted his hands into the air like a backwoods preacher. "Why the hell don't you spread out? There's more than enough out there for all of us!"

"Maybe we like it here," shot back the black-haired kid.

The blond man beside him stood. "Yeah—we were living here before you were!"

"You've got a new life now," spat the long-faced barkeep. He counted a dozen and a half of his new unchosen brethren. *"But you fuckers don't even deserve the lives you had!* Me and my boss stayed down at the border for years, just picking off the scum that walked into our hands. Some were greedier, though, like you dumb fucks, and they went other places, and none of 'em's around today. You gotta take those that won't be missed, or you gotta just take a little bit from as many as you can. It'll give you the same pleasure in the end, knowing how you've got 'em marked and that there's hardly a damn thing they can do about it! My boss—the old bastard who began *all* of us—could tell you *that.* He saw hundreds of our kind slaughtered in Europe! He came to this country and stayed on the outskirts, and we just took the ones that most didn't even know were there. He warned me I was moving up here too soon and that something like this would happen. I guess he was right."

The bar was silent.

"I was greedy, too, but I figured the desire for survival would be the first thing in everyone's head." The pale barman shook his fist angrily. "The ones *I* took first are out on their own. Them greasers are smarter than any of you bastards—they took to the bite like stink on shit. They spread out and they're everywhere now. But you just don't understand what will happen if they catch us, do you?" He clomped across the floor until he stood facing the blond dime-store cowpunk, and he rubbed his whiskery jaws dismally. "At least this way we can be free, and we can still *taste* life. If we're careful, we can do that forever, and we don't ever need to fear the Hell we did before. You assholes just don't know the difference between death and life. If they take our bodies, *we'll* be trapped. Every one of you'll be just as hungry as you were when you first woke up, *but you can't do a damn thing about it then*!"

A loud, hellish scream ripped through the sirens and shouts outside.

The red-haired hooker with them pushed her way to the bartender. "What do we do, then, huh?" she grumbled.

He took his worried gaze from the door and slid one of his long fingernails across her cheek. "You get the fuck out of here, bitch. *You all get the fuck out!*" he screamed. "You wanted to be like this so you could do what you wanted to—*so get out and do it!* I'm here for *me,* and I don't give a shit about anyone else! The night I came back I found my shitting wife and my brother moaning in my bed. I drank them dry and set a torch to them! You've got to make your own damn way in this fucking world!"

The blond cowpunk lit up a cigarette and exhaled smoke in the bartender's skinny face. "You take death too seriously. Come on, MaryAnn. Come on, Jerry." They pushed through the freak show of whiskery, T-shirted bums and floppy-bosomed women surrounding them, to the back door and the vacant lot next door.

"Good riddance and good hunting," bade the bartender, spitting his plug. The others began to shuffle out after them.

"Where are we going?" asked MaryAnn.

"We're going to do what we want like he said," Scott replied. "We're going to go hunting! Fuck him and his dip-shit boss. We'll drink this fucking town dry!"

19

The sirens finally stopped, but the night shook as they were replaced by the noise of shouts, shrieks, and new cries of pain. Sam peered over the window frame at the brightly lit street below. In the glow of flames and streetlights, she saw a mass of people burst out of the Corral bar across the way, then cross the vacant lot. A man in a uniform called to them to stop and shot into the air, then began to retreat as two bony forms broke from the others and went right for him. When he reached the center of the street, the two attackers whipped around with hideous laughter and ran back after the others, already scattered and disappearing into the lot's piles of discarded refuse.

"What are they?" Sam heard a thin voice. The man who'd been chased stared at the lot that was once more deserted. He took a position near the remnants of Mike's air conditioner below.

A trash can sat on the sidewalk on this side of the

street, filled with flames, and another stood across from it on the other side. Between them the police regrouped and began to walk back and forth in front of the apartment buildings, stores, and warehouses, revolvers in hand. Inching over the window frame, Sam looked more closely at the demolished air conditioner, and at the prostrate uniformed body beside it. The vampire that had attacked Mike had gotten that poor cop, and now a frightened co-worker was helping two men in white jumpers lift him onto a stretcher.

She desperately tried not to remember how she'd felt when that vampire-whore had frightened her and she'd tripped, dropping the holy water. Her eyes had shot to the locked door, and she'd known there was no way to get it open before the white, glistening teeth sank into her. And then she looked at those teeth, and into those red, terrible eyes that seemed to grow larger and larger until they were all she could see, exposing a vertigo of sensual pleasure like Walt had tried to disarm her.

But that temptation had been misguided, formed by Mike's lie. The sight of herself in an act of lesbian lust had made her stomach churn, leaving her empty and listless while her tormentor had returned to Mike. She'd tried to hold up her necklace, but her arms wouldn't budge, and the blond-haired monster had begun sucking him loudly.

Then she leapt through that window like she'd been stung by millions of wasps.

The whore was long gone. Sam had crawled over just in time to watch her attack another cop who was sitting in the ambulance, holding his bandaged thigh where she'd chewed him as he unloaded his pistol into her. Sam still heard the vampire's shrieks of hideous laughter as other policemen surrounded her. But those sounds cut off abruptly when the living cop now below her had picked up a piece of Mike's broken window frame and crept toward her uncertainly, aiming its jagged point at her breasts.

The creature had once more blistered the night with agitated screams, then left her prey to flee down the street into the shadows of that vacant lot. Sam had sighed with relief, knowing that she and Mike were no longer alone.

"Shit." Mike's thin voice came from the floor. "S-Sam?"

Sam turned and saw Mike finally open his eyes. She held her necklace before her, ready to run. His hand slid down to the rip that Mikie had torn in his stomach. He moaned.

"She bit you again," Sam muttered, inching closer.

He closed his eyes for a moment, then sighed. "I feel like I'm *dead*"—his voice cracked—"but my heart's going a mile a minute. What—where is she?"

Still holding the cross, Sam gestured at the shattered remnants of the window frame. "She bit you . . . then she jumped up screaming and threw herself right into that glass."

Mike's face clenched. "You destroyed her?"

But Sam shook her head. "You drank that water and she bit you. Some of it must have gotten into your veins, Mike. Hell, I don't know. All I can tell you is that she ran from you like you were on fire, and she jumped, and then she killed a man down there, and got away."

Pushing up on the hard floor with his elbows, Mike sat up as best he could. "I—I feel weak as shit." He gasped. "And I hurt . . . but somehow I feel *better*

too. I feel like I've passed stage one of cold turkey."
His mouth trembled into an exhausted grin.

Sam released the necklace and took his hands, huffing as she pulled him up and let him lean on her. She made sure the cross was between them and was hopeful when he didn't cringe. "I think the police might listen to what we have to tell them, now, Mike," she whispered, half dragging him to the door. She threw the dead bolt and pulled him into the dark, empty hall. "Come on," she urged, "there's some doctors down there."

He was heavy and not much help, but Sam got him to the stairway, inhaling a rising scent of burning garbage that she knew would be stronger outside. She did not think and did not want to think, but moved almost instinctively, backing down the eight-inch steps and letting Mike put most of his weight on her outstretched arms.

Halfway down the stairs Sam nearly lost her balance under Mike's weight. She shook the sweat away from her eyes and dropped her left foot down another step . . . then her right.

When she had gotten him to the bottom at last, Sam pushed Mike against the wall so he could keep his feet, and caught her breath. She went ahead to the outside door and saw one of the policeman pacing the sidewalk with his gun drawn. The putrid, saccharine smoke of wasted food from the trash cans stung her eyes and she coughed, barely able to make out the surrounding buildings or the other figures moving through the street. She croaked out a sound, swallowed, and leaned on the door. "I've got someone in here who needs medical attention!"

The young cop glanced up sharply, showing his

confused, oval face. "We got our hands full out here, lady."

"You've got an ambulance out here, and this man needs an ambulance!"

Hesitating, he glanced up and down the street, then pointed the gun muzzle at her and came forward, stopping a yard away. He licked his lips. "Don't try anything or I'll shoot you."

Sam held out her empty hands, then nodded her head back at the open door. "He's in *there*."

The young man looked over his shoulder at the nearest ambulance as voices rose down the block. "What's wrong with him?"

Several seconds passed.

"He was bitten," Sam admitted, "by a vampire."

The cop's eyes grew rounder and he looked at her sharply, but not disbelievingly.

"It was the one who jumped out the window and attacked you guys."

His finger circled the trigger of his pistol. "A *vampire*? Those guys are really—"

"You saw her!" Fingering her necklace and showing him its cross, Sam held it up to the cop. "Come on, this man needs medical help *now*."

"Medic over here!" shouted the cop, stepping to the door with the pistol in front of him.

Two of the white-suited men began to jog toward the building. Sam sighed. "That pistol won't do you a damn bit of good, you know."

The cop rubbed sweat off his forehead. "If they're really vampires, it'll do *me* just fine, lady. I saw what happened to Pete, and two of those creeps chased me —I couldn't believe it—b-but if one of those things comes on to me again, I'm going to stick this muzzle right in my mouth and pull the trigger, okay?" He raised the weapon to his lips with a frown. "When I die, I die a *man*." As if reminded of something, he took a step nearer—a very small step—and swept his eyes over her more cautiously. "Did any of them get you?"

She ignored him. "After we get Mike in the van, I want you to call your superior and let me talk to him."

He gulped again, pointing at a gray LTD that had pulled up beside the nearest ambulance. "I'll take you to him."

20

Brian Sunderman yawned, shifting on his seat and farting, liking the sound and the smell of the heavy Mexican dinner he'd gulped down. Despite the discomfort of gas with the long drive across town, he had loved every bite of it. The Brady account was his, and dinner with the big boss was that pat on the head he'd fought so hard for.

He'd kicked ass, corporately speaking, and the best part was that the boss knew it. Old man Tucker had even beamed at him, toasting his success and suggesting he might want to sleep in late as a bonus for his victory. Tucker had nudged him: *"And believe me, after eating those beans, you'll sleep like a baby until your old lady wakes you up with the can of Lysol she empties into the bedroom. Your sheets will stink so bad, she'll have to wash them twice!"*

Brian grinned to himself, then frowned as he thought of his wife and how this night would end. He would tell Donna the good news of his impending raise and promotion and wait for her to shower him with kisses.

When they dressed for bed with the kids safely tucked in an hour later, he would still be waiting, and he expected that when he awoke late in the morning, he would *still* be waiting, and would once again be forced to relieve his expectations of her with his own hand as he showered.

Donna would be too tired.

Donna was always too tired . . . except for that time when he came home from work with the flu and watched her and the divorcée who lived next door through the bedroom window. He remembered the sick twist he'd endured as he stared through the glass pane, soundlessly watching the naked bodies twisting the bedsheets and finally understanding that the woman he'd married ten years ago was a dyke. And felt sicker as he thought of that afternoon not too long before when he fucked her sultry partner himself.

Brian dropped his right hand from the steering wheel and rubbed it across his slacks, allowing the defeat of his married life to overcome the triumphs of business. A tall redhead stood on the median side of the expressway. His eyes grew big as she swung her hips back and forth under the orange expressway lights, taking off her shirt and exposing big pink breasts that jiggled. She laid the clothing on a skinny pole, then began unzipping her skirt.

Steering quickly ahead of a dented brown pickup into the far left lane, he ignored the loud blast of a warning honk, then hovered his foot over the brake pedal and licked his lips.

* * *

Headlights sprayed them from the fast-moving cars and semis blasting up and down the expressway, and MaryAnn removed her short black skirt, hanging it over her blouse on a median reflector pole. She sneered at Scott and Jerry as they stood ten feet ahead, their thumbs uplifted.

"Awright!" squealed Jerry as the passing Town and Country wagon flashed brake lights and its tires squealed. He and Scott started walking to it, then stopped dead as the car backed up and passed them again, stopping beside MaryAnn. Naked, she waited, standing casually as though she hitched rides like this every night. When the car with its metal woody-look sides was right next to her, she made a closed-mouth smile.

The window rolled down halfway and the middle-aged man inside waited for her to come nearer. "You with those guys?" he asked, pointing at Scott and Jerry ahead.

She shook her head.

The man looked at them through his windshield again. "Get in, then," he told her. "I'm celebrating tonight, and if you'll come with me, I'll give you something special."

"Thanks." MaryAnn chortled and grabbed her clothing. A car sped by on the station wagon's far side and she glared at it. "Why don't you get out so I can get in your side, huh? The cars are going awfully fast."

He took off his glasses and wiped them with a handkerchief while MaryAnn rubbed her bush against his door. She sniffed his scent of life. The blood tickled her nostrils.

He wore a dark suit coat and a bright blue tie that

was tight and straight. And in the shifting light, his face looked a bright pink. His gaze flickered from her to Scott and Jerry as they stopped and leaned on the car's hood.

He revved the engine loudly. "Hey—who are those guys? Is this some kind of a trick?"

MaryAnn licked a finger and circled it around a standing nipple. "I'm just *horny* and you're cute," she breathed. "These guys are bugging me. My boyfriend dumped me out of his car and they saw me and made me take off my clothes." She leaned against the window innocently. "Will you help me get away from them?"

He bit his lip, then unlocked his door. He pushed it wide and pulled her toward him fast, trying to speed her up by pulling the door into her ass. "Hurry up. Crawl over me."

"Ooooh," she whispered, bending down slowly, dropping her right hand over his crotch and squeezing —he was already hard as a rock. "Feels like you're horny, too, man!"

His squirming hands rose to her hanging breasts to urge her inside and she felt him harden still more.

"You want to fuck me, don't you?" giggled Mary-Ann, not moving. Instead, her hand moved to the ignition and switched off the motor, then touched the leather belt around his waist. "Let's do it *now*."

"Hey—"

He was strapped in by his seat belt and she wouldn't let his hand over to release its clasp, bringing it back to her breasts instead. A car horn honked behind them and lights flashed into the cab. Ignoring it, she worked her fingers harder until the leather belt holding tight to his waist came loose, and then his slacks were open and he helped her pull them down to his ankles. She touched the end of her tongue to his already wet pole. "You're nice and big . . . and *juicy*," she moaned, her teeth tingling violently.

Lights flashed in his eyes and he fought her to pull his pants back up. "N-not here." He panted, squirming again and trying to release the safety strap, but she firmly brought his fingers back to her nipples. *"Please—"*

She circled her lips and dropped her face, filling her mouth with his wriggling tool, and as she sank her razor teeth in fast, he jerked and she felt the sudden burst of his lust mixing with blood on her tongue, knowing that for at least that moment, he had enjoyed this as much as her.

"God!" He gasped, his hands on her shoulders.

She sucked him hard, laughing as he became limp and tried to push her away.

"Are you giving this man a bad time, MaryAnn?" asked Scott's voice as he pulled the door open wide.

"Looks like she's giving him a good one." Jerry chuckled. "Hey—my turn."

The man looked up dizzily at their teeth and screamed. He was still screaming as Jerry pushed in over MaryAnn and finally released the seat straps, and he and Scott pulled the convulsing man to the side of the road. Scott fastened his mouth onto one wrist while Jerry took the other, and MaryAnn didn't move from his crotch until the screams stopped . . . and finally even his weakening trembles were over. No other cars slowed down to investigate, and Scott pulled the half-nude businessman over into a ditch, pulled a torn box covered with dirt on top of him, and dropped his smoldering cigarette into that dust. "Ashes to ashes, big guy." He chuckled.

"After those cops, I can't believe I was *still* hungry," grunted Jerry, wiping his jaw with a sleeve. "Damn, it tastes good!"

Scott nodded. "Wait'll you try a wino whose veins are filled with booze. Man, that stuff is the best I've had so far. A helluva lot better than a bottle of Ripple!"

MaryAnn picked up her clothes and got dressed, ignoring the horns and catcalls from the speeding drivers. "Did you see the look on his face when he figured out what I was doing to him?"

Shrugging, Scott pushed her to the station wagon and urged her to the passenger's side, then unlocked the rear door to let Jerry in the back. "Well, we got a car now, gang, and it's hours before the sun comes up. Where you want to party next?"

MaryAnn turned the rearview mirror toward her automatically, then glared. "Shit," she muttered.

"Any ideas?" Scott asked again, twisting the keys and revving the motor.

Jerry was laughing hard.

Scott put the car into gear and squealed in front of an old Ford Pinto. "Well?"

"I'd love to meet the Dallas Cowboys cheerleaders!"

Scott laughed, too, and MaryAnn glared at the mirror.

PART IV

the hunt

1

Acrid smoke stung his eyes as it billowed against the walls of concrete, blurring the siren lights that danced on every side. The street looked, smelled, and sounded like a war zone in Vietnam. Golan wiped his forehead, reminded of that hell even by the summer heat. He had been drafted in 1973, arriving at the tail end of that decade-long conflict. Even as Richard Nixon was facing a long-overdue political castration, Golan had been sweltering and facing a more horrible death in the jungles of southeast Asia.

And whatever they were up against now reminded him of that—only the smell of napalm was missing. His mouth was bone dry at the verbal reports he'd heard, and at this point he wasn't at all ready to tell the woman sitting beside him in the car that she was crazy. From where he was, peering at the departing ambulances and the drifting, stinking smoke, the entire fucking world had gone bananas.

Again.

"Vampires," he muttered.

"That's right," Sam told him.

"Real honest-to-God storybook Draculas walking the streets of Dallas, huh?" His lip twitched with the pressure of his own faltering sanity as he peered at her smoke-blackened features. With her long neck she looked like a goose who'd just escaped the frying pan. "Or are they flying around like fucking bats?"

"With the damage they've already done on foot, I don't think they need to turn into bats."

The detective watched the first ambulance drive off, still surprised at her calm manner. In their few minutes of conversation Golan had decided that he liked Samantha Borden. When she'd first spoken to him he decided that, because she alone had the balls to say what everyone else had hinted at. He thought of what the patrolmen had said, and though none of them had dared to use the term *vampire*, the descriptions of the attacks that had killed an officer and wounded another, the *things* that had chased another, and the way those first two men had died, spoke that word in his mind constantly. He thought of Emily McDonald and Jay Adwon, and of all the recent, unexplained deaths and disappearances. "We need to powwow and this has got to stay *private*. The mayor has called in the feds and there's talk of closing this city up and declaring martial law. In the meantime I got you and some lady locked up in the hospital saying that vampires are all over the place, and one of my guys shot a minister in the cemetery last night who he says was trying to put a wooden stake into some girl's heart. The mayor says it's all some kind of mass hysteria and we're keeping a lid on it, but my gut tells me different. I've seen combat before, and I know the smell of a trap."

"A *minister* was killed?"

"Yeah, and his wife is the lady in the hospital. She told me he killed a vampire back in St. Louis—more than one, and she says they tracked them here."

Sam shivered.

"Your boyfriend's in the second ambulance?"

Sam nodded distantly. "He's not really my boy-friend."

"I'm glad to hear that, because he's got a record a mile and a half long."

"I know."

The second ambulance started its motor. "What are you doing with him, then?"

"He was bitten by that thing that killed one of your guys. I told you about that."

Golan started his engine and kicked the air condi-tioner up high. "Is *he* going to become one, too?"

"I don't think so if we can keep him alive. But he . . . somehow he can sort of communicate with them. Sometimes he says he knows where they are."

Golan raised his eyebrows.

"But he's *not* one."

The second ambulance backed up and turned, then started after the first one, and Golan turned to follow. "That's too bad. After the shit he's done, I'd love to put a fucking stake through *his* heart."

"It's not that easy."

Thinking of the dead bodies he had observed, of the cruel holes in their wrists, legs, and necks, Golan forced himself not to answer, and only trusted that his unthinking, mechanical killing-machine mind-set from the days of Vietnam would come back to him if any of this was really true. He once wasted three Charlies with his bare hands in a way that would have caused Rambo to shudder. Golan hadn't even fully realized that he'd done it until hours later, when the blood made his fingers stick together and he couldn't even pick his nose. Killing had become second nature, and he'd gotten so accustomed to the feel of guns and that power that he'd come back and enlisted as an officer in the police force, though he never felt the same scary thrill on the streets. Even with the pleasant bliss of his family, home, and TV sports, it was something that he slowly and grudgingly realized that he missed, and sometimes he even enjoyed the ghastly, sweating nightmares of those long-ago horrors as much as he once dreaded them.

"It's not that easy," the sweaty woman told him again.

"How do you mean that?" he asked.

Sam sat back into the seat, making it squeak. Her eyes darted to the dark buildings on either side of them and to the faces of the men being left here. They didn't look happy. "They make you see things that you *want*," Sam whispered. "When you look into their eyes, they show you the things you want . . . *or that they think you want.* Don't ask me how, but if these things can really exist, I don't see how anyone can let reality and certain knowledge make us disbelieve anything anymore—and they really do exist!"

Her words filled the cab as they drove behind the flashing lights ahead. "I told you that Mike and I tried to kill one of them last night!"

Reaching up to his visor, Golan pulled a cigarette out of the pack he had rubber-banded up there, fed it between his cracked lips, and lit it with the car lighter.

"I read the report on it this morning. What I want to know"—he spoke with more excitement than he let show, remembering his drill sergeant once saying that the best defense is a butt-kicking *offense*—that it might scare your enemy into just leaving you alone—"is why the hell they picked my tour of duty to show up? Do you think these . . . *things* . . . followed you back from that ghost town? Do you think that maybe they're coming after you, and maybe everyone else was some kind of a warning in case you decided to spill the beans and we decided to go after them?"

"No," she replied after a minute. "Mike said that they've always been here. He said he'd heard about them for years from older people, but that there weren't very many of those things." Sam wiped hair from her greasy forehead. "But maybe there are now."

"He said they've been *here* for years? Your friend, Mike, is a bigger dopehead than I thought." Golan sighed but felt uncomfortable under her gaze.

"How many missing people do you have in your files you can't account for, Lieutenant? How many people disappear every year and are never heard from again?"

He inhaled a lungful of smoke, needing the nicotine. "There's a lot. Seems like more every year," he admitted.

"Maybe now we know why."

Instead of answering, Golan stared out at the retiring city, listening to its ever-present hum. He followed the ambulances onto an expressway ramp. Already the slum area was far behind, hidden by the mind-splitting architecture of a dozen skyscrapers. Again, he mentally compared this place to Vietnam with its contradictory life-styles . . . the way people had walked the streets of Saigon about their everyday business and paused for only a few minutes when the shelling began, resuming their lives in the aftermath of flames and screams as if nothing had happened . . . *unless they were one of the unfortunates who were scattered in a dozen pieces.* If there were really such things as vampires . . . His hand dropped to the car radio as he struggled with the growing desire to call a squad car out to guard his own home and family, just in case.

But he would not do that. If it came to that point, he would go home to do that job himself. "Vampires, huh?" he muttered again.

"Yeah."

2

Sam's skin was peeling badly. It was just about painful, in fact. She hadn't used oil on her skin since before meeting Mike those twenty-four hours ago that seemed a thousand years. She followed the plainclothes lieutenant—*just call me Golan*, he'd told her—into the hospital and through the concrete-and-marble lobby that was crowded with so many green, leafy plants, it was nearly a jungle. Though she was surprised at his ready acceptance of her after the ridicule she'd undergone only days before, Sam knew the bodies of his men carried the weight her words hadn't. Voices rose and fell around her but she hardly looked up at the other visitors they passed. The conversations she caught and the sight of the smiles on too many faces was harsh proof of an ignorant population that was waiting for disaster.

"Just like 'Nam." They stopped in front of the elevator.

"What?"

"I said this is just like Vietnam. Everything is so normal here, and only five miles away . . ."

The elevator buzzed and opened.

"Come on," he urged her. Two older, somber-faced women stepped out. Sam met their tired eyes briefly as she followed Golan inside. He pressed the button marked eight.

"Where are we going?"

"I want you to talk to that minister's wife." He brushed a thread off his gray jacket, lowering his tone. "I think she believes in vampires too."

"After everything you saw and heard, don't *you*?" Sam asked, thinking of Mike somewhere else in the hospital. She wanted to see him again and know how he was doing.

Golan kneaded his knuckles, and they cracked noisily. "Maybe I do. But only if I can kill them. I don't believe in anything I can't kill. To tell you the truth, lady, nothing much surprises me anymore. The whole world is full of vampires as far as I'm concerned. You got greed and lust every way you look. We live off each other. But then, that's the American way, huh?"

"You don't sound like you believe in much of anything."

Golan grinned more softly as the elevator came to a stop. "Maybe I haven't seen much to believe in these past years, huh?" He took her elbow and they walked into a white corridor that was identical to the one they'd left except less traveled. An orderly pushing a squeaky cart was the only person in sight. "Maybe that's the whole problem. No one has anything to believe in, anymore . . . or anything to *disbelieve* in." Golan smiled nervously. "This way." His feet clapped the linoleum floor heavily. "Let's see if we can put some of this together."

As they walked past numbered doors, Sam yawned, feeling the exertion of these past hours pulling at her eyelids and muscles. She hadn't been home since yesterday, and the restless sleep in Mike's chair and in this hospital hardly seemed like sleep at all. "What are you trying to put together?"

They stopped. He looked at her with his chiseled brown eyes. "I'm not stupid," he told her quietly. "I'm not a scientist either. I know what I saw and I know what it looks like, no matter what I believe or what anyone else believes. I don't need to prove something to know it exists. I learned a long time ago that not accepting what I see and taking it for exactly what it appears to be could get me killed. I saw a lot of my buddies buried because they wouldn't believe old Charlie would wrap himself up in dynamite and then light the fuse and jump all over them in a kamikaze attack that makes the Japs in World War II look like rank amateurs. When the evidence piles up, I know better than to waste my time trying to figure out a way around it. When I've got three or four people who say they see vampires and I got a dozen bloodless bodies all over town, I gotta do something."

The hall air vents hissed faintly, and the now faraway cart squeaked noisily on a rough stretch of floor. The elevator hummed. "What are you going to do?"

Golan's ruddy face was inexpressive. "I'm going to take stock of our ammo and our wounds," he replied. "The first fact we face is that no one but that handful of patrolmen who actually saw what happened are going to believe a bit of this. In fact, the only good thing about any of it is that this crap is *so* unbelievable, the press won't dare print the truth. They'll probably get the damn sports- and weathercasters to write it up." He took her elbow again and started walking once more, only nodding at the greetings of the dour-faced nurse in her lonely station. He stopped at door 819 and tapped it lightly.

The door opened partway to reveal the blotchy face of a young woman. Her eyes narrowed as a cat's might, but after a moment she moved back and pulled the door wide, retreating into the hospital room that whispered sounds from the bright nineteen-inch TV bracketed to the wall. It threw colors over her and the other walls of the unlit room. Her thin lips twisted with a smile, and she closed her terry-cloth robe over a midlength nightgown. "It's after visiting hours."

Golan shrugged, flipping a light switch and turning away from the sudden fluorescent flash. "I should be off duty, then, Mrs. MacDonald, but I'm not. Can I talk to you?"

She shrugged this time, and Sam studied her in the light. She was as young as she first appeared, probably not even twenty yet, but her features bore ravages that spoke age beyond time's distortions. Her eyes were lined by circles like a student might bear after too many nights of late studies during finals week, and her blotchy cheeks were smeared with makeup streaked by innumerable lines of tears. Her hoarse and unsteady voice made that last conclusion certain. She peered at Sam briefly. "Have you brought in another psychiatrist?"

A high-pitched scream floated from the TV, and the dark-haired woman backed to it, not turning from the detective. She flipped the TV off. Golan took a deep breath. "What are you watching?"

"A vampire movie. That's what drives us nutty people crazy, didn't you know? Didn't you know that Charles Manson saw *Psycho* a thousand times before he got the idea to become one? Didn't the good doctor you sent up earlier tell you that? He told me that people can get so wrapped up in movies and things that they aren't even part of the real world anymore."

"I didn't send *anyone* up," Golan told her. "Please —I'm sorry about the crap you've been put through, okay? I just need to talk to you . . . about *vampires*."

"I think Warren will tell you all you want to know, Mr. Policeman."

Watching them both, Sam guessed at what she didn't know. Golan's clenched jaw told her as much as the young woman's hatred did. "I saw vampires too," Sam broke in. "They're all over this town now. I saw three people killed by them tonight. A friend of mine was attacked and he's down in the emergency room—"

Emily MacDonald walked to the bed slowly and sat. She was staring at Sam's necklace, and frowning, her smeared makeup not shielding her sudden paleness at all. She bowed her head tiredly, and Sam stiffened at her new sobs. Touching Golan's wrist, Sam nodded back at the doorway. He huffed and went out. Sam approached the shivering form that had bent over to its knees. When the door clicked shut, Sam licked dry lips and sat next to the woman, putting an arm around her. "I'm Samantha," she spoke softly.

Breaking a moan in half with effort, the black-haired woman sat up, exposing the new streaks dripping down her cheeks. "I'm Emily," she said.

3

Two figures in white pushed Mike's gurney down a long, cold hallway. The hard surface beneath him felt like ice. He stared up blearily at the round light fixtures that passed overhead, feeling the sick roller-coaster twists of motion. But even that couldn't overpower the sleepiness filling him since the man in the ambulance had given him a shot.

The gurney suddenly came to rest in a semidarkened room. The nurse's glasses flashed as they caught light and she fastened a plastic tag around his wrist. She held up a hypodermic, flipped it with her fingers, and waited as someone swabbed his arm.

Mike grunted as the sharp point poked in. Then the glasses flashed once more and the nurse withdrew the hypo. The figures withdrew behind shadowed curtains until Mike was alone.

But he was not alone.

He was surrounded.

By vampires?

Yes. They surrounded him. He hadn't been lying when he'd told Samantha that. He could feel them hovering around him and inside him, burning his veins hotter than the shot the nurse had just given him. He vacillated between longings growing stronger and stronger, and fading loyalty to the nearly buried self he'd sworn in his bleakest moments to one day return to.

The worst thing his heightened senses and desires brought back to him was the guilt of his more recent past: the young school boys and girls earnestly digging deep into their purses and jeans and giving him the dollars they stole from Daddy and Mommy for their fixes. A twelve-year-old blond babe who might be a cheerleader one day even tried to barter her body, but in his self-styled morality and mercy he shook his head and gave her two pills he couldn't even identify. When he saw the news story on TV the next night of the young preteen girl who overdosed on bad acid, his remorse was overcome in his joy that he hadn't taken the shit himself.

Why should *he* be afraid of vampires?

Drawing the truth of the indictments of his soul into the forefront of his soggy mind, Mike recalled how he had seduced and used Lynette, even as she was using him . . . as she did unto him as he did unto others and was trying to do unto her.

That was the part that frightened him about being a vampire. Nothing was certain. He'd told that fear to Samantha truthfully as he laid his plans to seduce her in the same way he had Lynette: *How could he be sure of getting what he wanted once he passed the threshold of death and became a bloodsucking creature who was as much an addict as those he addicted?*

He was not even certain that he had seduced Samantha, now, or if it was she who had seduced him . . . or maybe the need he could not really control.

The hungry desire for blood drooled in his thoughts, turning into MTV dreams as his breaths became deeper and he slipped into sleep. He saw himself parading through the dark, bottle-littered alleys and giving those big-eyed school kids a new lust and new high, this time taking the bodies of the half-formed precheerleaders as well, whether they were offered to him or not. He let the old trappings of every morality fall away, drinking them and seeking others, leading them in their new quest.

Sweat broke out on Mike's unconscious forehead as the blustery visions twisted and weaved from desire to desire: He marched into the police office with his herd of long-toothed converts, laughing at the bullets that riddled his body but couldn't stop him. He saw himself leading the very arm of the law as they rose from their graves afterward, following him too . . . until only one light in all of Dallas was burning.

The sedative wouldn't release him, and in the dream he walked to that last run-down apartment, followed by his horde. The old familiar door opened at his touch, and he saw his sister's terror-struck face as she brandished a stinking clove of garlic and stood between him and his glowering mother.

"I always knew you were shit, Michael," Ma's wispy voice chastised him that last time on the phone. She wiped a white lock from her disgusted face, holding up a glowing bottle in her hand. *"You were a bad boy. But now, I will baptize you—"*

He was screaming even before she smashed the glass over the crown of his skull, feeling the power of the blood she sang of in church that was flooding down in the holy water to destroy him—screaming as flames enveloped him—and then he was grabbing her in a fiendish hug to make her blaze with him.

She disappeared.

"Bad boys go to Hell, Michael," Ma's distant, disembodied voice spoke sadly, *"and Hell is forever."*

He screamed.

"What's wrong with him?" Sam yelled. Mike struggled, his frantic arms and legs bound to the bed. His mouth foamed and his eyes blazed as he shook uncontrollably. The doctor held up a needle as two orderlies held his right arm still. Sam tried to push past the skinny man blocking her entrance to the room. *"What the hell are you doing to him?"* she shouted.

The doctor examined the upper arm the orderlies offered him.

Sam grabbed Golan's wrist beside her. "Don't let them do it."

Golan tapped the skinny man blockading them and flashed his badge. "Don't touch him, Doc." He walked in.

The balding man glanced up with surprise, drawing back the needle and staring at it dumbly. His Adam's apple wobbled. "Who are *you*?"

Golan walked to the doctor's side, wrinkling his face at the curses and moans fleeing from Mike Hossiason. "What's wrong with him?"

Sam started after Golan, then hesitated and turned back to Emily. "You don't need to come in."

Emily's eyes glittered. "Is that your way of saying

I've been through enough?" She gripped Sam's hand and walked with her to the bed as Mike began to cough.

The doctor and Golan had stepped away from the bed and were whispering, and the two orderlies held Mike's arm tight as he shook it uselessly, whining.

Emily closed her eyes. "Give me your necklace," Emily murmured. Sam wordlessly unfastened it and gave it to her.

Emily held the necklace up in the light. After all Emily had been through, Sam could hardly believe the younger woman was still sane . . . or could at least act sane. She was anything but a stranger to death, or killing.

Emily pressed the silver cross over Mike's heart, and his sounds and thrashing struggle ceased instantly.

Silence. Golan's whispers to the doctor seemed to be loud, and then they stopped too.

"Shit," exclaimed the doctor, "is he dead?" He clutched Mike's wrist with his fingers.

"Is he?" Golan asked.

The doctor shook his head, but he continued to take Mike's pulse. After one minute had passed, he replaced that limb at Mike's side and nodded the two orderlies and nurse to the door. They all marched out without a word, but all of them turned their heads over their shoulders more than once.

"Shut the door, please," the doctor said.

The door clicked.

"What did you do to him?" asked the frowning doctor. He lifted Mike's right eyelid and bent over him. "Did you *say* something to him?"

"No," Emily answered.

The bald man's cheeks flushed red. "This is not funny, Detective Golan. I have people dying in this place and I don't have time for this sort of thing. After what I've heard happened on the other side of town, I'm damned surprised that you do. I intend to comment on this to your superiors."

Golan blushed himself but remained where he stood, blocking the doctor's way out. "You didn't answer my question, Doc."

"I was trying to. They brought this man in and he was given a sedative to relax him. Standard procedure. The men in the ambulance said he was babbling hysterically. They had given him a mild dose themselves but it was wearing off. The stuff my girl gave him should have knocked him out for hours, but ten minutes ago he was screaming so loud, you could hear him in the waiting room."

"That's still not the answer, Doc. *What's wrong with him?*"

The older man sniffed and ran a hand over the remaining hair above his ears. "We haven't had the opportunity for a full examination, but my, uh, estimate is that he is deep in shock."

Lieutenant Golan nodded and stepped back, letting the man pass around the bed. "And my other question?"

The doctor's eyes became small and he sneered. "Take a course in biology, Detective. Vampires can't exist—not real ones. Dead is dead, and pumping a dead body full of blood *can't* bring it back to life. Anyone who says he's a vampire is just a psychotic, but he's still got to be alive and, Detective, anyone who believes him is crazier than he is."

Golan cracked his knuckles and nodded, gazing at

the necklace on Mike's chest. "Thanks, Doc," he replied.

The doctor touched the doorknob. "And if this man's not sick, please get him the hell out of my bed. I have shit enough to deal with, okay? Burn victims are coming in from east Dallas. Some asshole set a whole city block on fire. And I *will* be speaking to your superiors, Detective."

Golan sighed as the door closed. He looked across the bed at Sam and Emily, then down at the cross and Mike, shaking his head. "I've got to go check out what he said about that fire, and see if it has anything to do with this, okay? Do you think he's all right?"

Sam had pulled up Mike's shirt to expose the gauze bandage taped to his stomach.

"Do you think he needs to stay here?"

Emily smiled. "These people can't help him, Mr. Policeman."

He nodded, then rubbed his eyes. After a long breath he took a card from his front pocket and gave it to Sam.

Sam squeezed his fingers.

"Call me at home later, and take these two out of here, okay?"

"I'll take them to my place."

He handed her another card and a pen. "Write down your address and stay there. Don't worry if you can't contact me because that'll mean I'm on my way over. I'm going to get my wife and kids on a plane out of this place and check out that fire, then I'll get back with you."

Emily took the necklace from Mike, and he remained still. She held it up to Golan, looking questioningly at Sam. Sam grit her teeth but nodded. "Take this, okay?" Emily offered.

Golan chuckled. "I'm Jewish," he said. "Besides, ask Samantha—I already told her I don't even believe in my own God anymore." He cracked his knuckles for emphasis and opened the door, then left.

Emily crossed herself with the necklace.

"Are you Catholic?" asked Sam with raised eyebrows.

The other woman shook her head, handing the tiny chain and cross to Sam as voices filtered in from the hallway. "Warren told me the symbolisms and protections of Christ go beyond religion," she said.

4

When the pathology lab finished with the bodies of Rick and Sherry North, they sent them down to the iceboxes that would be their coffins until all the asked questions were answered. Then, at last, they would be buried in peace.

Father Percival Tolbert sighed as he waited at the morgue's scarred front counter. The old wooden chairs lining the far wall were empty except for a couple of magazines. He clenched his fingers and glanced at the noisy clock behind the front desk, wishing he'd had the opportunity to say the last rites over Rick and Sherry before the forensic people had barricaded them in their labs for the untold investigations. He was glad that now, at last, he could look upon the faces of those strayed sheep from his flock and beg mercy for them. God would surely overlook his tardiness in view of the way it had happened, and perhaps this final act on their behalf would give both of them the absolution Tolbert earnestly prayed would bring them peace.

Though he didn't know the complete story of why Rick had murdered his ex–brother-in-law, and knew too many stories of Sherry's infidelities while Rick languished in prison, Tolbert didn't like to think of anyone spending eternity in Hell, especially when they had already spent their lives in its earthly counterpart. Neither Rick nor Sherry had strayed as far as others he knew, like the Mexican kid who hadn't come to confession in six years, Mike Hossiason. That young, pitiful jerk was breaking his mother's heart, not to mention the hearts of a lot of other mothers who watched their children going crazy under the control of his drugs.

That compassion he couldn't help feeling for others was why he had come to the old concrete building that smelled of formaldehyde and death at this late hour; as soon as he was notified that these bodies had been returned to the morgue—*made available,* as the calling police desk-jockey termed it—it was his duty to come, even though the sensible, enlightened part of him knew it could easily wait until morning.

Made available. Tolbert smiled sadly, clasping the rosary in his palm as he waited for the desk man to return and take him to the bodies. "Father in heaven," he muttered softly, "these two are made available for salvation at last."

Somehow the words smacked of blasphemy, and Tolbert swallowed them back up fast, licking his dry lips.

A gray-headed man with deep lines that made his tired face look even more exhausted closed the heavy metal door down the narrow hall behind the desk. "Come on back, Padre."

Dropping the beaded rosary in his pocket, Tolbert

advanced, pushing open the swinging half door with one knee. Passing a cluttered desk behind the high counter, he joined the uniformed man. "I appreciate this."

"Awful late to be calling, in my book."

"Yes."

The officer clicked his tongue across buck teeth. "I got them out so you can see them, Padre. Just let me know when you're done so I can close 'em back up, okay? They're already spoiling, and I don't need this place to smell any riper than it already does."

Tolbert nodded and twisted the lever until the door clanked and swung open on its own. He shivered at the chill and fought the desire to hold his nose at the bad odor that swept out to greet him.

"If you don't mind," the man called behind him, "I'll shut this up until you're done. Got to keep it cold. I just got word that we're having more visitors coming in from that fire."

"Yes."

The door clanked again, and Tolbert stood in the silence, examining the numbers on the drawers lining the wall.

The air was very cold.

At the farthest end of the twenty-foot room, two drawers were pulled out like the file cabinets at his church, burdened by prostrate statues. He walked around the steel table bolted to the floor and took out his rosary again, then looked down first at the icy face of Sherry North. Her open mouth and the dull lack of expression in her frozen eyes twisted his heart. Her skin was no longer the pale chocolate it once had been, but the sickly color of a tan wall with the handprints and dust of a dozen years embedded in it. He laid the rosary over a naked stomach that already showed her ribs, and wanted to close those dead eyes, though he knew that it was impossible. The sweat of thaw was already trickling over her hard flesh, but it would take an hour for the eyelids to soften enough to hide her staring pupils.

Since he was old, almost sixty-one, and still primarily traditional in his beliefs, Tolbert laid his hand over the rosary, ignoring the temperature of her body, and said the last rites for her in Latin. The words were certain, even though he nearly stumbled as he recalled the day thirty years ago when he had baptized her. As he finished, he glanced sadly into her eyes once more, and his heart skipped uneasily at the bright red glint he thought he saw in their blackness.

But it was just the light.

Walking on to the far side of the next drawer, Tolbert gazed at Rick North.

Rick's face was twisted, and his sightless eyes nearly bugged out of their sockets. Tolbert wondered what had so frightened the big man. Rick had just left prison, and Tolbert knew that not many things would be able to drag out this kind of an expression from anyone who'd stayed inside the penitentiary walls. He'd listened to too many confessions from cruel guards who didn't seem able to control their fury, and from too many inmates who had endured it, and harbored their own secret sins.

The rosary flowed from Tolbert's hand onto Rick's hairless chest, the beads making a kind of circle there. "Whatever you saw that scared you, Ricky, it's not as bad as Hell, and I pray to God in Heaven that you weren't so far from the Gates that He won't let you in."

Rick's eyes stared at him as though Tolbert himself were some ghastly demon from Hell, and Tolbert laid his fingers on the rosary chain, staring back as he chanted his ceremony slowly and earnestly.

At the last word, when Tolbert crossed himself and lifted the rosary, Rick's eyes flashed red as Sherry's had, and Tolbert's skin crawled with goose bumps. He studied the man's thawing face, his neck and wrists, then his abdomen, tightening his jaw as he saw the solid circumcised penis women other than Sherry had long ago confessed to welcoming. They never used names, of course, but he had come to know the regulars in the congregation so well by then that his guesses as to the identities of the confessing voices and of who they spoke was usually on target. It used to make him grin behind the wall of his confessional booth when Rick came to confess his sins and left some of those sexual forays out. He would remind Rick that he must confess *every* sin.

As though videotaped with his hand in the cookie jar, Rick always did.

"You never really found *love,* did you, Ricky?" Tolbert muttered sadly, touching the chilly flesh of the man's forehead. "You and Sherry were always searching for it, but no matter whose bed you lay in, you still kept looking. You never took the time to understand that maybe love was only waiting for you to invite *it* in." He sighed, wishing that he had been able to get the meanings he preached through to the burly man, and studied the part of Rick's anatomy that had so hindered his life. Even Rick's imprisonment was due to an ironic misuse of sex, and he had murdered a man for committing a sin he might easily have been guilty of himself.

But for the grace of God.

The big penis that had found so many places to rest was wet with dissolving crystals of ice, and Tolbert saw the imprints of toothmarks at its base—at the root of Rick's root. Suppressing the crudity of more such thoughts, Tolbert leaned closer and felt his jaw tremble, certain of his deduction.

And Sherry?

Tightening his fingers around the rosary beads, the old man took quicker steps to get to the other side of her drawer. He barely heard his footsteps on the concrete, or the moisture that dripped on the floor. Not touching her, he bent low again, staring into her bristly pubic hair like a desperate bum searching the pages of a pornographic magazine. He found similar markings hidden from casual view.

Tolbert checked his watch. About fifteen minutes had passed. He remembered that awful night, twenty years ago, when he had last put one of these creatures to its end. There were few left in Dallas who remembered those days now, when vampires had roamed the slums, and of course, the white men who were finally losing their grip on supremacy at that time didn't believe it could happen. They searched for drugged-up Black Panthers or stoned white hippies to blame for the disappearances and murders. The insanity of a society torn by war protests, the assassination of Martin Luther King and Bobby Kennedy, and morality gone berserk had hidden the true meaning of the threats and crimes, and few white men had accepted the truth they saw.

Back then it had been up to him and the outcasts he ministered to overcome the danger, and he could never forget any of those awful nights, waiting in cemeteries as they destroyed each one. The dead he and his brethren of different faiths buried were examined for marks like these on Sherry and Rick, and when the signs were found, the fiends were impaled or sprinkled heavily with holy water, and their coffins sealed with prayer.

The impending holocaust back then ended as suddenly as it had begun, with no one the wiser. The white authorities blamed it on radicals, and their blame wasn't far from the truth.

But he was old now, as were the others who'd fought with him.

Whistling softly, Tolbert fished in his jacket for the small vial of the holy water he'd carried every day since, and wished he had some of the Host too. Even with the last rites said, his previous experience told him that these two might rise up tonight, frozen or not.

Sherry's thumb twitched and Tolbert opened the vial of water, then dabbed drops on her eyes and over her heart, pouring half into her mouth. Her thumb shivered madly for long seconds, then grew still. He clutched for the words:

"I cast you out, unclean spirit, along with every satanic power of the enemy, every specter from Hell, and all your fell companions, in the name of our Lord, Jesus Christ."

The frozen eyes blazed; then, dismally, that fire faltered.

Tolbert didn't wait to be sure. Swiftly now, he moved back to Rick and followed the same ritual, then replaced the empty vial in his pocket. *"Vivit agnus noster, eum sequamur,"* the old man breathed, walking back to the door.

When these bodies were returned to him for the funeral, he would deal with them more properly, but for now he wanted to get out and call those who'd helped him before. Someone had done this to Rick and Sherry.

Where there was smoke there was fire.

Tolbert remembered what he'd heard on TV about the victims of the fire burning on the east side of town.

5

Warren was dead.

Emily had stared at the hole in his forehead as he lay motionless on the ground with horrid emptiness, feeling a loneliness that she had not remembered since they met and learned to love each other.

But now he was dead, and she was *alone*.

Why?

Why did it happen?

Shaking her head numbly, she touched the split ends of her hair and ignored the television Samantha and Mike were watching intently. Samantha's tiny apartment was silent but for that, and Emily gripped the arms of the chair, glancing at those two sitting close together on the sofa. She felt much older than her twenty years and wanted to hate the God that had spit in her eye with this most recent betrayal: being separated from the man who had cared so much for her and whom she had truly *loved*—maybe the first love she had ever really known. They had come through so much, and now he was dead.

And she still lived.

"Goddammit," she whispered. *Because God had betrayed her.* After the hell of her younger years and the self-loathing her parents had induced, she had wished them dead. But events had finally released and destroyed the animosity and insanity that had violated her. Warren and their friend, Ben Dixon, had taught her the meaning of love through their determination and concern as they had tracked down and destroyed the vampires, and she knew she had helped them too.

They'd made her feel needed.

But then Ben's haunting warning from months before came back to her—*that they had destroyed the vampires her parents became with unblessed stakes.* He told her that their spirits could come back again to inhabit another vampire's body.

And he said that the only way to destroy them forever was through faith.

Now Ben was almost seven months dead, and Warren's lifeless body lay frozen in the city morgue. Without Warren, Emily felt very much alone, even if these other people surrounded her. But she still had the desire to be *needed.* Emily had helped Mike and Sam so that Warren wouldn't be always in the forefront of her mind, and not for the companionship that always seemed to twist and crush her. Still, she felt a strange kinship to Samantha. They had a grim bond because they both hated—and feared—the bloodsucking creatures that had invaded their lives.

A commercial for McDonald's blitzed into the news scene of flaring Dallas homes, replacing their smoldering shingles with the newest rock version of Ronald's happy song, and Emily salivated at the sight of the golden french fries.

"God." Samantha sighed sharply. "I can't believe they pick a *food ad* to run after just showing us those ambulances and body bags." She faced Mike beside her. "Are you feeling okay? Do you need another drink?"

"If you've got beer," he muttered, sinking back in the cushions.

"No way. How about you?"

Emily nodded. "A Coke if you have it. What I'd really like is some of those McFries on TV."

"And four or five burgers," Sam said.

"Gag."

They both stared at Mike. "What's wrong with *you?*" Sam asked. You haven't eaten anything for hours. I'm growling like crazy."

"Please, I'm serious. *Don't.*" He brushed black hair from his eyes. "Even *hearing* about food makes me want to throw up. It makes me hungry . . . but then I want to barf."

"Shit," Sam said.

"That's just how I feel."

Emily went to him and touched his hand, angry that she had forgotten his condition in her bitter self-sympathy. "You're cold. How are you doing?"

"I just told you that." He laid his head on the back of the sofa and coughed raggedly.

Emily sighed again, seeing his glazed eyes. "You're pretty far gone."

He pointed at the television screen which was listing a phone number to call for companionship; a woman in a negligée was stroking the phone blatantly and licking her lips as she urged lonely men to ring her. "So's half of fucking east Dallas," he grumbled.

As though listening, the station programmer faded the woman kissing the phone and returned to those streets, filling the nineteen-inch screen with flames and the face of a local anchorman:

"Welcome back. We are still covering on the spot the incredible inferno that has become a funeral pyre for at least twelve Texans tonight. An unknown number of unidentified hoodlums attacked a car in the residential neighborhood only a block from where I'm standing earlier this evening, dragging out both passenger and driver and murdering them. Several homeowners came out into their yards and tried to intervene, and two of them were also killed. Others bolted their doors and called the police. Reports have it that when the band of hoodlums had set the car on fire, they began setting fire to all the houses, too, ignoring the screams of the homeowners inside. One resident fired several shots at the attackers, witnesses say, but apparently missed every time. When the first police car arrived, it was overturned by the marauding gang and set afire, but authorities are declining to give any further information on the officers who were inside the car at this time. Other squad cars arrived a few minutes later, and witnesses who managed to escape from their burning homes estimate that they saw at least three policemen killed in hand-to-hand combat after the bullets they fired seemed to have no effect. Fire trucks are still trying to put out this blaze that has spread to the two apartment complexes behind me, and even to the surrounding stores. The area has been blockaded and everyone with business in this section of Dallas is urged to remain *home*." The newsman barely smiled. "And that goes for you sightseers, too. Just stay in your home and we'll show you everything that happens here with *Our Eye on Dallas* on Channel 9. Further reports will continue to break in on our regularly scheduled programming throughout the night of this terrible tragedy, and we will try to bring you a live report examining a similar disaster that occurred earlier this evening. Police authorities are now confirming reports of a conflict in south Dallas where it is believed these hoodlums fled from. . . ."

Emily turned back to Mike, trying to forget the interruption. "Uh . . . Mike . . . I *know* what you're going through," she said. "My husband, Warren, was bitten once too. He said he could feel the others—the other vampires—through some kind of a *bloodlink*."

Mike swallowed, then coughed again, staring at the interrupted rerun of *Star Trek* that replaced the newsbreak. *"I'm a doctor, not a bricklayer,"* Dr. McCoy told Captain Kirk.

Emily squeezed Mike's wrist. "You're still a man, not a vampire," she said softly.

He balled his hands into fists. "I don't want to touch them, damn you! That's what happened to me back at the hospital. The damn nurse gave me something to make me sleep, and all I could feel was *them*, all around me and inside me. That damn doctor was trying to give me another shot."

When Sam came back with the drinks, Emily gave Mike's hand to her. "It's okay, now. Samantha's here and you're safe, but you have to tell us where to find them so we can make you well, okay?"

"No." His dark face was wet and he grabbed a handful of hair and pulled it. "Wh-when I touch them, they don't want to let me go, damn it. They make me see things that I want . . . and *feel* them! I'm like one of those school kids to them, and they just want to take me and suck me dry and make me like they are."

"Stay with him," Emily said, nudging Samantha down to the sofa beside Mike. "I'll get some cold water. Then we need to do something. We need to get *moving*."

"Lieutenant Golan is going to meet us here."

Emily frowned, glaring at the TV, then her watch.

"Mike," Samantha whispered. She sat beside him.

Emily retrieved her suitcase from beside the door. It sat beside a blooming peace lily in one of Samantha's half-dozen brick plant-pots. She put the suitcase down on the nook table in the dining area. Emily dug out one of Warren's studded crosses and a plastic Coke liter bottle full of water he'd blessed. She carried them both through folding bamboo doors into the kitchenette. The wood-look counter and cabinets were clean, orderly.

She went through the cupboards, found sugary breakfast-cereal boxes, and smiled in surprise, finding a new link of kinship between her and Samantha. In the next cabinet she found a glass and filled it with Holy Water. It was so clear it looked syrupy.

Mike was coughing louder.

Wishing for Warren so badly that it made her spit sour, Emily resisted tears and hurried back to Samantha and Mike. She handed him the glass and stood back as Samantha helped him. His eyes widened with pain and he pushed her back. "It doesn't work!" he snarled. "I already tried *this*!"

Bending until their faces were level, Emily pushed the glass to his lips. "Try it again," she said. "It'll make it better for a while. If you *did* try it, you know I'm right."

Mike squinted at her, then slowly drank the entire contents. A wisp of steam rose up from his tongue, but none of them said anything about it. When he was finished, Sam let him lean against her. She yawned.

Emily went back to the kitchen and retrieved the studded cross, then brought it to the coffee table. Despite her anxiousness, she felt their exhaustion. She gave a tired smile. "Strange bedfellows." She sighed.

"Huh?" Samantha asked, blinking heavy eyes.

"Nothing. Come on, you two need to lie down and I want to get some things together. The night is still young and if you're going to get any sleep at all, you'd better do it now. If Mr. Policeman doesn't get here before long, we'll have to go on without him."

6

The cars sped by on the expressway, and no one noticed the body on the shoulder that was nearly covered by a flattened, dirt-caked cardboard refrigerator box. Peter Collins, a truck driver who'd been speeding his load for fifteen hours now, scratched his head dully when he saw it move, but decided to look away and just keep going when a hand crept out from underneath and started sliding the box to the side. He figured maybe he was just seeing things, and stopping to investigate would only waste precious time that was slipping away. He wanted to get to Oke City by dawn, collect his pay, and look up his ex-wife, who spread her legs for him far more often now than she had when they were married.

Peter Collins pushed down harder on his gas pedal and kept the semi in high gear, not looking back as Brian Sunderman crawled out from under the cardboard and knelt in the tall grass and dirt, blinking as he wiped the dust off his blue suit coat and stood up. When Peter finally did peer into his rearview mirror, he saw nothing unusual anyway, though Brian Sunderman still stood there. Peter didn't worry at all about the hand he thought he had seen—fifteen hours behind the wheel did funny things to a man, but not nearly as funny or pleasurable as the things he planned to do with his ex.

The unfastened slacks slipped down Brian's hairy legs when he got to his feet, and after brushing off his coat he bent and pulled them back up, and the old spotted boxer shorts under them too. In the artificial glare of the scattered late-night traffic, he saw the blood clotted in his lower hair, but didn't care.

He felt good, and despite the huge helping of Mexican delicacies hours before, he was *hungry*.

What the hell had happened to him?

But he *knew*, didn't he?

Yes, he knew, even though he still didn't believe it. But then, how could he deny the orgasm that naked red-haired girl forced from him that was the best come he had ever known, even as sudden and short as it had been?

How could he deny it when he knew he was dead?

"I'm *dead*," Brian whispered to himself, buckling his belt and watching an old Buick Skylark that had pulled into the lane nearest him *and was slowing down.* He touched his chest under his coat, surprised that he did not feel hysteria or even a sadness when the silent icy flesh under his shirt confirmed his thoughts.

He *was* stone cold dead.

The red car crunched gravel on the shoulder of the road and stopped. "Need a ride, mistuh?" drawled the unshaven youth whose patches of bristle made him look like his electric razor had gone berserk. "You look pretty fucked up."

Brian stared at him with his first feeling of real surprise, feeling the tingle in his throat that worked up to his teeth until his mouth was practically shaking. Self-consciously, he covered that mouth with his hand.

"Are you okay?"

Hunger. Every thought inside him disappeared except that one, and he felt saliva dripping on his palm as the kid opened his door and got out.

"Hey . . . I ain't a taxi, but if you got some gas money, I'll take ya' where you wanna go. You got some *money*?"

It was uncontrollable, and he went for the young man's throat just as he'd seen vampires do in the movies, feeling his long teeth sink into the soft neck as the kid tried to turn around and run. Brian held the boy's arms with suddenly powerful fingers and sucked him like he used to suck on cherry Slurpees from the store, except this drink was warm and almost hot and without a straw, and some of it spilled and trickled on his chin. It tasted damn good, anyway, and made him feel even better . . . it made his heart begin to beat in an odd rhythm; bumpa-bump-bump-bumpa-bump.

New blood whistled in his collapsed veins.

Minutes passed as headlights flashed them and passed on, and the infrequent car hums did nothing to distract him. At last he released the still body he was holding like a big fluffy sack of cotton, and forced himself to burp even though he didn't need to. It was damn fine—better even than that dinner with the boss. "Pour me another." Brian licked his lips, then pulled the scraggly teenager's body back to the flat refrigerator box. He dragged the box over the kid's frayed jeans and black Aliester C. T-shirt, taking a long look at that silk-screened rock star licking the blood from a head impaled on his guitar.

The sight of the T-shirt made Brian lick his lips again. He wondered if his wife was entertaining their divorcée neighbor in his absence tonight. He slid into the still-running Skylark, pushing aside an empty beer bottle and a package of smokes, then jerked the car back onto the highway. He bet to himself that no dyke had ever eaten Donna the way he was going to.

Twenty minutes later waves of heat flushed through the car's interior. Brian no longer felt uncomfortable in the temperature and didn't sweat, but he remembered that he once had, and that memory *did* make him uncomfortable. At first he was pleased that in death such things no longer affected him, but then he began to miss the sweet-rank odors of his own body. Fire trucks and police cars and sawhorses blocked a side street, and he drove through a cloud of thick smoke, coughing habitually even though he no longer had to breathe. A cop in a dirty uniform swung him to the left with a red-rimmed flashlight, and he obeyed, but only because this was nearly his turnoff anyway. He saw more police cars cruising up and down this new street and pressed the gas pedal until he was swerving and dashing around them at a speed well over the limit. He grinned sassily at the faces he passed, daring them to come after him, but each looked up, studied him, and let him go his way.

That made Brian a bit nervous, and he slowed down, even after the police were all well behind him. The air was clear now, and he turned twice more, watching the duplexes change into single-family homes that looked so much alike . . . as if they should be his *own*. He was glad he would no longer have to stay in that shoebox anymore, and thought of how his boss's smile would change to a frown when he didn't just come in late tomorrow, *but never even came in at all.* The eight-to-five world was history now. He had entered a sudden, unexpected retirement.

It was a relief. His son and daughter would wonder what had happened to him, but eventually he would come for them, because the love he'd once felt for them both was gone now. He even laughed at those vanished emotions that everyone took so seriously. People always said that love lasted forever, but it was bullshit, because once you were dead, your love and concerns were dead too.

He knew that because he was dead.

And hungry. Hungry for the lives that he detected all around him just as he once had been able to smell baking bread in the factory when still a block away.

Brian passed Donna's Oldsmobile parked on the street and pulled into the single-car driveway, smirking at the flaking paint on the small house he would never have to sand away and replace. He walked to the side of the house and pushed into the stickery holly branches until his nose was pressed against the wire screen, searching the darkened bedroom, the empty bed.

Nothing. He could not even *feel* her in there.

Glancing at his watch, Brian thought with irritation that it would be typically careless of Donna to leave their children alone in the house. But then, why should he care? He backed out of the bush. *It would take a while to get used to the idea of being dead.*

Besides, she wasn't far off. He crossed to the house next door, crossed lightly in front of the garage, and ignored the Doberman that had begun to bark frantically in the divorcée's backyard. Elaine, the woman's name was. She had told him that after he'd fucked her the afternoon he helped her move a divan into her house. They had broken in the divan right there and then, with his wife less than thirty feet away as she cooked dinner in their own home.

Tonight he would fuck them both, side by side, and watch them as they dropped all their pretenses. They would die side by side, naked, so that their hidden secrets would be common knowledge. He would satisfy himself and enjoy the revenge he still desired even after death. He opened the screen and rattled the doorknob.

It was locked.

"Shit," he breathed, trying to summon up his new power so that he could force the door open, but the door wouldn't budge. He blinked with surprise and tried to force the heavy wood again, feeling slow and confused.

Thoughts squirted in his head, and then he remembered how that red-haired knockout had not so much as touched him until he had opened his car door for her and invited her in. It struck a note with the memories of the movies he'd seen as a kid; that he would have to be *invited* inside. Backing away with anger, Brian stomped down the concrete steps to the side of this house and peered into the first side window. Between tangled curtains a red strobe light was flashing on those interior walls, the bed, and the two naked female bodies locked together on top of it. Loud rock 'n' roll pounded inside, and though the sound was faint out here, he could feel the fast rhythm keeping time with his heart. Brian growled.

He watched them, feeling a vengeful anger grow until it churned his stomach with a growing, insatiable lust even harsher than when he'd sucked the life from that teenager on the road. He beat his fists on the screen and wall.

The women's faces jerked up together, and Donna crawled off Elaine, wiping her chin and staring at him through the window. She squinted her beady eyes and grabbed a pillow, holding it up in front of her. Elaine did the same with another pillow and scooted to the bedstand, picking up the phone.

"Donna! Goddammit—it's *me*!" he squealed with a sudden aggravation.

The two women faced each other, and he saw Donna mouth the word *husband*. Elaine put the phone down and slipped on a robe. She kept her face from the window as she walked out of the room.

Brian snarled at Donna. She backed up to the headboard, her eyes big in fright. She doubled over the pillow.

The front door opened and slammed closed. He backed away from the window.

"Brian?"

Elaine walked around the overgrown bush at the corner of the house and stood before him, holding up her hands. Her face was dark in the shadows and the long robe swayed in the night's breeze. He tried to form words, but the scent of her so close made a moan overcome them.

"Brian, stand back and calm down. I know you're mad, okay? But please, just calm down."

He smiled.

"This is all my fault, Brian, okay? Just calm down and don't be thinking of taking this out on Donna. You know how it is, because *you* fucked me too." She moved closer, her feet making soft swishing noises on the grass, and then she touched him with hands cold as ice. He felt—

Elaine stared blankly for an instant, then recovered. "You're just a little late, Brian, but I'm glad you understand." She smiled, the lights of her bedroom showing her features, the red stains on her mouth that had leaked down to discolor her pointy chin. "I learned the secret at a bar a couple of nights ago, but Donna will be disappointed because I know she wanted to be the one to give it to *you*. At least this has brought us all out into the open, huh?"

At last comprehending, Brian staggered a step back, and realized that his teeth were no longer tingling. A jealous irritation flooded him and he shoved her away, snarling. "You bitch—you fucking *bitch dyke*. You fucked me and then you started screwing my wife! What the hell gives you the right to break up our family like that?"

"Hey." Elaine grabbed his shivering hand. "Cool it and come help me finish her off, okay? We'll get the kiddoes next. . . . Then maybe you'd like to try doing your thing to a man for a change—we can fuck around with anyone and everyone we want to, Brian. We'll all be just like one big, happy family." She pulled him along after her, her bare feet gliding over the grass. The streetlight shone on her, but she didn't cast a shadow, and when he looked behind himself, neither did he.

Elaine laughed. "We're all in this together, okay?"

7

Mike tossed and turned, and Sam could barely rest after she lay down with him on her double bed. Emily paced the floor noisily in the living room, opening and closing her suitcase constantly. It made Sam nervous, especially with the signs of the infection in Mike.

She knew his disease was spreading.

After a while the sounds in the next room stopped, but Sam still couldn't sleep. When another half hour passed, she let go of her necklace and pushed off the sheets. She went to the doorway and scanned the dusky space lit only by her fifteen-gallon aquarium. Emily was curled catlike in the center of the sofa, finally asleep.

Emily was weird, even under *these* circumstances. Her characteristic calm sadness seemed at odds with the way she had banged around in here until a few minutes ago. In the hospital Emily's attitude had been almost cold when she placed Sam's cross on Mike.

Sam couldn't comprehend how anger could flare in her face and voice one minute, and how she could quell that violence the next.

Sam didn't understand the religious fervor that had driven her husband after these creatures.

But she did not doubt the danger, or the evil, of what they faced . . . of what they all faced. The cruelty she had glimpsed in that faraway bar was more than enough.

Vampires existed . . . but they did not live. That sense had weighed in on her at the beginning. They did not seem to comprehend compassion or progress, and with the bodies piling up, she suspected that their thirst was something never quenched.

That knowledge frightened her most of all, confirmed and underlined by Mike's own descriptions of it. It was like the tequila she drank and drank but that never completely satisfied.

No one can eat just one. Sam shivered. Her tired thoughts swam back and forth between the ridiculous impossibilities of the situation and fear. The fear that had never left her since that night in Las Bocas—a dead town empty of anything but death.

She wanted to be, as Walt first accused her and then Mike, a world saver. She at least wanted to save herself from the running and hiding of her nightmares, and somehow make up for the death of her brother in that useless jungle struggle so long ago.

Going to the armchair in front of the dark TV, Sam sat quietly with an eye on Emily. She drew up her legs, thinking of Mark and that long-ago night when his army friend had come to see her parents, bringing the sketches Mark had done, his last works as the artist he'd dreamed of being. The tears from the past curled hot in her eyes.

"You would have been very proud," the young ex-soldier had told Mom and Dad. *"It was so crazy over there, and one night one of our guys just went nuts. He woke up screaming and started to shoot anything that moved. He tried to kill us all, but your son stopped him. He gave the rest of us our chance to grab that crazy bastard and tie him up. But when we got to him, he'd already put his bayonet into Mark's heart."*

The tears ran through her drooping eyelids, and laying her cheek on the back of the chair, Sam closed her eyes tight. In a minute she was sound asleep.

Thirty minutes later, pounding at the front door brought Sam awake. She was trying to shut it out when a hand tagged her shoulder. "Samantha?" Emily spoke lowly.

She rubbed her eyes as Emily leaned against the door. "Who's there?"

"It's Golan—open up."

Emily opened the door and Golan pushed in with the acrid scent of thick smoke. He wiped a dark smudge on his wide forehead, smearing it into the lines there, and adjusted the stubby cigarette in his mouth. His slumped shoulders spoke of exhaustion. "Hi."

"You stink." Emily told him.

"That ain't the half of it," he said hoarsely. "We got a big problem on our hands. The fire's under control, but the feds have hit the city and that fire's just begun. Fifteen people are numbered dead already, and I counted seven dead of 'unknown causes' "—he spoke with unhidden bleakness—"which means they were drained of blood. They're moving the bodies to the morgue for examination." He tossed his cigarette butt out on the landing and slammed the door.

"That's good," Emily said.

Sam pushed herself up and went to turn on the overhead lights.

"How's that?" he asked sharply.

"Warren and Ben said the victims couldn't turn and come back until they were returned to the ground or until funeral vows were said over them. If we could get into the morgue, we could stop the new ones now. We can fix it so they can't come back."

"You want to tell me about all this?"

"Do you believe what's happening, then?" Sam asked Golan.

"I told you, Samantha," he said, "I never disbelieved it. I got too much army drilled into me to disbelieve anything. I'm just tired of reacting and I want to start making the waves myself. My blood's pounding and I want to move before the guys in charge put the clamps on me. I'll need to do some headwork so we can figure where to hunt first—but I have to know what we're up against, okay?" He pointed a dirty thumb at Emily. "And you're Miss Know-it-all."

Emily spoke coldly. *"Mrs., thank you."*

Golan turned red.

"The first thing," she said after a strained moment, "is to find out who has died recently, and then track their bodies to their graves and consecrate them. We can do it in the daylight." She and the detective exchanged a look. "Mr. Policeman will be able to get us that information easily."

"Okay. Then what do I do?"

Emily's thin lips turned up viciously, but her voice stayed icily controlled. "Nothing," she said. "I've never heard of a vampire being turned back by a Star of David. I think we should talk to some of the ministers around here. We'll have to get some Holy Water and sacraments to consecrate the graves—"

"Shit! What about all the missing people who haven't even been found?" Samantha blurted suddenly. "We don't have any idea where they might be."

Emily glanced back at Sam's bedroom, and her dark grin grew wider. "That's where your friend will come in. He'll know. There's some kind of a telepathy among them. We can use him to guide us."

The living room light spilled into the bedroom and outlined Mike's twisting body, revealing him in the throes of another nightmare. Sam didn't like the idea of using him through those awful visions that resembled her own dreams of fleeing. "We can't ask him to do that!"

"We won't ask him." Golan patted his shoulder holster. "He owes it and he won't have any choice. This will be a down payment on his debt to society." He glared at Emily with hot mirth. "And I don't give a shit about what religion your ammo is as long as it kills . . . and I give you ten to one that I do just fine."

Another moment passed while her lips twitched, then: "Sorry."

The brawny plainclothesman walked to face Sam. "How about something to wet my whistle? I wasn't born to be a fireman, and eating smoke's got me real thirsty."

With a last look at Mike, Sam led Golan into the kitchen.

"Just water."

She served it to him as Emily closed up her suitcase and set it beside the table. She sat beside Golan.

"Did you get your family on a plane?" Sam asked him, thinking of her own parents who lived on the outskirts of the city.

"Yeah."

Emily cleared her throat. "We need to get moving. Wake up Mike and bring him in. We may not get a chance to go over all this again."

8

 "There's something wrong with you, Miriam."

"There's something wrong with *you,* Ed—I can't believe you're acting like this. It's a miracle!"

Snorting, he kept his eyes on the living-room doorway. "We haven't been to church in five frigging years and now all of a sudden, you're into miracles. It's *not* Kathy. We buried her. We had to identify her and you know as well as I do that it was her!"

"Maybe we made a mistake." Miriam Conway clasped her hands together and breathed deep. "She was so pale and sick looking. Maybe it was Tammy, the one they say they can't find. *Maybe it was really Kathy who was missing all along!*"

Stoking his pipe with a calloused finger, Ed shook his head and wiped that digit on his undershirt, which bulged over his huge beer-fed tummy. He crossed the room from his lumpy easy chair and flipped off the TV, then examined her hopeful, overjoyed face. Her smiling lips disappeared into flabby, colorless cheeks. "Tammy's parents were there too. Don't you think they would have said something if they thought that our girl was theirs?"

Miriam shook her head, making her nightrobe shimmer. "This is our Kathy," she answered. "You know she's ours!"

Fitting the pipe's chewed black stem between his teeth, Ed grunted. The house had been so sad the past week since the van's wreck. They'd both tried to cling to the possibility of an identity mix-up until the bodies were shipped up and they went with the police to view them. Then the cold sight of their dead daughter had released the agony they'd tried to deny.

It had been Kathy, and she had been dead.

But tonight, only a half hour ago, Kathy had come to the door and knocked. Ed got up from the late-night *Playboy* channel offering, and his pipe nearly slipped out of his mouth. There was no doubt it was Kathy, and though she was pale, his own pleasure had nearly overcome the impossibility, especially when he invited her in and Miriam saw her too.

But Kathy was *dead.* "It *can't* be her," he moaned under his breath.

"Mom?"

Miriam jerked around and held her arms out to the young blond woman. Kathy had gone into her room and changed out of the dusty shorts and T-shirt. She was wearing the slinky, tight dress Miriam had let her buy three months ago. Ed frowned at the low-cut top and high hemline. He had wanted to take it back to the store the first time he saw it, when he spied so much of the little girl he'd raised that he had wanted to forget who she was. For a moment he'd imagined her as one of the airbrushed beauties in the magazines he kept in the garage. It wasn't right for a daughter to make her own dad feel that way about her. Especially when she swung her hips in a way that made his pants too small.

She swung them like that now.

"Who are you, *really*?" he managed, ignoring the his wife's anger. "Did you plan this out because you looked like Kathy and wanted to cheat us out of our money?" He knew that old plot from a hundred TV shows but still felt hot under her chilly eyes. *"Who the hell are you?"*

Breaking away from Miriam, Kathy came forward like a *Penthouse* girl, pouting her lower lip and licking it with the end of her tongue. "I'm your dear little baby, Daddy. I've come to give you birth, like you and Mom did for me." She winked. "Momma," she continued, "will you let Daddy and me talk alone for a minute?"

"But, honey—"

The woman who said she was Kathy and looked a hell of a lot like Kathy glimmered a smile at the older woman and winked at her once more. "Just a few minutes, Momma, then I've got a lot to talk to you about." She paced around her and glided past an antique Singer sewing machine Miriam had varnished and put in here like a museum piece.

"Ed," Miriam warned, but he turned away from her to stare at the yellowing drapes that covered their big picture window. Kathy whispered something, and then he listened to his wife's house-shoe slippers flop down the hallway carpet until the bedroom door closed.

His head throbbed with contradictory emotions,

from the unexpected rapture of his daughter's reappearance, to the crushing confusion that it was not possible; to the dread he was slick and dripping with now—that if this was a dream, it was the most vivid, Technicolor 3-D extravaganza he'd ever met. It was even more potent than his half-drunk imaginings out in the workshop, when he guzzled a six-pack and stared at those Forum letters, then gazed at the bare models who looked like they wanted *him*. Those fantasies were almost as good as the real thing, and he always pretended that a thousand other guys weren't salivating over those poses too—that the girls were naked just for *him*. Ed swallowed hard, shutting his eyelids until he was staring into darkness, seeing those waiting women.

"Daddy?"

Her fingers danced up his bare shoulder and touched his thick neck, rubbing on the day's whiskery growth. "You're . . . not real." He forced out the words, remembering how he'd always tried to give her everything her more well-to-do friends had—even sending her to that goddammed hot-shit Texas A & M College. It had been his fucking credit card that paid for the shimmering dress she wore now.

"Daddy?" She pressed her cool body against him.

"You *can't* be *Kathy*," he whined as new sweat lined his forehead. Her fingernails drifted down his undershirt and she moved right up against his chest. He bit his lip. Those wintry digits went lower, hesitated, then stroked him through his polyester pants, making his teeth bite into his lip deeper as he felt himself firming in her touch. This time his pipe did drop out of his mouth, but he barely noticed it.

He heard her through his heavy breath. "I can be

anyone you want me to be." She sighed, unzipping him and pushing her cold hand in. "I can be every one of those sluts I watched you jerk off to in the garage, Daddy. They were just pictures, and if you can want them, I know you can want *me.*"

"K-Kathy—"

She pulled his trembling lips to hers, gliding her body up and down.

Ed moaned, midway between despair and making every forbidden fantasy he had ever masturbated to come true. He started at the bad taste of her tongue, but that discomfort disappeared when she stepped back with a lovely smile that asked him what he was waiting for. She reached up to the silver snap that held her nothing dress together and pulled it apart. The material flowed down her naked, perfectly tuned body to the carpet. Her standing breasts were so much like the ones he'd sucked on Miriam before Kathy had been born and made them misshapen. Her slender stomach led to a jungle of shiny blond hair that was asking his entrance into the treasure it hid.

"Fuck me, Daddy. Fuck me like you fucked Momma the night you made me, and I'll make you too. Fuck me like you dreamed of fucking those girls in the magazines, 'cause I'm real and I'm here just like in your dreams, just like you always wanted when you cracked open the bathroom door and watched me in the shower . . . *like the time you hid in the doorway and watched Scott fuck me on the couch.*"

Ed grit his teeth, startled at her knowledge and feeling the blood rise hotter into his face. *This wasn't right.* The blush ran through him but couldn't stop the way her words made him stiffen, and he remembered when he had felt this way before, time and again, staring at her growing body that was everything he wanted but must never have. He could see her and that boy, Scott, wrestling on the couch naked and panting as that young man forced his way inside her. The chastising words Ed had first intended died in his throat, and he felt each stroke, wishing it were him inside her.

"Fuck me, Daddy. Stick that big honker into me and call me your little girl."

Her lips parted as she lowered herself to the carpet at his feet, and the sight of her long teeth made him struggle to regain willpower. He tried to remember the stench of her baby diapers.

But he couldn't. Her eyes drew him into her already, and he could not deny the future she was unfolding in them. She spread her long legs wide and squeezed her breasts together. "Suck my tits and fuck me good, Daddy dear. Lick my juices and I'll *swallow* yours. . . ."

It was too much and he didn't want to hold back even one more second. Weakly, he got to his knees and unbuckled his trousers. She pulled them down and he laid on top of her. Sliding up sleek, cold flesh, he entered her tightness, freed from guilt by her eyes. They moaned together and moved furiously until he was limp. Then she got up from under him and bent over his fatigue, and her tongue returned that spent life until he was breathless . . . until he was coming again into the mouth that she had once kissed him with innocently when he tucked her in bed.

Fucked her into bed.

At the height of ecstasy, he groaned from the mixtures of hot pain and pleasure, feeling sharp teeth dig deep, lips sucking and sucking and sucking until he could only smile at the black unconsciousness drifting through him and over him.

9

"Ben told us the only way to really destroy them permanently was through faith in God," Emily was saying, her eyes on Golan, "but there's a lot of other ways to get rid of them. I killed my mother with a wooden stake through her heart, and even Ben killed my dad the same way. The only bad thing about doing it that way is that Ben said the spirits that reanimated the bodies might return in another body later, and if that spirit remembered, it might come after you—"

"Mumbo-jumbo," said Golan. "Look, I personally know I'd have a hell of a lot more *faith* at the sight of a stake in one of those things. My only problem with doing that in the morgue is that the powers that be might raise their eyebrows at it. If you think it will really work, why don't you get some of your precious holy water and try it? I think I can get you into that place even with the feds swarming down, and like you said, that can be done during the day, anyhow. These

other creeps are what I'm worried about." Golan
drove his wiry eyes into Mike. "So where the hell are
they now?"

"All over the place. . . ."

Sam clutched Mike's shaky fist as the hoarse words
crept out, holding as strongly as she could even
though she felt as if she was about to drop. It was half
past three. "Mike, you said you could *feel* them, remember? Where did you feel them?"

The brown-skinned man stood. Emily sat in an eerie, stiff calm at his right; Golan hunkered over the
table, his cheeks in big hands. Sam stared nervously at
Emily's big cross. "I can feel them but I can't see
them," Mike croaked. "I know they're out there, and
sometimes I can even get glimpses of what I think
they're doing. I think I know when they're getting
close to me. But that's it, okay? It—it's like some kind
of a radar—but it's limited, okay? It's real limited!"

"Are they close to us now?" Sam asked.

Mike shut his eyes for a short moment, then sighed.
"No. But a few minutes ago when I jumped like I did,
I felt like someone had just tried to rip out part of my
heart, and I think it was because one of *them* got hurt
pretty bad."

Golan's stony features flickered. "Hurt?"

Laying his index finger on his neck, Mike slid it
across his throat with a whistle.

"One of them was killed?" Emily asked.

"I'm not sure. It hurt really bad. But that's why I
don't like thinking about them and letting them into
my brain." He sat back down and let his head roll
back. "They make me want to hurt *you*."

"Like all the kids you've hurt by passing around
your shit, huh?"

Mike's head flipped back and he leaned forward dangerously. His narrow eyes were filled with heat. "But that's why you need me, cop! I know things you need to know—just the way your fucking prosecutors need guys like me to put other guys that are no worse than they are in jail. And I know that the only difference between me and the geeks you give a suspended sentence to is you're not offering me a damn thing."

"I'm offering you a chance to be free. You help me, and I'll personally kill the bitch who did this to you."

"They're offering me freedom too, and, Cop, their freedom looks a lot nicer than yours. The thing that stops me from going to them is that I've already been too near that road once. It scares me, because I know if I let them get me, I can never come back."

Golan yawned.

"And another reason is that maybe . . . I'm *ashamed* of the things I used to do." Mike grabbed the detective's arm. His urgent fingers turned Golan's wrist white. "I never really understood what I was doing to those dumb-shit kids who came and groveled at my door with their twenty-dollar bills, and how it wasn't really *them,* but that it was what *I* had turned them *into.*"

"My heart bleeds!" Golan tore his arm free. "Unfortunately, I just don't give a shit. Go into your trance or whatever it is and—"

A steady, shrill bleat broke in with an unexpected punctuation.

"I—" Golan dropped his hand under the table and cut the beeper off. "They're calling me from the station. Can I use your phone?"

Sam pointed at the phone in the kitchenette.

As he rose, he leaned across the table, hands planted

firmly in its center, until his face was only inches from Mike's. "I don't care why or how you can do what you do or why you *will* do it, Hossiason. What I want to know is when you're going to shut your big mouth and show us where these guys are, and if you really do think you give a shit, then let's start now, okay?" Without waiting for a reply he pulled back and laid a straight line down between himself and the phone, then closed the bamboo doors behind him.

Emily stroked Mike's knuckles.

"It's not so easy." His voice trembled.

"I know."

"I mean, I think I know where a lot of them are, but I don't want to get close to them. It—it makes it worse. When they get near, I just think of the things I've done—they show me those things so I'll know that I'm already a lot like them. They offer me more. They offer everything I thought I ever wanted. But I don't think it is what I want. It's getting worse. I'm getting worse."

Emily crossed her arms. "That's why you have to do it. We're all like they are. *They come from us.* For right now, only you can take us to them. Warren, my husband, once said that the true mark of repentance is facing your past to overcome it. By accepting the forgiveness for what you've done, you put an end to what you *were.*"

Sam took Mike's hand. His fingers were warm and smooth.

"They've split up," Mike finally whispered. "Those things really *are* all over the place, but I think I know where most of them rest. I think they're right in the neighborhood where I live."

The kitchen door opened, and Golan looked right at

Mike. "I got to go, but I want every one of you to stay around here, okay? The shit's really hitting the fan. Some preacher called the precinct on the south side going on about vampires, and we've got four more bodies. On top of that, that bastard doctor called and laid it into them about me too. I'm going to talk to the feds and see what they want, then try to get some sleep. After that I'm going to round up a couple of guys to help us out. I'll be back here by noon."

Emily exploded. "We don't have that kind of time. We need to be out in the graveyards at dawn to sanctify the graves, if nothing else!"

"Hey, I'm in charge here, okay? Do you have any idea how many cemeteries there are in this town? Sawed-off mavericks who jump out on their own just make matters worse. That's exactly why your husband got killed."

Emily picked the studded cross up from the table as though to ward the detective off. She raised it, then her body trembled in a sigh. She put the cross back down and dropped her head. "What about the bodies in the morgue?"

Golan shrugged. "If what you say is true, lady, then they're not going anywhere yet. The big brass is having a group of specialists brought in to study them, but I'm hoping we can get to them within a couple of days. Right now, we want to worry about these other things still roaming the streets." His smile was thin. "And tomorrow Mr. Hossiason is going play *blood*-hound."

10

"This is boring," MaryAnn grunted, watching stores and houses pass by. The bank time-sign on the corner displayed the hour as three o'clock. "Everyplace is closed and everyone's gone to bed."

"Not everyone." Scott hummed along with Elton John as his old song about fighting on Saturday nights ripped through a scratchy radio speaker. "I keep thinking of that asshole back in that bar. He pissed me off and he plays shitty music. He's in there grabbing easy lunches while we gotta go out and find ours. Can you believe the way he was trying to tell us how much and *whose* blood to suck?" He turned the car onto a smaller, two lane street, passing a greasy-spoon diner that was just closing. "Who elected him king, huh?"

Jerry nodded and leaned up against the back of the front seat, sticking his head between them. "What can you do to him, huh? He's already dead."

"Shit. We can take his customers before they ever

get inside—how about that? We can make him have to go out like we do."

"Hey, slow down." MaryAnn was studying the night-owl diners as they rubbed their bellies and hitched up their pants, or dangled their purses and swiveled lazily toward their cars. The lighted sign above the hexagonal building flashed TEX-MEX, HOT —AND LIP-SMACKING GOOD!

"So?" drawled Scott. "You wanna bite these guys?"

Jerry stared out his window, wrinkling his nose with a superior air. "Doesn't look that appetizing to me. Why don't we just keep going? I know some junior high creeps that live on the west side. We could really freak them out. Then, I think it might be fun to do something like that bartender dick was talking about."

"Oh, yeah? *You* were *thinking*?"

"Eat me, Scott. Just listen: We can find everyone who ever pissed us off, okay? There's this prick who used to beat the shit out of me after class in elementary school. I want to give him the bite and just set him on fire like the bartender did to his wife and brother. Just think of the expression on his face when he wakes up in Hell or wherever he'll go."

Scott had stopped the car in the middle of the street and creased his brow thoughtfully. "Might work. We could find all the jocks and dopeheads we used to go to school with and do it to them, and fuck up the other frat-houses and sor-whores. I know a lot of pricks and pussies I'd love to do it to." He grinned suddenly, his lips curling back to reveal the pointed top teeth. "Shit, we could even give that fucking bartender a taste of his own medicine."

"You two are like a couple of old yearbooks. I think it would be funnier to eat these guys right after they've just eaten. I like Mexican food! We can do the other stuff anytime."

Scott followed MaryAnn's gaze, then shook his head. "You've got no ambition."

"Sure I do, but what's the hurry? We've got all the time in the world now."

Finally, he shrugged, and she glanced at Jerry.

"Yeah, okay," Jerry finally agreed. "There's some jigs over there who look like they want a good scare, anyhow. Let's go fuck 'em up until their skin turns white, and split. Driving and dreaming is bullshit, Scott. *Let's do it!*"

" '. . . *get a little action in,*' " sang Elton, backed by his banging piano.

Scott steered into the lot. The station wagon rumbled over the cracked asphalt and past the big windows where lights were going off inside the building. Busboys were putting the chairs on top of tables and sweeping around them.

"Let's get the niggers," Jerry whispered, pointing at the three slumping black men who had reached a green LTD at the far end of the lot. They were all older, two of them with salt-and-pepper hair. The tallest still had a curly mop that was as jet-black as his skin, but the light pole they stood beside showed the deep lines etched in his face. "Let's see if they taste as good as a white man. Maybe they're flavored *chocolate.*"

"I'd rather have a chocolate woman," Scott mumbled, stopping in front of the LTD. He sighed. "Okay, Jer, let's do it."

Jerry snickered and got out. He grinned when MaryAnn stood beside him.

" 'Scuse me," the tallest man said mildly, "you need to move your car."

"Nigger."

The tall man frowned, then squared his shoulders and shook his head.

"You want to make us move?" Jerry sniffed, hands on his hips.

One of the other men stepped up beside the first. "Man, cool it."

Jerry cackled and shoved him back easily. The tall man flinched and jumped back. "I scare you that bad already, huh? Well, you want to see something really scary?"

The tall man was pointing behind Jerry. *"He ain't got a shadow."* His hand flew down in his jacket pocket, and MaryAnn laughed, wriggling forward like a dance queen and unzipping her skirt.

"How about some of this white pussy my daddy says you people dream for?" she asked in a mockery of sweetness. The skirt dropped down to her ankles and the warm breeze licked at her thighs as she pushed her pelvis toward them and kicked the garment away. "I want to see if you darkies all got the big cocks you brag about."

The tall man's eyes grew, and his hand sprang back out of his pocket with the clatter of hanging beads. He leapt forward, shoving that hand into Jerry's face. *"Now do you believe me, you stupid niggers?"* he hollered at his friends. He clutched Jerry's arm as Jerry shrieked with pain. A fiery yellow steam exploded from Jerry's face where the shiny crucifix torched him, and his cry blasted louder, riding across the lot to the departing cars.

MaryAnn stopped dazedly, her legs separated

lewdly. A whine hurtled up from her own lips as Jerry struggled against the man who wouldn't let go. The shining cross ignited his dry skin.

"NO—"

She stared and remembered the fear she'd felt that first night in the cemetery, when that man had popped up from nowhere and come at her with a cross. "No."

Jerry fell to the pavement and the big black man dropped with him, using the rosary crucifix as a knife and driving it into his forehead, making Jerry's burning flesh crack and split apart down to his nose, exposing his skull, cracking that bony protection and bringing up a stinking mist from the slimy brains that exploded out of that hole like a shaken bottle of cola.

A hand grabbed MaryAnn's wrist and she shrieked. *She wanted this new existence to go on!* She wanted to have *fun!*

Jerry's entire body was steaming now, bathing the black man bent over him.

"She don't have a shadow too," one of the other two men gasped.

The man who'd destroyed Jerry glared right into MaryAnn. *"I told you they were back!"*

MaryAnn shrieked again, trying to get free of the sudden grip tugging her backward. She beat hysterically at the hands dragging her into the car, grinding her long fingernails into an arm as it reached across her and slammed the door shut. Her head jerked with the movement of the car, and she remembered what terror was and how this terror was worse and more bitter than any other even in those faraway memories of life. "No!" she was screaming, over and over again.

The parking lot was spinning. She heard squealing tires and wanted to cry the tears she could no longer create. Her fingers clutched the dashboard so tightly, she heard it crack, saw it splitting under her pressure, just as Jerry's face had split open.

"Cool it, MaryAnn," Scott hissed, speeding the station wagon along the silent, night street. He raised a fist and socked her cheek. "Cool it right *now*! If you hadn't flipped out, we could be eating those black motherfuckers."

Dropping her hands to her naked legs, MaryAnn forced herself to look back at the three black men and the mist rolling around them formlessly. It was her last look at Jerry. For the first time since she'd awakened into this new reality, she was really and truly scared, because she knew that mist could be *her*.

It nearly destroyed her appetite.

"Motherfuckers," said Scott again. "They got him, and they were just fucking niggers!"

"They *know*," whined MaryAnn. "They know how to kill us!"

Scott's laughter was brutal. "We got to kill them first, then. We'll make those niggers back into our slaves."

The wind from the open window made MaryAnn's red hair fly; finally the bad feelings flew away too. Scott turned the radio back up and she touched her aching teeth.

"We've got to be careful from now on. Shit, maybe that cocksucker in the bar was right. We got to be more careful!" Scott began slowing down, and he glanced out at the warehouses they'd come to. "I don't know where the fuck Kathy is, so it's just you and me now, MaryAnn." He drifted his right hand onto her bare leg. "But that's okay with me. Jerry even found us a snack earlier, when he was wandering down that old alley." Scott handed her a soiled sack, taking out a well-used tampon. He sniffed it and made a face.

MaryAnn made a face too. Her hand dropped into the sack and she brought out a dark napkin, remembering how she'd once set the table at home with sanitary napkins as a joke. She recalled the pain and cramps she associated with these things, how they stank after she pulled them out of her panties and dropped them in the wastebasket.

They smelled good now. As Scott touched the tip of his tongue to the tampon in his hand, she couldn't help but lick her lips.

After a brief initial repugnance she was crunching the plastic and cotton like a hungry dog and relishing its taste of blood. The thrill of this moment made her remember the only other time when she and Scott had been alone. It was one night back in College Station when Kathy was sick and Maury's mom had made him drive home, keeping him from their usual Friday-night outing. Scott and she and Jerry and Tammy had gone out to a movie, and when the latter two had retired into Tammy's sorority room for a nightcap of sex, Scott had invited MaryAnn into his fraternity house. They made love twice in the space of an hour, though she understood better than ever now that the love they'd made was lust. But it had been good. Better than sex with Maury, really, because it was so sudden and unplanned, and after the first few minutes, uninhibited.

The memory of Jerry's loss slipped away in the understanding of the no-holds-barred terms for that lust now. Scott stopped the wagon in front of a dark building and they both crawled into the back, venting their frustrations on each other, snacking on the remaining

tampons, and then returning to the cemetery just before dawn.

MaryAnn was smiling as she stood on the dirt before her tombstone, and she disappeared into the
ground as pink daylight streaked the morning sky.

11

 After giving Mike another glass of the holy water, Sam decided to lie down beside him again.

Detective Golan had gone, and Emily was in the bathroom. Mike had begun snoring as soon as he hit the mattress. Sam sat down on the bed's end, then stretched out.

Despite the exhaustion tenanted inside her, her eyes didn't want to close. She watched Mike in the shadows.

According to Golan, he'd not only been an addict and pusher but was one of those creeps who transformed kids into hideous, cocaine-snorting freaks.

Mike was a bad guy.

His shoulder twitched, and Sam scooted another inch away. Emily had said that the vampires came from *all* of them, implying that everyone had a vampire locked up somewhere among the skeletons in his closet.

Sam sighed in that truth: in their most self-serving moments there was very little difference between a living human being and a vampire, and she saw that only the sense of caring most people tried to hide separated them from the undead. Only the ability to love unselfishly proved the existence of that chasm, like the love her own brother had shown when he sacrificed himself to save the other soldiers in his platoon.

Sam scooted closer to Mike's warm body again and laid her hand on his stomach, feeling the snores that built up from there and spilled out his open mouth. Lying against him, she closed her eyes at last, and drifted into sleep.

"Shit!"

Sam jerked up, blinking the sleep from her eyes. It was daylight. Mike darted wildly to the open window curtains. Raising an arm to shield himself from the sunlight, he grabbed the curtain tassel and yanked it, closing the drapes.

"What's wrong?" Sam asked, jumping out of bed.

He shook his head, grunting, then shifted his narrow eyes to Emily at the doorway. Emily was yawning and slump shouldered and wore a rumpled cotton nightgown. "The sun won't even kill a real vampire," Emily said. "Unless it's a psychosomatic reaction from seeing too many movies."

"It hurt." He walked to the far corner and rubbed his bare forearms as though they'd been burned.

"That's because vampires lose their supernatural talents under the sun. Warren and I read a lot about it. Direct sunlight makes the undead very uncomfortable, too, kind of like sunbathing in the middle of a scorching day without tanning oil."

He was shivering. "That doesn't make me feel better. Shit—maybe I died in my sleep and I'm one of them now!"

Sam raised her hand to the cross around her neck.

"I think it's just that the infection is spreading," Emily replied. "You're still breathing; your heart's still beating, right?" She smirked, then tapped her forehead. "Just like the psychiatrist used to tell me: You've seen too many movies for your own good."

"It's not funny and it's not a joke, goddammit!"

Emily drew back the heavy curtain and peered out the window. "The sun's been shining in this room for a while, Mike. If you were on the bed, it was on you the whole time."

"It hurt!"

Emily shrugged. "You're a good alarm clock, anyway." She checked her watch. "It's getting late. Do you mind if I use the shower? We need to be ready."

"Yeah," Sam said. "I'm after you. I'm going to get something to eat."

"I get the Froot Loops," Emily said and went out almost pleasantly. A minute later the bathroom door closed, and Sam heard the sound of running water.

"She thinks I'm cracking up," Mike said in a low voice. He was cowering in the corner, his eyes dull.

"Maybe—"

"Maybe, nothing. She thinks I'm losing it and so does Golan. And I think maybe they're right." He clutched at his arms with restless hands. "I know they're right. This is bad, Samantha. You guys just don't understand what I'm going through. I can't just let that cop lead me around town on a leash while we find every one of those damned bloodsuckers. The closer I get to them the crazier I get. I—I see things in my dreams."

"You're not the only one who's in danger, Mike."

"No. But maybe I'm the only one who understands the danger. If you use me like that, I think I may flip out completely. They want you, but they really want me, because they already know about me. I've got to find the bitch who did this to me and kill her, or I won't be able to go on." His teeth clamped and he ground them noisily, lowering himself until he was sitting on the floor. "You said you'd help me!"

"I know. But I want you to try to help us first—please? If—if you really *can't* . . ." She grit her teeth, too, feeling the meaning their history gave them, no matter how meaningless either of them had tried to make it.

"I don't know if I can," his thin voice whispered. "I don't want to."

"Please?"

Mike sighed.

"If you promise to help me get her, even if I can't help, I'll try."

Pity.

She pitied him, and herself. Deep down, the vampire in them both was struggling desperately to get out, growing out of his greed and her desires for Walt and success that had driven her to drink. Their separate darknesses had gained footholds in pleasure, then steadily warped into single-minded cravings. Though their purposes had been diverse, the circle of obsession was a single unbroken line.

When Emily was through, Sam took her place in the shower. She stood under the beating stream and soaped herself over and over.

When she dried off, Sam still felt dirty.

12

Once again Mike didn't want to eat or even talk about it. As Sam and Emily made up for his lack of appetite, he sat in front of the TV, watching a news piece on the aftermath of the inferno that had destroyed three small businesses and ten homes, and severely damaged others. Sam hungrily devoured two bowls of Lucky Charms and three pieces of toast, rinsing it all down with her second glass of milk. She was still hungry.

Emily was too. "How about some Froot Loops and eggs? I'll cook them."

"How about not talking about it?"

Sam frowned at Mike. "Why don't you take a shower, and we'll promise to be finished by the time you're done."

"The water *burns*," he muttered, "like the damn sun. I'm fine—just, *please*, don't talk about food. I *am* hungry, but I know if I even try to eat, it'll make me puke. My stomach's flipping like crazy just thinking about it. Okay?"

"He's probably right about the water," whispered Emily. "Running water is supposed to paralyze and sometimes even kill a vampire." She took her bowl to the kitchen and started work on some eggs.

"How come?" Sam asked.

"Purity, I think. Warren understood that part of it pretty well. Kind of Old Testament stuff. You know, sacrifices, kosher food. . . . He said a stream of living water represented a *living purity.*"

"I can't believe anyone would call the water here in Dallas pure."

"It doesn't have anything to do with that," Emily replied. "Warren was strong and had a lot of faith, and he said things like crosses were only a means of focusing faith for the person holding it, enhancing a *purity* of *belief.* Holy water has to be blessed by someone with faith in God, but the person using it only has to believe that the water is Holy. He said natural things, such as running water or something else representing purity, like silver, didn't need faith at all because they were under a natural blessing." She dropped a glob of margarine into the frying pan.

"What about garlic?"

"Anyone would be offended at that smell! Warren said that the natural protections like that were here for people who weren't Christians—which includes most everyone these days—because God loved everyone."

Love. Sam felt her face twist. *God.*

"Before you go thinking I was married to some kind of fruitcake fanatic, remember that Warren was a minister, okay?"

"You've got to admit it sounds kind of crazy," Sam said.

For a moment Emily's eyes narrowed, but then her face resumed its inexpressiveness. "It's all right, Samantha." Emily spoke dispassionately. "Vampires sound kind of crazy too."

"I didn't mean—"

"At least Warren's at peace now."

Sam let the uncomfortable moment pass. She glanced at Mike in the armchair. "So . . . could some of those 'natural blessings' help Mike? Is killing that vampire the only way to save him?"

Emily let the eggs simmer and looked with her. "I don't know. Some of the books mention that there might be other methods. Self-sacrifice was about the only one any of them agreed on. *It requires a denial of self for the welfare of others and the choice of God . . . to the point of death.* Like Jesus on the cross." She tightened her jaw. "But because of a vampire's selfish instincts that method is nearly impossible.

Though Sam raised her eyebrows, neither of them said anything more, and they ate the eggs in silence. They were just putting up the dirty dishes when a sharp knock sounded on the front door. Sam answered, and it was Detective Golan with two other men. One was a sour-lipped black man so tall, he might have been a basketball player in younger years, the other a chubby man with round cheeks who was vaguely familiar. She stared at him another second and remembered him at the precinct station when he'd given her Mike's address. He was out of uniform now.

"Hi, Samantha. I hope you people got more sleep than I did." The chubby cop closed the door on the hot air billowing inside. "This is Officer Jay Adwon and Father Tolbert."

Suddenly Emily was at Sam's side. *"Why the hell did you bring him?"*

The chubby man seemed to shrink inside his checkered shirt and faded jeans. Golan stayed between him and Emily. "Because he *killed* one of these vampires. He's been suspended from the force for what happened to your husband, Mrs. MacDonald, but from what he's told me, I don't know that I might not have done the same thing if I'd been him. In my book Adwon's only mistake was in not telling anyone what he was doing or where he was going. He should have had backup, because if your husband had been the lunatic Adwon thought he was, *he* might've been killed."

Emily crossed her arms, her face red. "Warren *tried* to explain it. Warren told him to call squad cars to the cemetery. We had read about the deaths of people here and that's why we came."

Adwon peered from behind Golan's big shoulder. "I —I'm sorry, ma'am. I'm . . . sorry. I thought you two were crazy with all that stuff you were saying, and—"

"And he wanted to play the big hero," Golan cut in. "But he knows better now."

Adwon watched Emily. "I was on the east side last night when that fire started up. I saw one of those *things* run into a 7-Eleven and grab an old woman. The store clerk ran into the back room, and I ran in to help her, and God help me, that son of a bitch was chewing into her throat and . . . *drinking her blood.* I had already been dismissed, so I didn't have my gun, but I tried to stop that thing. I hit it over the head

with a bottle, and when it turned around I saw its
teeth—"

Emily's face stayed stony.

"It tried to bite me!"

"What did you do?" Sam asked.

Adwon pushed damp hair from his forehead.
"There . . . was a broom beside the door, and I
grabbed it when he charged me. The son of a bitch ran
right into it. I fell down and the broom cracked in two,
and I pushed what was left of that broom right into his
chest. It went into him. God, he was cold. Even his
blood was cold. He screamed and started running in
circles, and the blood just kept spraying. I just about
shit my pants, and then he fell down. He shriveled up
and turned into the worst stinking smoke I ever
smelled! Then there was only a pile of dust on the
floor." Adwon squeezed his eyes shut. "I called the
precinct. Then about an hour ago, Lieutenant Golan
showed up at my door." His voice was thin. "I—I'm
really sorry about what happened with your husband,
Mrs. MacDonald. I guess you two were *right*."

Emily's gaze stayed on him another second, then
shifted to the tall black man. His hair was pure black,
but the lines on his face were the deep crevices of long
years. His round jaw moved idly as he chewed gum.

"And you?" she asked.

"I killed one too," Tolbert said in a low voice. "Last
night. A long time back I killed a lot more. This isn't
the first time this has happened around here."

Golan sniffed the air. "You all eaten?" Golan
walked warily around Mike into the kitchen. For his
part, Mike kept his eyes on the TV set. "I'm still going
on some hash browns I gulped down last night, and
we've got a long day and night ahead of us. It doesn't

look like our side's going to make it any easier: some of the hotshots in D.C. have taken a real dim view of any talk about vampires, and they want every one of these freaks captured . . . *alive*." Golan snorted. "The FBI have taken over and they've dropped a curtain over this place. Martial law and confinement is enacted as soon as they can get the airlines, and every road out of this city closed down and blockaded; probably sometime tomorrow. People are going to have to get special clearance and health exams to leave—plus, every patrolman who participated in that fiasco where I met Samantha has been temporarily relieved of duty. In a way, you might say that Officer Adwon and I are in the same boat. I've been dismissed too."

Finally, Mike looked up with glassy eyes. His stomach growled so deeply that no one in the room missed it. "You might say we're all in that boat then, Cop. If we can't kill those things and we can't get out, we'll all be on that boat until it goes down faster than the *Titanic*."

Golan didn't even turn. "I've called a few of the other guys who were dismissed and most of them are willing to help. And our pastor here has a few *veterans* to advise us."

Emily had gotten up. "What are you going to do?"

The broad man snorted fitfully. "As George Bush once put it, darlin', we're gonna kick a little ass."

13

The whore was the only one who'd come back to the bar, and the bartender watched her sitting at one of the lonely tables. He didn't mind her being here, because he had picked her himself. The others had gone, all right, but in just the space of last night, they had fucked up his plans almost as badly as if they'd stayed. There hadn't been a customer since he opened the front doors at one this afternoon, and when he saw that the street was still cordoned off and guarded by fresh cops, he doubted that there would be any tonight. That tangled bunch of undead half-wits had blown the cover he'd expected to keep going for several more months, until he made his army so strong that nothing could stop them. . . .

A tough, lean army with all the assholes weeded out from their mistakes. He'd had hopes of being a cattle baron, herding humans and carefully selecting the choicest blood for his table each night. He was tired of running and hiding, and dreamed of beginning a new age for the undead by scattering ranches of penned-up humans throughout the state.

Now, even though he was certain that the powers that be would never actually admit to the existence of himself and his kind, they were alerted, and dangerous things were happening. The dumbfuck newborns had no vision for the future. Curfews were going into effect and the city around him was being closed off like a wild river—dammed up until it became a stagnant pool that could be tamed.

Even more startling, word had passed to him that there were some out there who *already* knew . . . and it was only a matter of time before they came after *him*. The gossip was that two of the newest vampires had been destroyed in last night's holocaust—and he believed it, feeling their destruction through the tendrils that had connected them.

The bartender licked his pointy teeth and went to sit beside the whore, studying the damage done to her. She had crept in here an hour after dawn, and he guessed that the police had kept her from reentering her grave before the light broke over the sky. Her lips were blistered and cracked, and her face surly and brittle looking, scraped in several places so badly that some of her skin hung loose. "The Boss told me I was moving too soon," he ventured quietly, "and it seems he was right. I can't stay here now."

"I'm hungry," she whispered.

"I'm going to try to make it back to the border and leave these other fucks to go to Hell on their own. I don't want them with me, but maybe you will come, huh?" He laid a hand on hers. "I received so much when I took you. You are the only true follower I have found. You knew the meaning before I even came to you."

"I'm hungry."

"There's not a big selection where I'm going," he said. "But I think it will satisfy you. Will you go back with me?"

They stared at each other, and he felt a yearning for the true life he'd given away so many years before. "I've been alone a long time."

Her face tightened. "We are all alone except for the life we take inside us."

The barman made a crooked grin. "But perhaps two can pretend better than one alone, huh? After all, we are only hiding from death ourselves."

"I'm hungry," she said again.

14

Father Tolbert and the other cop left for the south end of town. Golan took Mike, Sam, and Emily to his Chevrolet Blazer, then to a lumberyard to buy a gross of wood pickets and several heavy mallets.

With the back of Golan's Blazer full they returned to the detective's house and Sam made a quick lunch. Mike watched them eat while the gruff cop spoke vibrantly of how his renegade band would use the pickets tonight. The vision of death and gore Golan imagined made Mike's stomach flighty and he felt a strange antagonism . . . nearly as though he ought to warn the night creatures.

Pushing aside the plates, Golan bent over his police maps carefully while Sam and Emily double-checked their supplies. The two women came back in and watched as he made markings with a felt-tip pen. They took his place when he left the police charts an hour later. Emily groaned as she counted the area graveyards. Chuckling with a dark humor, Golan grabbed a couple of beers and led Mike onto his shady porch.

Staying in the shadow of the modern brick home, Mike sipped his brew warily, sweating in the jacket he'd put on to protect his arms from the sunlight. Emily had been right that the exposure wouldn't actually hurt him, but it sure as hell felt like it did. A picnic table stood before them, and beyond that a silver swing-set sat in the middle of the fenced backyard. Sparrows, robins, and blue jays swooped down to its bent frame and rested, then flew back into the hazy sky.

The sun was very low.

He adjusted his sunglasses and grimaced as he made himself turn toward the swelling, fiery orb beyond the trees. It was red.

Red like the blood he could not resist thinking of.

Red.

Blood.

"It's getting close to dusk," Golan said. "Can you feel any of them yet?"

He shook his head, trying to ignore the headache that wouldn't leave even after six aspirins. "I don't feel them much until the sun is all the way down," Mike told him. "You don't want to know what I'm feeling."

"Try me."

"I don't think you'd understand, Cop. It's like needing a drug."

"Yeah? Well, I might better than you think. I did my time in Southeast Asia."

Mike brushed away a fly.

"Try me," repeated Golan.

One of the pine stakes lay before him on the table and Mike picked it up, sliding his fingers over its rough surface. The desires were growing so powerful in him that he did feel one of them now—*wanted to be one of them.*

Golan thumped the wood in Mike's hand.

"You're going to enjoy this," Mike said.

Golan shrugged. He took a deep swig of Carta Blanca. Mike licked his lips and did the same with his own can, but he no longer felt the old pleasure. He tried to pretend it was blood. . . .

"Nothing wrong with enjoying your job, Druggie."

Mike looked at the sun again, lower now. "The only difference between you and them, Cop, is that you don't drink the blood you spill."

The big man's face grew bright pink; he laughed uneasily, then heartily. "Is that a sin? Waste not, want not?" His roar sent a new flock of birds into the air all at once, and he gave the picket stake in Mike's hand another playful sock. "Hey, greaser, don't talk morality to me, 'cause I got an earful of that shit when I got back from laying my ass on the line in 'Nam, okay? I was a good guy there, and I'm a good guy now, but this time we good guys are going to wax the floor with the bad guys."

"I don't know if there are any good guys," Mike said. He thought of his own life, selling pleasure and taking away much more. But was it wrong? He had sold his pleasure, after all, to people more than willing.

It made Mike's head pound harder.

Golan finished his beer and crushed the can with a loud, metallic crunch, then tossed it at a bird that had returned to roost on the swing-set. "It's seven-thirty. Come on, hound, time to muster camp and hit the trail."

* * *

Sam was thumbing through Emily's Bible with a frown, and Emily was trying to convince someone about the vampires over the phone when Golan pushed open the sliding glass door.

Golan said nothing when Emily dropped the receiver in its cradle and looked up at him. "I've called ten churches and no one believes me."

"You tried," he said too cheerfully. "Come on."

Emily glanced back at the phone, then at her watch. She nodded with resignation.

They gathered their things quickly and got into the big four-wheel-drive vehicle. As Mike sat in the front seat beside Golan, the sun touched the horizon. Mike shut his eyes as the whistling Golan started the engine and backed out of his driveway. The rear of the vehicle was filled with the stakes and mallets, and Emily held her cross and the bottle of holy water between her legs. They looked like a fruitcake family preparing for a camp-out; no tent but plenty of stakes.

"There's a lot at stake here," Golan had punned as he glanced over their supplies.

Mike kept his mouth shut. Samantha had tried to speak to him, but he'd walked away, refusing to admit the grip of the lust that was making his teeth sore and a spot ache somewhere above his stomach. Somehow, the way Samantha had taken his hand when she tried to talk to him burned him with guilt for his growing desires. *There are no good guys,* he continued to tell himself.

But what about her? Even with what she knew of his past, even though he'd admitted using her and lying to her, she still cared about him.

Why?

Emily had seen him push away from Samantha, and even without her words he could feel her empathy. Somehow, she came closer to understanding him than the others.

But even that wasn't really so. She understood some of it, but the only one of them who really comprehended his thoughts completely was Golan. Golan didn't drink blood, but he thirsted for it nonetheless.

"Looks raunchy," Emily said from the backseat as the Blazer crept away from the nicer neighborhoods. She pressed her face against the window and stared at the yards of long grass and weeds, decorated by scattered old tires, rusty car parts, or derelict dolls and Tonka trucks. "This whole place looks like a cemetery."

Golan smirked and glanced at her in the rearview mirror. "Maybe the welfare checks haven't come in this month."

"Mr. Policeman," Emily said calmly, "if you'd listen to me, you'd know that this isn't going to do more than give us some extra time. I told you that the stakes will only kill the *bodies*. The spirits will be free to find somewhere else to go. They can enter someone infected—"

"Then we'll fucking kill them *all*." He lit a cigarette and filled the interior with his tobacco-laced bad breath, stilling further conversation as he drove on. Fifteen minutes later he slowed the vehicle at the sight of parked police cars only two blocks away. He cut the engine and rolled down his window, letting the moist hot air into the car. "If they can't enter anyone who's not infected, we'll just make sure that there ain't no one left to be infected . . . uh, no one left to *infect* anyone, I mean."

Twitching filled Mike's brain, and he felt its urge drive into his muscles. He didn't need to look to know that the sun was down. Somewhere close he felt a tugging of relief . . . of fingers clawing at the dirt covering them. Taking off the sunglasses, he closed his eyes for a moment, sighing. He flinched at Samantha's touch.

"You feel them, don't you?" she asked.

Mike nodded. He couldn't keep from licking his lips. Nightfall made his new senses buzz, and he felt as though he was awakening *from* bad dreams instead of entering them. He smelled the life-giving blood inside Sam.

His teeth were tingling and sore.

"Come on," said the cop, opening his door. "I see the guys across the street." He waved his hand at the half-dozen men who looked like fish out of water in their civilian clothing, a couple of them with guns strapped to their waists. As Golan opened the back of the Blazer, the men gathered behind the vehicle, their voices and salutations loud.

Mike shivered at the nervous laughter and off-color jokes as the men sorted through the back of the car. He felt Sam's hand touch his shoulder, then felt another hand that he knew was Emily's. She held the open Coke bottle out to him.

Mike shook his head.

"Drink it." Emily pushed it to his lips. "I don't think it'll help much now, but it will a little."

His desires shrank at the touch of the wet plastic and he yelped as it stung his chapped lower lip.

"Drink it," she insisted.

Slowly, he gripped the container, shaking.

"No way," puffed Golan as he suddenly threw open

the driver's door again. "Get that shit away from him! *You don't fuck up a hunting dog's senses when you're loading your fucking gun!*" He reached in fast and grabbed one of Mike's trembling arms, throwing the bottle from his hands and onto the back floor as Emily cried out.

"You bastard!" She hauled the half-empty liter back into her lap, her face livid. "You *bastard!*"

The voices from the back grew silent. Golan dragged Mike over the space between the two captain's chairs and the gearshift, ignoring his grunts. He pulled him out onto the street and pushed the quivering man up against the car body. "You're the bastard," he whispered to Mike, wrinkling his nose as though he were cleaning up dog turds. "If you're suffering, just think of all those damn kids you made suffer when you dealt out your *shit.* Then if you're a fucking *good* dog and give me what I want, I'll put a stake in you when we're done."

Though his legs were Jell-O weak, Mike stared back into the big man's brown hollow eyes, feeling only hate and a wish that his hungry teeth would sharpen so he could tear them into the man's throat. "I—I'm not one of them . . . yet."

"Yet," Golan spat, grabbing his collar and tugging him to the men at the back. They were filling paper sacks with the pickets and brandishing the wooden mallets like Indians with tomahawks. "This is *Rover,* boys." Golan grinned. "Rover's gonna lead us to our game, but first we got to get around our friends up there." He nodded at the police cars blocking the street ahead. An oncoming car pulled up behind the Blazer.

"Right on time," Golan said. "Jay—you know a

way onto that street so we don't disturb our commanding officers?"

Jay Adwon whistled at the sight of his friends and fellows with the ludicrous new weapons. "Holy shit." He stood beside his car. "There's an alley back there that will take us to the vacant lot and the Corral bar."

Between the secondhand shops and the dreary apartment buildings, Golan spotted the narrow alley and nodded, then pushed Mike toward it roughly. He grabbed Mike's earlobe the way an angry mother holds her disobedient child. "You smell 'em, Rover?"

Sam, Emily, and the bizarre platoon followed.

15

Letting her essence drift up through the dirt, Kirsten created the image of herself as a big-bosomed bitch in *short* white shorts and a silver sequined cowboy top with fringes lining the bust so that when she moved, the leather strings would jiggle mercilessly, drawing her prey as a spider's web drew flies.

She would make men's flies bulge.

Then she would bulge with their *blood*.

Kirsten cackled dryly as other cloudy shapes emerged from the graves the bartender had dug in the rocky ground all around her. She wondered if her brother had awakened yet. Last night it had almost seemed that she could feel him joining the ranks that were growing each hour. But then, nothing.

"Bubba." She mouthed the name she'd had for him in life, barely recalling why she'd called him that.

But she was hungry, and forgot Bubba quickly with memories of the taste of the two rich white men she had last night. Their dainty white pricks were so small that she had been able to bite their abdomens both in turn even after they hardened into her mouth. But when those two awoke next they could be as large as they wanted to be—just as her cup size had grown from a 34B to 38C.

"Good fucking shit."

The voice broke past her dreamy thoughts and urged her toward it. She broke past the others of her kind that were still forming and deciding how to form, like a woman presented a fashion store as a wardrobe closet. Kirsten smelled the sweet scent of life blossom and dove for its source. Her lusting heart hammered at the sight of the group of clean white men who looked like a squad of vacationing armchair quarterbacks in the dusk's final illumination. With a shrill cry of glee she jumped over a pile of rusted kitchen pipes and grabbed the first man she came to, filling his large blue eyes with her offerings and shaking the fringes on her tits as he struggled to look away. His small mouth flew open and he dropped a threatening stick and hammer from his shivering hands, and then she slammed into him hard, knocking him back to a pile of discarded cardboard. Her hands trembled with urgency as they tore at his khaki slacks and pulled his straining member out of his jockey shorts with a violence that made him shriek.

"It'll be better in a minute, baby," she said, and sank her mouth over his meat fast, smelling more such life all around her and wanting a chance at it too. Salty ejaculation filled her throat as her teeth tore into soft flesh, bringing the taste of his acidy blood. Kirsten sucked deep, faintly hearing other cries and shouts as

the undead who shared the ground with her hurried to share this unexpected, quick meal.

Kirsten gorged herself as fast as she could, then sprang to her feet and left the dying man's remaining drops for the greasy wino who had already chomped yellowed fangs into his wrist. She leapt high over a ruined stereo cabinet in the alley where three men were holding more sharp sticks. Behind her, five more of the men were covered by her gurgling companions. Kirsten picked out a small stocky man entering the alley and sank her vision deep into him, showing him the pleasures in his imagination, then darted to him, smacking into him and knocking aside the sharp wood he tried to force into her.

The man screamed, and the other two who'd been beside him pulled back. She fed them a dark grin, laughing at the way the bigger one was protecting himself with the thin, greasy Hispanic he held tight, like a crook with his kidnap victim.

"Help me!" blubbered the porky man underneath her as she ripped his shirt apart and dug her nails into his potbelly, slicing them down into his jeans. The wino suddenly appeared at her side and dug his fangs deep into the roll of that shivering flesh. Kirsten growled and knocked him aside. This man was hers!

"In the name of Jesus Christ!"

Kirsten's teeth slid down toward twisting flesh with the shrill, woman's screech blasting in her ear. As she jerked her head up, the woman forced her fists into the sides of a plastic Coke bottle, and the contents exploded from its neck. The stream of the bottle's oncoming liquid danced over her.

It *hurt*.

Bubbles popped up on her face, neck, and back

where the hot, fiery moisture splashed onto her, and even as her tongue licked at his first spray of blood, those bubbles expanded and filled her with agony. The liquid broke through her skin and the boiling purity spread into her, making her reformed flesh drop off and sizzle. Driven on mindlessly, as though unaware of this horror, Kirsten's tongue darted back and forth into the blood flooding from her victim's torn stomach. Then she screeched and fell back from him at last.

Dazed and not even hearing her own cries of agony, Kirsten realized that the liquid had washed all over the man's wound and she had sucked it up inside her. Jerking like a lunatic string puppet, she vomited out the scalding gore. The woman's shadow fell over her. Kirsten tried to push herself backward. The bottle dropped closer and she snarled, struggling to make her arms obey her. The white bitch bent low, and the mouth of the bottle connected with Kirsten's shriveling lips, pouring its hideous, choking contents into her. It spilled down her throat, pumping disintegration through each vein and capillary.

Her heart exploded.

The last thing she saw was the gravity-defying shower of blood she let loose into the night's air.

16

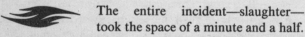 The entire incident—slaughter—
took the space of a minute and a half.

Sam felt shock waves of nausea. Vampires scattered
through the lot like rabid lemmings into darkness. Sirens had broken the air as the first screams began—
less than thirty seconds ago—but it seemed they had
been sounding for hours. In front of her, surrounded
by the dirt and trash of soggy mattresses, red-rusted
cans and junk, lay seven men, and only one was
breathing.

The cops came, saw, and got their asses kicked.

Kicked hard.

And Sam had just stood there, wide eyed, and
watched.

"Fucking shit!"

She turned to Golan and saw that he had finally
released Mike. Mike was still, hunkered over, and Golan ignored him as he pushed beyond Sam and onto
the scene of his fallen comrades. *"Fuck."*

A spotlight flashed onto the vacant lot and the siren was almost on them.

"They—they're *dead*!"

Emily tugged Mike back to the alley and then shoved Golan harshly. "*Worse* than that,'" she hissed. "We've got to get out. Help me get Adwon!"

Golan blinked at her as she tossed aside the empty Coke liter and bent over Jay Adwon's groans. Emily took an arm and tried to lift him. "Help me, you bastard!"

Sam brushed past Mike and knelt, taking Adwon's arm and helping Emily get him to his feet. Golan was still staring at the battlefield dumbly. "It was so fucking fast," he gasped.

Sam and Emily struggled under the limp man's weight, crunching glass and unnameable items under their shoes. Emily glanced back at Golan. "Come on!"

Shouts from the street tried to overcome the siren. Golan finally came to life and ran to them. The searchlight swept over his back. "Hurry!"

"Give us some help, then," Emily shot back.

"Goddammit, leave him!" Golan pushed past. "I'm gone!"

"I've got the keys you left in your . . . car," she panted. He stopped.

"Bitch!" hissed Golan.

Sam wanted to slug him, but the shouts behind were louder and the alley stretched on twenty more feet.

"*Help us!*" Emily yelled.

Another second dragged as he stood there, and then Golan knocked Emily aside, crooking an arm under Adwon's knees and another around his shoulders. "I fucked up," he whispered, lunging ahead as though his burden were a sackful of feathers.

They made it to the sidewalk a minute later and crossed the street. They reached the Blazer just as another siren exploded without warning. A new police car started up the street toward them, its colored lights flashing. Regaining his speed and ruthless dexterity, Golan opened the back door and tossed Adwon inside, then opened the front door and dived over the gearshift into the driver's seat. Emily and Sam jumped inside, and they slammed their doors at the same instant. All ducked instinctively as the police lights drew nearer, splattering the tired, cracking walls of the surrounding buildings.

Their urgent, tired breaths filled the Blazer. The lights passed.

A small flame flared across from her with the click of Golan's lighter.

"Fucking *shit*," Golan grumbled, touching the flame to his cigarette. "Now what the fuck do we do?"

Emily mumbled something from the backseat.

"What?"

"I said, you must have been a real ass-kicker back in your precious Vietnam, General Policeman. No wonder we lost the frigging war!"

"Shut the fuck up! Just shut the fuck up and give me my damn keys!"

A key ring flew over the seat, smacking Golan on the cheek. He stuck one in the ignition and gunned the motor noisily. "We got to figure something out. We got to regroup and figure out a way to hit 'em hard! They —they're so fucking *fast*!"

Sam sat up, glancing into the backseat. "Where's Mike?"

"We don't need him, now, sister," Golan said. "We know where they are."

"Where is he?"

Golan pulled the Blazer onto the street and cruised up to the police blockade at the next intersection. From there they could see the vacant lot. "He went into the bar back there, I think. While you bitches were yelling at me, he took off. I think that must be their headquarters. We gotta figure out a way to take it down and them with it."

Sam couldn't believe Mike was stupid enough to try to face his nemesis on his own. She knew that he wouldn't be strong enough to go against *her*. The vampire-whore's fiery eyes lit her mind.

The vacant lot was quiet now, and beyond it the sign, CORRAL, glowed bright in red letters. The bar door was shut, and the sidewalk around it empty but for a few patrolmen passing by in a hurry. Except for the police vehicles the street in front was empty of cars too. Only an elderly pickup truck covered in dirt waited nearby. "Where are all the people?" Sam whispered.

"They cleared out during the day and last night," Golan explained in a slower voice. "The fed boys drove out the few that didn't want to leave. They checked them all out and relocated them in the Y and a couple of churches. This block is as vacant as a ghost town."

Ghost town. Sam thought all of Dallas might be like that soon. With silent stone and brick towers rising into the night sky around her, she imagined the darkened metropolis, falling to ruin and decay as the years destroyed its concrete and glass the way the vampires had destroyed its inhabitants. And then, when all the streets were as wasted as this one, they would move on, driven by their insatiable appetites.

It was numbing, because, as Golan had repeated over and over, they were *fast.* Only days ago the idea of vampires had been like a bad dream. Now, as in her childhood nightmares, the horror was pursuing her, gaining strength, unstoppable. "Good God," Sam moaned. "Maybe I *did* bring them here!"

Emily and Golan both stared at her.

"From that border town. Maybe they're following me!"

Emily eased Adwon onto the seat. "Don't put on airs, Samantha. You were just in the wrong place at the wrong time—or maybe even just the opposite. Without you we might still be back at square one, with me locked up in the hospital and our General pushing papers trying to figure out what's wrong. Mike might even be *dead* without your help."

Sam fingered her necklace. "He might be dead right now."

No one answered.

They had fucked without love, but somehow, even in greed, they had shared. Mike was a human being like she was. They had *shared.*

It was the difference between herself and a vampire: *They* took, giving nothing in return. Mike had brought her a feeling of warmth that she was no longer alone, giving her a bizarre sensation of belonging, and she hoped she had done as much for him.

It made him part of her. They had shared life.

It was the same love her brother had died for.

Sam grabbed Golan's wrist. "We've got to help Mike! We promised. *I promised!*"

"Bullshit. Time to regroup our forces."

"Pull over down the street," Emily said.

"Bullshit!"

"Do it, General Policeman. You want to stop them and I've got a way. We'll cover you with glory in spite of yourself. I've got an idea that will bring us *all* what we want."

Golan stiffened.

"Do it. Drive past these police cars and park. I've got an idea."

17

When the darkness fell, MaryAnn slithered up from the confines of her coffin through the dirt with the ease of practice and the authority of her own Darkness. Images clouded her, and somewhere in them she knew that this new existence wasn't all fun and games anymore. As she solidified in front of her marker, the street sign of her new residence, she clothed herself like an Amazon in hot pants that were designer battle fatigues and a color-coordinated bra top. She admired the vision of herself in her mind, though she suddenly worried that the camouflage colors of her brief clothing wouldn't be much good with the expanse of skin she displayed.

It was the thought that counted anyway. This was war.

Picking up the chewed tampon she'd dropped on the grass early this morning, MaryAnn licked the stale, dried menses staining it, waiting for Scott.

It was war, and tonight she and her new lover

would reverse the Emancipation Proclamation and begin to enslave the *darkies* once more. She tittered at the thought of herself as Scarlett O'Hara, watching over a plantation as the niggers worked the harvest of souls, bringing trembling bodies to her so she could sip their blood like a mint julep.

"Fucking niggers wouldn't even show me their precious cocks!" she grumbled, sniffing the perfume she'd imagined for her body, pretending she couldn't detect the stink of decay underneath it.

A squeaky whistle stung the air, and MaryAnn, with her supercharged senses, flinched. "Scott?" she whispered cautiously.

Silence. The wind danced on the leaves and made the fluttering sound of a thousand birds.

"Scott?"

"Boo!" Scott's laughter came from behind a nearby mausoleum.

"You dick." MaryAnn giggled nervously. "You're a vampire—not a *ghost*!"

"Yeah? Well, who are you tonight? Rambetta?"

He was dressed in his sequined cowboy togs again but had added a bullet-filled holster and pearl-handled six-shooter. She shrugged. "Better than a long-toothed John Wayne. *God damn!*"

"Ain't that the truth." He rubbed the pointy toe of a boot against his faded blue jeans, then tipped his wide-brimmed hat. "Let's go get some *niggers*!"

Father Percival Tolbert wiped his nose with the tail of his white shirt. That white made his skin seem really black—especially in the bad light of the church outbuilding. He smacked his gum idly and peered at the older faces that made up his small following. They

stood among rakes and the two church lawn mowers.
He was glad that they were joining up for this, hopefully the last hurrah. Luke was here, his balding head
shiny as new tar, and James, his short goatee framing
his chin in white. The fat ball of blubber beside Luke
had put on a good hundred pounds in the long years
that had passed and his name was forgotten, but the
skinny one with hair crawling from his nose was Ja-
cob, and the muscular man standing behind them all
had gone by the nickname "Coffee" even after the civil
rights movement.

"What about those Porky Pigs you was talking
about, Percy?" asked Luke Smithey. "Thought you
said the arm of the law was on our side this time."

"Shhee." Tolbert stopped, not finishing the word
with the *t* it begged for. "The law is on its *own* side.
The law is the law, and even though the Book says we
need to obey it unless it conflicts with God's Law, that
police lieutenant told me that the government doesn't
want to kill these demons." He chewed loudly.
"That's a conflict, I think, so we got to make our own
way again. The policeguy wants to get rid of them,
too, but he's a loner and I figure we'll do better on our
own, just like last time. That man's got more balls
than brains." He peered at the younger men now,
three black boys he thought he recognized from the
masses they infrequently attended, two Mexicans, and
the white man who was the only Caucasian that regularly came to his church. They and the older gentle-
men brought their numbers to twelve, ten short of that
last crusade.

"I'll tell you now," Tolbert said. "There's a lot more
of them than there are of us."

"Not after tonight," one of the younger Hispanics

said with a grin. He was almost as tall as Tolbert, but much heavier, and his striped orange-and-brown T-shirt showed muscles underneath it.

Tolbert dipped an army surplus canteen into the dented tin basin of Holy Water he'd prepared. "If that's your faith in Mary and the Saints and Jesus Christ our Lord, you may be right, man, but if that's *you* talking, then you better spend some time confessing your pride to me before you go with us. Because a notion like that from your own heart will get you killed, and if *they* kill you, your resurrection won't be into the arms of the Lord." Tolbert fixed him with his eyes.

Silence.

"Forgive me, Father." The strong man bowed his head uncertainly. "What . . . must I do for . . . penance?"

The priest put the canteen on the warped table they surrounded like King Arthur's knights. Tolbert stared into the shadows. "Do you know the twenty-third psalm?" he asked the young man, submerging another canteen in the clear water.

He blushed and nodded.

"Then I want you to stand by me through the night and repeat it as we work. *Constantly.* Think of what the words mean . . . especially when you come to the part about the 'valley of the shadow of death.' " He shook his angular head. "All of you repeat the psalm now as our prayer into battle. Some of you are here because you saw the horror last night, but you don't fully understand it or believe in it even yet. You must believe . . . and be afraid, and remember that only the Blessed Virgin will guide your steps in safety as we separate and walk this night; if God is merciful, *she* will protect us from the filth of these demons. . . ."

". . . thy kingdom come, thy will be done, on earth as it is in Heaven . . ."

MaryAnn cringed behind the bushes in the church courtyard. The words she herself had once been able to speak at a furious pace to get the Sunday School memory prize burned her ears.

"These niggers are full of bullshit," whispered Scott beside her. His teeth flashed in the light from the shed, and his pale flesh virtually glowed.

"What are we going to do?"

". . . lead us not into temptation, but deliver us from evil, for thine is the kingdom, the power, and the glory forever. Amen."

"I'm going to scare Jesus, Mary, and Joseph out of them—*watch this*!"

He leapt up to his feet, and MaryAnn tried to pull him back into the leaves. "Scott!"

"Only a couple of them even believe in that bullshit, MaryAnn. And no one ever made the rule that we can't use the weapons of this world—watch!" He strolled casually toward the unpainted shed, waddling with exaggeration like a bow-legged cowpoke as the shiny sequins of his shirt caught the light and reflected a thousand pinpoints onto the rough building's walls. His fingers stroked the gun handle in his holster. He stopped when he was less than ten paces from the shed's doorway. Inside, the tall black preacher had finished filling almost two dozen canteens and passed them out, and was now unfolding a big city map. Scott listened to him giving his followers directions as to where they should go. He paired them up like a black Noah sending out animals to replenish the earth.

As the men listened offhandedly, Scott grasped their thoughts, feeling their cockiness. The preacher and a couple of the older men were the only ones who understood the gravity of their situation.

"Let's go!" said the only white man. He held up his canteen and a makeshift wooden cross and went with a black man wearing an orange-striped shirt into the yard. The others were still talking and gathering their weapons.

"You'll *go*—to *Hell!*" yowled Scott. His sequins dazzled the night. Floating over the lush grass, he dashed in front of them and raised his arms high over his head, the revolver in his left hand.

"Shit." The white man hopped back, colliding with another black man trying to exit through the door. The young black beside him jerked to the side, dropping his canteen and cross. The white man stumbled forward, then fell on his face in the dirt and dropped his own canteen and cross. Quick as a firefly Scott fired his pistol into the doorway and a voice cried out. He dropped to one knee and lifted the white man's hand as though to help him up, then wrapped his lips over the man's bony wrist. MaryAnn saw blood spurt and darken Scott's cheeks . . . and heard the sound of suction.

Overcome by the smell, MaryAnn forgot her caution and pushed through the bush half covering her. She was at the fallen black man's side in a second, following Scott's lead and raising a wrist to her tingling teeth. The warm, lively tang of blood filled her mouth and dripped over her lips as the victim gave a ghastly wail, echoed by the paralyzed form under

Scott and even by the men inside the shed. Scott raised the pistol at them again and fired twice. She listened to their scattering feet.

Swallowing as fast as she could, MaryAnn filled shrunken veins with her victim's essence, half watching the astonished party as they shrank back and forgot their holy instruments. When the black priest pushed the others aside, she released the wrist. "This is *sacred* ground!" he proclaimed.

Scott threw the spasming white-skinned vessel aside, cackling at the dry sound his bones made when they hit the ground. Scott aimed the gun. *"You nigger son of God! Come to me!* No tar baby like you can waste a *white* man!"

"Mary, Mother of God." The priest stared down at the night's first two casualties.

Scott stepped forward cautiously, waving the revolver. "Better run, nigger priest."

The other men in the shed were advancing again, slowly, holding up their wounded comrades and crowding in the open doorway.

The black priest squared his shoulders, showing the glistening tears on his cheeks, and MaryAnn scooted farther back from the body she'd feasted on, feeling a danger in his fearless sorrow. "There is no love in you," he said in a cracked voice. "No *Love!* Your life is a lie and your god is the father of lies!" He took a solid step forward, and the ground seemed to tremble under his weight.

"Scott!" MaryAnn warned, not understanding the priest's strength. *"Scott!"*

"Y-you're *black*!" Scott blustered. He pulled his trigger twice, missing and stumbling back over the body he'd emptied.

"All children of God are white as snow in *His* eyes," spoke the priest, coming nearer. *"You're the only dark man here."*

Scott turned desperately to MaryAnn and dropped his gun. The powerful black hand grabbed his neck and drove him down to the dirt. MaryAnn saw the rosary from the night before appear in the man's other fist. It moved quickly up to Scott's bone-white face. His wide mouth was open in a silent scream of terror that crackled over his features like an astronaut pulling too many G's.

"In the name of *Jesus!*" howled the tall man, gawky and yet graceful as his skinny knees bent to hold Scott to the ground. Then he drove the crucifix into Scott's flapping mouth and past the gasping curses that were escaping, replacing them with an explosion of white light that was filled quickly by the dark red blood spilling up Scott's throat.

Terrified and fighting her own paralysis, MaryAnn fled back to the street.

She was on her own now, but following instinct, she turned in the direction of the other undead creatures that were alone like her, back to that far-off vampire bar.

18

Ducking the bright light that shone against the piles of broken, disintegrating furniture, household goods, and cardboard Mike gritted his sore teeth and cleared himself a space to huddle. He cringed at the shouts and surprised exclamations behind him, forcing himself not to look back at the cops and the bodies they had found. Ahead was a side entrance in the cracked wall of concrete. Every nerve under his sweaty skin was tingling, and his mind throbbed in the midst of the singular thoughts overtaking it.

They were here. The vampires were in the bar and all around him, hiding in the shadows.

But most of them had gotten into the bar.

She was in the bar.

His heart pounded hard as he looked at the chipped gray blocks, and his brain pulsed with the desires inside those walls.

She was in there. The blond lady of the night who

was most truly a lady of the night now. She wore his name, calling herself Mikie, and he wore her mark that was fairly burning under his jeans, making him hard in the need for her and what she would give him.

What she would take from him.

Pushing his face into the ground, he worked his mouth, tasting the gritty dirt and feeling it coat his tongue and teeth. He started to rise, but his fingers sank into the dirt and didn't want to let go.

She would take away his life, imprisoning him in a bleak sameness that might be worse than any jail cell.

But it was little different from his current existence.

"Shit—there's another one over here," rang out a shocked drawl, making *shit* sound like *shee-it.*

He squinted through the piles of garbage in the direction Sam had gone. Somehow he knew that she would be upset that he was not still with them. For some reason she seemed to care.

"This one is Tom Haney," burst out the drawling voice again. "These guys are all ours!"

Ours. The suggestion of belonging stung Mike hard. He did not understand the feelings for Samantha that trickled into his mind now, and he didn't want them because they made him dread the other things he wanted.

"Let's check out the rest of this place," called out a new voice against approaching sirens. "No telling who we're going to find, but it looks like the bad guys won this one."

Good guys, bad guys. There are no good guys.

Filling himself with that thought alone, Mike got to his knees. A *new* life awaited him behind the bar's side door that was only ten feet away . . . *a life of saturating his every want.*

Keeping his head low, Mike waited until the four men in uniforms all had their backs to him, then darted raggedly ahead. The thoughts of Samantha were pushed out of him by a sudden urgency. His shoulder banged into the ancient wall. His fingers clawed the door handle.

The door opened. After a moment's hesitation he forced his feet into the Corral's back hallway. It was dark except for the bar light ahead.

19

The bartender worked his tobacco and watched the slobbering blood-suckers he'd helped create. The nine of them had been cowering in the corner since they'd charged in ten minutes before. When their sensitive ears all heard the back door click open, they turned their fear-filled eyes at him. He took the blond whore back to the cup-boards of liquor bottles, then pulled out his long-un-used holster and strapped it on, eyeing the entrance to the back hallway cautiously. He smelled blood but wasn't sure if it was from the yelling dick brains out-side or if one or more of them had gotten in.

If they had, it could mean a quick, easy meal.

Or a slow, painful disintegration as he was pulled down to the Hellfire he had escaped so long. That was the problem: He didn't know who or how many he might be dealing with, and worse yet, he didn't know how much they *knew*. It made existence as bad as if he were still only a human and living by the sweat of his balls, because when your potential victims knew what they were up against, they could fight back. The man you counted on for your next feast might pull a long wooden stake out of his coat and drive it through your heart, turning the tables and gloating over your confirmed damnation.

He allowed his cowardly brethren to continue their whining noises, counting on their sounds to cover his surpise. They had really pulled the lid off this time, and pretty soon the entire outside world would know there was something odd breeding in this little corner of Dallas. That meant it was time to move the fuck out and leave these whimpering peasants to the demise they richly deserved. His boots moved silently over the floorboards, and pulling his six-shooter, the barman pressed against the wall. He ducked his face into the hallway and saw the hulking man leaning on the adjoining wall, their eyes only separated by inches.

"Who in the fuck are you?" The barman brought the pistol's muzzle to the intruder's nose, cocking back the trigger.

The man's mouth trembled. The bartender almost squeezed the trigger when he dropped to his knees.

"I—I need Mikie," he whispered, hanging his head until only his greasy black hair showed. *"Mikie."*

Gruffly, the vampire grabbed his jacket collar and hauled him back up. "Texas is inhabited by pansies these days. None of you got the cocks you was born with—be you living or dead!" He hauled the cringing fraidy-cat into the barroom. "Everything was going fine until you assholes decided that being dead meant your brains were dead too!"

The pansie undead didn't move. They didn't even try to leap at this shaking man he held immobile, though the blood coursing in the living veins was nearly driving the barman himself crazy with fever. He licked his teeth, then brought the breathing jackal back behind the bar. The whore grinned.

"You change your mind about coming into my place?" he asked the cowering greaser. "We're all *afraid*. That's all you're ever gonna know again after me and my bitch gets done with you, Mex. *Fear and hunger*. You get the pleasure from time to time, but it gets fucking boring after a while. Everyone starts to taste the same."

"Shit," the man moaned, barely struggling against the bartender's western-styled shirt.

"*Shit*'s the word. Glad as hell you dropped in, though, boy, 'cause I got a long haul ahead of me tonight. Got to get the fuck outa this turkey town and get some rest. I might get hungry along the way and for some reason or another, your modern fast-food places don't serve it *my* way like the commercials promise. They don't serve it my way at all, and I hate to stop in a place I don't know and find a meal." He glared at the frightened vampires that had begun to lick their lips at his prize. "Never can tell what kind of asshole you got your teeth in."

Mikie pushed up against the barman, reaching out a long nail and running it through the man's hair. "He's mine, okay? I already got him swimming around inside me, half made. He and his slut are the ones who fucked up my face last night."

The bartender snorted. "You just come with me, babe, and we'll share him before the night's over. But for now you practice some of that restraint I told you about in the beginning. I want to save him for the road and some celebration when we get to my place. You gotta learn to hold back sometimes, 'cause the Boss won't let no one do to him what these dickbites have done to me."

Mike shivered and the barman's nails bit him deeper. "You hear that, dickbites?" he called into the corner, then he turned back to Mikie. "We got to get out soon, though. It's a drive. I already got some of your dirt in the back of the truck. The next time the shit flies, we're outa here." He glared at the other vampires studiously. "And if the shit don't fly soon, I'll kick these animals outa here and *make* it fly."

But a few minutes later the shit flew fast.

20

The police car drove past the Blazer once more. Tires crunched the pavement and its glare flashed into the cab, then continued along the street. The patrol car killed its siren and stopped at the blockade, leaving an open space between itself and another marked car. Five minutes passed as a distant siren grew gradually louder, and then was joined by other sirens. Three ambulances pulled up in front of the vacant lot, bathing the area in their lights that made a crazy dawn. Policemen and medics stood all around them.

In the backseat beside Emily, Adwon had regained consciousness. His breathing was raspy, hesitant. Emily leaned over the front seat.

"I think you're right, General," she said with dulled sarcasm. "I think they are in that bar—some of them, anyway. Warren and I guessed that this was the area they were concentrating on. The only reason we went to the damned cemetery was because one of the hookers was buried there. She was the one that rose, the one my husband was trying to kill."

Adwon groaned.

The interior of the car was close, even with Golan's open window, and Sam unrolled hers, too, breathing a little easier when a warm, silent breeze bathed her forehead. The new sirens finally ceased. Golan raised his head higher, looking back at Emily. "We know they're here. They must've been planting all those missing people right there in that damn vacant lot!"

"And they know we know. The legend has it that to rest and revitalize any damage done to its body, a vampire must return to the dirt it was buried in . . . but they can take that dirt anywhere and find a new resting place. I think they'll do that now! They can carry a handful of that dirt in their pockets and go anywhere they want."

"How is that going to help us kill them, damn it!"

"Just listen. I told Samantha that the purification of *running* water could paralyze and sometimes even destroy vampires—not just Holy Water, but *any* stream of moving water."

Golan puffed his cigarette angrily.

The medics were scattered over the littered lot, lifting fallen bodies onto stretchers and carting them back to the ambulances. A couple of short-haired men in conservative civvies had joined them. They looked like FBI agents straight out of a movie.

"You wanted to be Rambo, General, and I want to give you your chance. There's a five-gallon can of gasoline back here. We can use a piece of this old blanket as a fuse. At dawn, when the vampires are returning to their graves, all you have to do is drive this overgrown car right into the middle of that lot and dump that can out. I'll try to make the fuse long enough to give you time to get away. With all the junk around, the whole place will catch fire, and it might even ignite that bar. When the firemen start to hose the blaze down, maybe the water will take a lot of those monsters back to the Hell they come from. We won't get them all, but it'll give us a fighting chance to knock out a lot of their numbers."

"But we can't just sit here until dawn," Sam said. "What about Mike?"

Emily's dark smile faded. "You and I are going to have to find a way into that bar."

"Kamikaze attack," whispered Golan, flipping a long ash out his window. "Fight Charlie on his own terms." His mouth formed a twisted grin in the shadows. "That's what I always said we should do. An eye for an eye and a tooth"—he chuckled—"for a fucking sharp tooth."

"You'll do it?"

"With bells on, sister, and I bet I got a better chance of making it out alive than you do."

"You may be right about that," Emily replied, staring at Sam.

They held each other's eyes for a moment, then each turned away at the same instant to watch the chaos of shouting medics and cops. A few minutes later the ambulances buzzed away into the night, leaving the neighborhood in an aftermath of silence that seemed abnormal. Emily tore a long, narrow strip from the blanket in the back of the Blazer. She had already torn two other strips, and bandaged Adwon's wound with them. He leaned against the door now, his eyes shut, but Emily knew by his rapid breaths that he was far from rest.

"Son of a bitch," Golan murmured, "it's just nine-thirty!"

Emily's smile was almost wicked. "Sit in your trench, trooper. Take a rest. There's a lot of hours between now and dawn. Just now, I'm worried about Adwon. We need to get him out of this place or he won't stand a chance. He's in no shape to be running and jumping."

Golan raised an eyebrow. "I'm surprised you give a shit."

"The only reason I'm even in this *fucking* town is because I give a shit, General!" she spat out with the hottest anger Sam had seen in the woman. "And you don't fool me for a second that you don't give a shit, too, 'cause if you don't, you better hightail it back to Momma instead of risking your ass for someone else."

"Shut up."

"Maybe you could take him back to my place," Sam offered. "Emily and I can get out and try to figure our way into the bar."

"That's going to be hard to do, the way they're guarding this place."

"They're not watching shit," said Golan. "They've got their guns on and they aren't even scared—won't be until they taste this kind of combat, and then it's too late. All those guys are doing is telling dirty stories about their girlfriends and how they're gonna stick it into them. One of those pricks is even drinking a beer." He pointed at a scarecrow whose uniform dangled around him like a flag on a windless day. He and the other policemen and FBI agents stood out against the Corral's red light. Their wired postures had relaxed in the space of time since their fellows were found and driven to the hospital.

"Well, let's do *something*," Sam said. "My bladder's about to let loose."

"Bitch, bitch, bitch," Golan grumbled.

She spared a mean glance at the big detective. "Let's at least drive around and see if we can find another way into the bar!"

Still grumbling, Golan twisted his key and the motor jumped to life. Sam saw the scarecrow and a couple of others look up briefly, but as the Blazer pulled onto the street, they went on as before.

The tires hopped over a pothole and Adwon groaned. Emily put her hand on his cheek and he quieted, but she was biting her lip so hard, it began to bleed. She propped Adwon back against the door.

Golan circled slowly around the buildings that hid the alley and the battleground they'd faced half an hour before. There was no easy way in.

Golan turned back toward the street they'd started from. In the middle of the block he rolled to a stop, straining his face.

Sam shoved him. "Hey, wake up. Move this heap before we get pulled over, huh?"

"Listen."

"I hear it," Emily said breathlessly.

Sam leaned out into the muggy air, hearing distant traffic and car horns. Somewhere nearer by, the out-of-place strains of Beethoven's "Ode to Joy" caroled. "What?" The dim street ahead was lined by warehouses and now-deserted office buildings.

"Feet. Someone's running up there. A lot of feet are running up there, and God damn, *they're coming right to us.*"

Listening harder, Sam squinted at the light pole on the corner and past it.

"Motherfucker," Golan breathed. "What the hell is going on?"

"We're going to find out pretty quick," Emily said. "Turn left."

Golan twisted the wheel. "What's your idea now?"

"Stop. Didn't Adwon drive up here in that blue car over there?" Emily hopped out of the Blazer and went around the front.

Golan jumped out after her. "Good thinking. Let's get him into it."

Golan gathered the man in his arms and carted him to the Chevrolet Celebrity. Emily dug into Adwon's pockets for the keys and opened his back door. Golan shoved him in.

"Watch it!" Emily yelled. "You almost broke his arm!"

Watching from the Blazer, Sam's mouth dropped as she finally heard the pounding of many feet against pavement, and twisted to see a mob of blacks and Mexicans running beneath the streetlight. A pale girl in sexy combat fatigues kept several yards ahead of them.

"Hey!" she screamed out. They were headed straight toward Sam, Golan, and Emily.

The Celebrity's door slammed. Golan and Emily ran for the Blazer, but not as fast as the girl whose red hair streaked out behind her. For a moment, Sam thought that she was fleeing from an army of vampires. Obviously sharing her thoughts, Emily stopped and held out her arms to the girl.

But a jolt of terror shocked through Sam as she recognized the young woman from Las Bocas. She'd given herself to the boss vampire. Those full lips and cocky eyes were the same.

"Emily!"

As Sam screamed, Golan slammed into the side of the Blazer and wheeled around, and they both watched the redheaded woman dive into Emily's arms and sink her hideous, shining teeth into Emily's neck, dragging her along with gurgling sounds while she continued to run.

"Shit!" cried Golan, hesitating, then jumping inside the Blazer as the mob came closer. The tall man leading them held out a wood cross. Their faces were exhausted, frantic. Golan gunned the engine and spun the Blazer into a sharp U-turn, catching the vampire and Emily's struggling form in his headlights. The running men moved alongside the car for a moment, then the car pulled ahead. "Get over the seat and open the gas can. Drop the fuse down here beside me—then open your door and be ready to jump!"

Obeying the authority that had returned to the detective, Sam climbed over the seat, falling into the back. Knocked back and forth, she got the top off the gas can and fit the torn blanket into its hole. She dropped the end of the fuse onto the front seat beside the gearshift. The heavy fumes made her gag, but she climbed back over the front seat and pulled up on her door handle, gripping the dashboard tight as the vehicle lurched. They passed Emily and the vampire on the right, then Golan skidded to a sudden stop and flung out his door in front of them. They slammed into it, and Golan hooted in victory. He jumped from the Blazer, grabbed Emily's twisting body under her armpits, and hauled her inside, throwing her over his lap and at Sam. Knocked out of breath, Sam gripped Emily fast, then screamed as the vampire pulled up her combat-bikini top and smothered Golan with her naked breasts, leaping on top of him.

"Out! Now!" He hit Sam hard, throwing her back against the door. It swung open with her weight, and Emily spilled out on top of Sam. The Blazer's motor raced, and Golan's grin spread high. His cigarette lighter flared, and dropped down to the fuse. The old blanket flamed immediately, and Golan laughed even as the girl's red hair covered his chest and her needle teeth broke the skin of his throat. The Blazer's wheels were spinning wildly. Then he let up the brake and it jumped through the air like a jackrabbit.

The tangled group of vampire hunters hadn't stopped, and those tired footsteps were upon them now. The tall man holding the cross grinned at Sam for an instant, and they went on, following the Blazer that was already glowing fire through its windows. Golan made a wide turn at the end of the next block, plowing into the sawhorses and a police car blocking the way. Several uniformed men had dashed into the middle of the street, and Golan took one of them with him as the rear end of the police car wheeled sideways. The Blazer crushed the sawhorses beneath it. Sirens had started up again, and Sam tried hard to sit up on her bruises. She heard tires squeal, and then a loud metallic crash.

Ten seconds later, the loudest noise she had ever heard rocked the air, and a sudden heat baked her skin as a brightness sprayed up taller than the buildings.

21

"Shit!" Emily said.

Sam turned stunned eyes down at the woman she was dragging along. "Emily?"

"Shit!" Emily MacDonald blinked, then reached up to the open wound on her throat. She wiped the wetness, then gazed at the dark smear on her palm. "Shit, shit, *shit!"*

"Hey . . . it's okay. What's wrong?"

Holding up her hand, Emily yelled, "God, are you a dumb shit or what? *She bit me!"* She rubbed her neck again, and her eyes widened. "But . . . the mark is *gone!"* With Sam's help she staggered to her feet. The street echoed in flames, screams, and fire-truck sirens. A gunshot blasted through it all.

Emily sagged. "Where's the General?"

"He grabbed the redhead that attacked you. He lit the gas and he"—she raised her dry voice over the crescendo of sirens as their dazzling lights appeared down two streets—"he drove *there*!" She pointed at the smoke and fire.

"He blew up the lot?"

"And the one that bit you, and himself. It's been about five minutes." Sam pulled Emily down the street that led to the alley. "Can you move?" she asked belatedly.

"That idiot," Emily said. "That gung-ho son of a bitch!"

They stumbled down the street, driving hard to beat the fire trucks that bathed them with light. "He . . . saved . . . your *life*!" gasped Sam.

"But not my *soul*!"

The plate glass window beside them was alive in reflections of multicolored lights. Sam and Emily went on in silence, moving toward the noise, then disappearing down the dark alley. Sam winced with every movement, and they both stumbled in the darkness. Sam braced herself on a trash can.

Their ragged breaths formed a hellish harmony.

"That bitch is destroyed," Emily whispered desperately, "but not her fucking *soul*! Her mark is off my flesh, but she bit deeper than that. Her evil is inside me! *"Goddammit!"*

Alarmed by the change in Emily, Sam leaned away. "Mike—" she blurted.

"I used up all the damn Holy Water! What the hell can we do now?"

Sam touched her shoulder. "We have to help Mike. I *promised* him."

"We're all dead meat!" Emily shrieked, knocking over the trash can as she pushed away from it. Her eyes shone with an inferno of terror that made Sam flinch. A sob wrenched her and she kicked the fallen

can so hard that garbage shot out the top like shotgun pellets.

"Get your shit together and come on!" Sam shouted. "If it's that bad, *we haven't got a damn thing to lose!*"

Balling her fists, Emily leapt over the trash can. She eyed Sam angrily. But at last her shoulders slumped. She touched her sticky neck and took a deep breath, then sighed it out like a frustrated child. Together they shuffled through the tunnel of darkness.

PART V

Back
to hell

1

The vacant lot had become an ocean of fire. The Chevrolet Blazer was overturned in the center. Flames shot up highest from its twisted metal, and the heat dried the surface of Sam's eyes. From the alley she heard the shouts of the firemen fifty feet away as though over a longer distance. It seemed hopeless from here. Devastated.

Emily pulled Sam back into the alley's safety. "That stupid, heroic son of a bitch!" Her voice was trembling. "He was *supposed* to *wait* so we could get the others!"

Pushing back into the searing heat, Sam strained her eyes through the rippling, bright colors. The crackle and sound of them made a wall against all but the loudest sounds of the firemen as they hooked up their hoses and started fighting the angry flames. They stretched all the way to the side wall of the bar.

"Shit." Sam gasped.

Emily came to her side as the bar's side door bulleted open. Though it was hard to be certain in the heat-warped air, it looked as though three men and two women were being pushed into the flames. Faint screeching wails reached them. Sam covered her hot face. The fireman turned his hose toward the group that had begun to run right through the fire. The water blasted into them, knocking one down and stopping the others. Their bodies squirmed as other hoses began to spray the area. They dropped to their knees.

The fireman struggled closer, keeping the flames away from the men and women he thought he was saving.

But he was killing them instead. The rivulets beat into the group like acid. One of the men's arms fell off in a blood spray. Two women disintegrated under the wet fury—the head of one shriveling and dropping off in an aftermath of squirting red slime. Smoke was replacing the flames, leaving only small patches of fire around the still-swelling rage that bathed the Blazer— truly a *blazer*, now. The smoke clouded the final demise of the vampires who had tried to escape.

But even as Sam searched for their remains, she saw four other figures dash into the street from the front of the smoldering bar. They were screaming like a thousand maniacal banshees as they swooped straight for the firemen and the police.

The noble fireman was down, two of the howling bloodsuckers tearing their teeth into him. The firefighter beside him backed away, started to drop his hose and run, and then turned that sudden weapon upon the three of them. Two other vampires, once a man and a woman, had made it to the center of the street and were forcing an FBI agent to the ground. A third fireman flipped his hose around at them, knock-

ing them back and paralyzing them as the drenching
power made their flesh drool around them in muddy
red clumps.

"Holy . . . *shit*," Emily said.

Movement at the front of the bar drew Sam's attention back. She expected a new surge of creatures to
make their dash for freedom. But instead a thin man
in a cowboy hat and a tall blonde hurried for the old
pickup parked on the street. They were dragging
something heavy between them. Her skin tingled with
goose bumps as she saw that the thing they were dragging had two arms and two legs.

Even through the twists of smoke Sam knew their
captive was Mike.

"I . . . *holy shit is right*." Sam grabbed Emily,
forcing her back into the alley. "They're going—
they've got Mike! They're taking him with them!"

"We got a lot of them," Emily said.

"They've got Mike!"

They kept going, but Emily was moving more
slowly now. Sam tried to pull her faster.

"We haven't even got any stakes. I can't make any
Holy Water, not after being bitten!"

"Then what can we do?" Sam's urgent question echoed on the brick walls. "I've got to go after him! I have
to try."

Sighing, the younger woman began to move more
quickly. They broke onto the street, the streetlights
dimmed by spreading smoke. Emily turned an exhausted expression to Sam and bit her lip. "It never
ends, you know that? It just never fucking ends.
They're everywhere, but no one knows or even cares
until they have no choice, and then most of them still

don't care, *because their souls are already as dead as mine is now.*"

A new rush of ambulances and police vehicles flooded the road before them. The vampire-hunting troop was milling around. The tall leader had his eye on the pickup Mike was in. It sped to the far end of the street and screeched through a turn. Two police cars chased after it, but they hit some debris at the turn and ended up in a pileup.

The tall black man shook his head and approached them. "You two ladies okay?" he asked.

Sam shrugged, finally recognizing the priest, Tolbert, but feeling a ball forming in her throat. She wanted tears to fill her eyes, but none came, as though the fire had boiled all the moisture in her body away.

Tolbert pulled back Emily's collar.

"They got you."

Emily nodded dully.

"And the vampire who did it was in that car that blew. She's dust now, you know. That means you gotta get free the hard way, little girl." He reached under his skinny arm and handed his canteen to Sam. "Make her drink some of this. It's Blessed Water. It won't cure her, but it will make her strong when she gets the chance for salvation. You get the bite all the way into you, you gotta be strong when that time comes, 'cause you gotta be like Jesus and die on the cross, even though every bone in your body wants to turn away."

Emily blinked.

Sam touched him. "Will you help us?" she asked. "The truck that got away—we have to go after it. My friend was *with* them."

The priest glanced back. The cops had managed to

start one of their dented cars and were backing it away from the others. "I think you probably know that your friend is dead already."

Sam gritted her teeth.

"I got to stay here, young lady. The work's just begun, but I'll give you something if you're set to try."

She nodded.

Eyeing Emily again for a moment, he gave Sam another canteen, then put his wood cross in Sam's arms. After a moment he pushed his fingers into his pants pocket and hauled out a string of beads attached to a shiny golden crucifix. He hung it around Emily's neck, frowning when she flinched. "I give you my prayers too," he told them. "I got a lot to pray over and a lot to do to get these demons out of this town, but I know God has time to listen to another one for you two. Go in His Grace, and may the Blessed Virgin light your way."

Sam felt the disappearing hope in her blossom. The tears finally did spill out and made her cheeks wet. "Thank you," she said.

Already heading back to his group, the priest just raised his arm, pointing a finger at the sky.

"Thank *God*," Emily interpreted. "Come on, we need to check on Adwon and get on the road. I can *feel* those bastards now and I know which way they're going."

Sam nodded as they limped toward the blue Chevrolet, thinking of her experiences in the desert. "So do I."

Emily handed Sam the keys and they climbed in. Adwon lay still in the backseat. Sweat streaked his cheeks and there were dark circles under his eyes. Emily took his wrist. "His heart is still pretty strong. We can either dump him at a hospital or take him with us, but my guess is that he should go. He's got the same problems I have, and I don't think any doctor's going to help a bit."

Emily's attitude toward Adwon seemed callous to Sam. "Do you really think it's the best thing for him?"

"I don't know if there is a best thing for anyone, anymore, okay? But I heard what the priest said, and what's true for me is true for him. Holy water destroyed the bitch who bit him—but that other creep got away." She dropped his hand back onto his chest and sat. "Let's go."

"South?" Sam asked.

"South," repeated Emily.

Driving to the corner, Sam headed for Interstate 35 West. It would take them to Austin and Highway 87. From there she would turn off onto Interstate 10, dropping south again after Fort Stockton onto Highway 67. After that it was west once more on Highway 90 to Alpine, and south on road 118 past Sheriff Bill's snug home to the dirt road ending at Las Bocas. Somehow she was certain of that destination.

Sheriff Bill. The thought of that rough, superstitious man brought a hesitant smile.

She wanted to stop and ask him to help. Emily and Adwon were walking wounded. The priest had armed them, but she feared she might be the only one strong enough to use those weapons.

She would need Sheriff Bill.

Or maybe what she really needed was a good stiff kick in her ass, for being so impulsive and stupid to even do this. The good thing was that it would be damn close to sunrise when they made it to Las Bocas. The bad was that if they missed that dawn by even a few minutes, she knew it would be impossible to find their quarry. The vampires would be resting in their hidden places, and Mike would be dead. *And who the hell was he anyway, that three people who would have little to do with him otherwise were risking their butts for him?*

It would be a hell of a lot easier just to turn around and drive the other way, then start her life over elsewhere . . . except that Emily had come from elsewhere and the vampires had been there too. She had told Sam they were everywhere.

There was more to it than whether or not Mike deserved their help.

Her jaw tight, Sam found the expressway sign she wanted, turned onto Interstate 35E, and kept the speedometer pegged at seventy-five.

2

"Shit," Sam muttered. Austin was still ten miles on, and four hours had passed. It was two o'clock—maybe five and a half hours until dawn. She had stopped for gas once, and the rest of the long minutes had been spent doing seventy to eighty-five on the road. She could hardly believe she hadn't been pulled over by a hypo. She'd passed two black-and-whites, but they hadn't pulled her over.

The second patrol car, which she'd seen three miles before the last turnoff, had been parked on the shoulder. One uniformed man lay motionless on the car's far side. Sam veered to the right of Austin's glare and caught the exit to Highway 67 and Interstate 10. She kicked up the air-conditioning another notch. Sweat had begun to form all over her. She had not seen a glimpse of the pickup yet, and only Emily's intense perceptions and her own inner certainty kept her from letting up. She prayed that they would have time to stop and convince Sheriff Bill to go with them.

In the Celebrity's mirrors the Austin city lights shrank behind her. "Emily?" Sam said.

Emily uncurled on the seat. She licked her lips and reopened one of the canteens. Every half hour she took a sip and shared it with the semiconscious policeman in the back. Swallowing, she dipped it to his mouth again. He sputtered.

"Are they still ahead?" Sam asked.

Emily nodded and offered the canteen to Sam. As before when Sam had drunk its contents, she was choked and stunned by its purity . . . by a sweet thickness that invigorated her.

"We're even gaining on them," Emily said. "Remember those highway patrol cars we passed? They stopped the vampires. Each one held that truck up for only a minute or two, but we've almost caught up now. I've felt them close for a long time. They're not more than a mile ahead."

"They bit those cops?"

"One of them in the last car," Emily whispered. "I think. I can't feel them too clearly except for *where* they are. I don't think they took that time with the rest. They just killed them."

"What—what about Mike?"

Emily sighed, took the canteen and closed it. "I don't know. But I think they feel me too. They know we're getting near."

"That makes me feel real good." Sam slid into the next lane, squeezing the steering wheel as the car hit eighty-five and began to shake like it wanted to come apart. The camel emblem on the side of the semi she was passing tried to keep up for ten seconds, then lagged behind. When the trucker flashed his brights on her, she pulled back into the lane in front of him.

"Do you really think *you* know where they're going?" Emily asked.

"I think they're going to the ghost town."

"What the hell can we do when we catch them, though, Samantha?"

"It'll be almost sunrise."

Emily's voice was hollow. "I don't have a plan either."

3

Tires squealed. For the third time in the last half hour some asshole was showing off to his gal, or had filled himself full of so much booze that he was taking the time trying to impress himself.

And once more the loud sounds tore Bill back from the edge of slumber. Dorothy, his wife, muttered in her rest, but when he looked at her in the bluish starlight, Bill could see she was still fast asleep.

Rolling over, Bill tried to regain the lullabyes that were slipping farther and farther from his grasp.

Ten minutes later another car, or the same one, revved its engine as it passed Bill's sheepdogs, Bubba and Bimbo. They barked wildly.

"Son of a bitch," he whispered, staring through the window at the pickup screaming by. He pulled on his uniform slacks and boots, grabbed his shirt and holster from the dresser as he passed, and slipped into the dark hall.

Bill walked through the dark, finding his keys on the hall credenza, and passed through the front door quietly for Dorothy's sake. Reaching for the chewing tobacco in his holster's flap, he took out a twist and bit into it. Outside, the heat still lingered. He yawned and went down the creaky porch steps, then crossed the dry lawn to his Jeep.

The next time that speedy ass licker whipped down this way, he was going to give him a new hole to shit from.

Smacking his chaw, Bill looked down the old highway, listening. A *loud* motor, coming fast.

"Dipshit."

He saw nothing in the direction the pickup had gone, and turned the other way. Bill chewed faster when he saw the new noise-maker, rattling and vrooming as it kicked stray rocks into the roadside ditches. Cursing under his breath, he opened the door to his Jeep. A scarred star was painted on the door in dust-clouded yellow. His son had done it ten years ago, two months before he had disappeared into the hills near Las Bocas. The report on Johnny read that he was missing and presumed dead down one of those mine shafts. Bill hoped it was true and guessed it probably was, since Johnny had never come back for either him or Dorothy. Vampires tended to come after family first.

But that white truck he'd seen in that damned ghost town looked just like the one Johnny had spent two years fixing up.

Live and let die.

The pale blue Chevrolet Celebrity was kicking up a growing thunderhead of dirt, and though it seemed to be slowing, Bill got into the Jeep and flipped on his dazzling red-and-white display housed in the dome on top of the cab. He left the siren off in consideration of Dorothy.

The Chevy's brakes shrilled and more rocks flew as it came to a skidding stop. Bill heard the hiss of steam under the car's hood and spat as one of the pebbles rang against his grill. He slipped out of the Jeep and stood with his hands on his hips, shaking his head. He had taken a step forward when the door nearest him shot open, and a bobbing head of tangled brown hair popped out behind it.

"Sheriff Bill!" screamed the high, cracking voice. A woman's body followed. The shadowy figure staggered to keep its feet, holding out her hands. *"Sheriff Bill!"* she called again.

Nearly swallowing the bittersweet lump in his teeth, Bill marched forward; slow at first, then faster. "Missy Sam?" He spat again, reaching out to grip her elbow as her knees buckled and she knelt on the dirt and grass of his scraggly lawn.

"Help us," she moaned, her fingers dancing crazily along his wrists. *"Please.* There's not much time."

"Help you *what*? What in the hell is going on?" He stopped short, spying more movement inside the car. Another woman emerged, pale and drawn, her blood-less face exaggerated by black hair that hung down in stringy clumps.

"Samantha—come on! They're moving fast!"

"Who?" Bill asked with a sudden tremble. "What the hell is happening?"

"The vampires." Sam gasped. "They fucked over Dallas and my friends. Will—will you help?"

There had been contradictory reports on the evening news. Looking back at the star his son had made for him, Bill took a hand away from her and wiped his slick forehead. His mind balked against the confrontation he'd avoided for over twenty years. The disease he dreaded had sprung past him, spreading its trail of destruction.

"Please?" She pulled herself up. He began to shake as he thought of all the missing people he'd written off as having fallen down collapsing mines.

Live and let die. If you don't bother them, they won't bother you, right? Just like bees and wasps. You leave them be . . . and they let you be. . . .

Wrong.

Bill sucked in a hard breath. "What the hell's the hurry? It's sunup in a couple of hours. Can't we wait?"

Sam was shaking her head and stumbled back to the blue car as if she were drunk. She took a splintery cross from the other woman and faced him. "They have our friend," she told him breathlessly, as though she'd run all the way from Dallas instead of driven. "They . . . kidnapped a man . . . who was with us. I promised him I'd help him!" Sam was crying. "They're taking him to that place—that fucking place that shouldn't even be here!"

His face went tight, every furrow in his forehead filled by the blush of his past. "Get everyone into my Jeep," he whispered.

Sam was wiping her face and taking deep breaths, but she forced a smile.

The black-haired woman came forward. "This is judgment day, Mr. Sheriff. One of your kind got himself killed back in Dallas helping us, but I think it may have saved his soul. You may never get this chance again." She gathered some canteens from the car, took the rough pine cross back from Sam, and climbed into the Jeep.

Tobacco juice drooled a sour path down his throat when he swallowed. The woman returned to face him. "Now, help me get our passenger and we'll go."

"Go where?" He gulped at the dark east sky.

The woman opened the Chevy's back door. Sam came up beside them. "Don't be an asshole," she said. "Come on."

His stomach doing sick rolls, Bill helped them carry the ashen-skinned man. When he was propped in the backseat, the woman got in beside him. Bill looked back at his front door and thought of Dorothy, then got in behind the steering wheel. Their urgency kept him from awakening his wife and giving her the last kiss he might ever give. Instead, he started the engine and they bolted out of his drive onto the highway.

"We've got to hurry," Sam gasped.

"I know a shortcut, missy." The night spoke of terrors he never wanted to imagine or face, and three miles farther on, he turned off onto a gravel road with scattered bushes and dehydrated grass.

She was taking him back to Hell.

4

 The bartender wanted a drink.

"Pour the bartender a drink," he muttered.

"Pour one yourself." Mikie giggled, her ruby lips fastened noisily to the man between them.

"Hey!" He slapped her cheek. "Go easy on him. We're going to share him, remember? I can't drink and drive at the same time, okay?"

Mikie glared with red eyes and scooted farther toward the door, dragging Mike's shuddering limbs after. "He's mine. You did that cop back there. This one is mine. I started him and I want to finish him. I got him right inside of me!"

Flipping his eyes up to the rearview mirror that didn't reflect either of them, he found the road empty behind. Still, he detected a pursuit somewhere . . . a woman named Emily reaching into him and knowing his movements. He slapped the whore harder, jerking the living man back to the seat's center, then let up on

the gas. Holding back mounting desire, he brought up
the skinny brown arm she'd dropped and licked at the
trickles on the greaser's wrist. He dropped the arm
and pushed the pedal to the metal once more, feeling
the rush of the night air spray his cheek.

"You greedy bastard," Mikie whimpered. "You got
the guy at the gas station and the fucking cop, and I
just barely tasted them at all, and now you want to
take away this one too!"

His headlights flashed the pavement ahead and he
growled at her, though mostly in the anger that he'd
missed the turnoff onto that shitty gravel road miles
back. It would have brought them to their destination
fifteen minutes sooner. It had been too late to back-
track when he'd realized his mistake, though. "Dog
eat dog is the name of the game, bitch," he said with
surly aggravation, "and I'm a big old dog. You just
count your lucky shakes that I shared at all, and that
I'm taking you with me." He tried to recall the strange
emotions that had drawn him to take this blond slut
along.

But with the smell of this man's blood so close, he
couldn't. He could only envision himself sucking the
last drops away and then lying down in the space he'd
left under the Hotel los Vampiros for a long-needed
vacation from the hustle and bustle of city life.

"You just be fucking glad I don't throw you out of
here," he muttered.

5

"I've only been out here once after dark," Bill murmured, jerking the wheel to miss a sharp rock. The gloomy gravel road sloped up before them endlessly.

"What happened?" Sam asked.

"One of my deputies followed a carload of kids here. They'd been tearing up the highway, knocking over signs and playing chicken with truckers and cars. He chased them all the way to Las Bocas—said they were all stoned and started to beat the shit out of him. Then, he said some guys came out of that hotel and stopped the shenanigans. They told him they'd take care of his problem and all he had to do was get back into his car . . . *and never come back*."

"Bullshit."

Bill glanced at her sharply. "Jimmy got the hell out and called me. I got there before the sun was up. I found the car, with five dead kids inside—like that van we passed when you were here before, missy. They were locals, though. The preacher here took care of them before they was buried. No lawman's stepped too close to this place until our little visit the other day. We all got families, Missy Sam."

"So . . . why are you taking *us*?"

Bill chewed noisily, and his words became a whisper: "I think they lied. Jimmy and his family moved out of the area, but not before his little girl died of a sudden blood loss. My own boy turned up missing soon after. Nobody said it, but we all took it as an added warning." He swerved the car angrily. "Still, they lied."

"Are you sure this is the right way?" Emily asked.

"I'm sure," Bill replied tightly. "The question to ask is, what the hell we're going to do when we get to this place?"

Sam glanced at Emily. Adwon's head lay on her lap. "Can't this thing go any faster?" Emily grumbled.

In reply the gravel road became a ragged dirt trail, and the vehicle pitched. Emily held Adwon tight while Bill wrestled the steering wheel; then, at last, they topped the slope and started down into the valley he'd once described as the inside of an ancient volcano. Sam thought that, with its size, it had to be the mother of all such hells.

"I can't go any faster. Can't afford to have a crash out here. That damn dynamite back there would blow us clear to kingdom come."

Sam's eyes shot to him and she remembered his telling her of the dynamite. *To blow the mines closed.* "Shit," Sam said.

He grunted again.

The mines were silver mines.

Sam turned anxiously to Emily. "What was it that you said about silver and vampires?"

The tired woman blinked. "What about it? Silver is a natural purity and robs a vampire of every supernatural power except for its existence. It can't kill them." She laughed. "The only silver we have is your little cross, anyway."

The idea grew in Sam. "That town is crawling with tunnels, Emily. It was a mining town and they were mining silver ore."

Her eyes narrowed, but Sam caught a flicker of interest even in the darkness. "So?"

"Sheriff Bill has dynamite in this Jeep to bring those mines down. If we could get those things down into the mines—"

"They couldn't get out," Emily finished for her. "Right. They'd be trapped there for eternity, but how can you convince them to go along with that? I'll give you ten to one that they know better than to hide in those tunnels if there's silver in them. You'd have to lure them down, and I don't know if they'd be tricked even for an easy meal. I think you'd have to really piss them off so that they wouldn't rest until you were dead."

Sam slid her hands over her knees. "How do you piss a vampire off?"

The Jeep bucked high, then bounced on its destroyed shocks. The Sheriff said "Shit" again.

"I guess we already have." Emily leaned forward, sliding Adwon's head to the seat. "I can feel more hate in my head than I ever thought existed. It makes my brain throb so bad, I just want to die." Emily retrieved one of the canteens from the floor, unscrewed the cap, and brought it to her mouth. She took a long swallow.

"You think they'll follow me into those tunnels, then? I—I could wrap some of that dynamite around me like Golan said the Viet Cong used to do when they attacked him and his men . . . and lead them in."

"They don't know you. They're pissed off with me because they think I'm leading us to them. I can feel those thoughts. They want *me*."

Though she tried to keep back her relief, Sam couldn't hide it from herself.

"It still might not work, though," Emily whispered. She reached into the back of the Jeep and opened a heavy pine box. She lifted out a faded pink stick that was ten inches long and an inch thick. As she handled it, new energy seemed to flow into her voice. "I think we need to blow up their hideout first. When the whole place goes up, they won't be thinking of anything but revenge."

"Heads up," called out Bill. "We're a mile away. They can probably hear the Jeep already. I'm going to stop behind some boulders before we reach the town. Stay inside until I tell you. This whole damn place is crawling with holes and rattlers, okay?"

Sam turned to Bill. "Did you hear our plan?"

He spat down into the cup between the seats, missed, tried again. The ball of brown juice slapped its rim and drooled down the side. "Missy," he drawled, "this is exactly what I've been telling myself I ought to do for the last ten years. I bought that shit the summer my boy died and it's been sitting there ever since, because I was too afraid to use it." His voice trembled. "They're gonna be after every damn one of us. *Every damn one.*"

"But you'll help us?"

"I already chickened out on you once, missy, and I've been red from that embarrassment ever since. Live and let die, remember? Maybe we'll live . . . and they'll die." He spat, and this time his dark spittle shot into his target.

The headlights splashed over a solid barrier of copper rocks ahead. Bill pressed the brakes, concentrating on guiding the Jeep to a stop in the powdery dirt. The motor cut off into silence.

Sam felt the stillness drape them and was brought completely back into the nightmare of her last visit. No sounds. Just as though the world had disappeared, leaving their little band as completely alone as they felt.

Bill stepped out, letting in cool, dry air. "Come on back here and help me get this stuff so we can get going!" Emily called. "It's only forty-five minutes before dawn!"

"Watch your step," Bill advised. He opened up the back of the Jeep and lugged the box out to rest on the ground. His face was immobile in the red rear lights as he began to stuff the sticks into his pockets, and when they were full, he dragged out a dirty tarp and began piling the dynamite on it. He pulled the corners together, making a bulky sack. Sam helped him pull it over his shoulder.

Emily found Bill's spare holster and strapped it around her, then poked some escaped dynamite sticks between her clothing and the leather belt. Sam had stuffed four sticks in her pockets, so now they were all deadly. Bill had some heavy-duty matches in the glove compartment, and he divided them among the three of them.

Emily took the wooden cross and one of the canteens.

"What about the guy in the Jeep?" Bill asked.

Emily started to walk into the jumble of boulders. *Come on*—show me where we're going."

Squeezing between the rocks with difficulty, the sheriff grabbed Emily. "You want to get there, follow me, okay?"

He led them into a gully and back out, staring at the black ground, then paused behind another boulder and spit out his chew. He went to the right, his steps slow and nearly silent.

Sam and Emily followed, and the three of them stared at the square structures that almost seemed a part of the battered landscape. But straight ahead rose the one unmistakable man-made form: a two-story building, its windows dim with lantern light.

"That's it."

Emily's jaw hung low. "I *feel* . . . them."

Bill marched stiffly to the dirt road running through the middle of the opposing lines of adobe and stone huts. "I *hear* them." He let the makeshift bag drop from his shoulder and began to drag it, walking faster as it crackled in the dirt. He motioned them back.

"I think they know we're here." Emily leaned against a rock, her face tight.

Stopping in the center of the road, Bill brought out a single stick, then struck a match, and touched the flame to the dynamite. He waited and through the night Sam heard indiscernible counts under his breath, then he pulled back his arm like a pro-ball pitcher—

—*and blew up.* The stick in his hand fizzed and flared, and as Sam opened her mouth to shout, the flare enveloped the entire stick, and suddenly her eyes were blinded by a red, yellow, and purple white blaze. In that split second Sam thought she heard Bill's gravelly vocal chords scream, *"Shit!"* one last time, and she would never forget the sight of his arm splitting wide open to the muscle and spitting veins . . .

   . . . *as long as she lived.*

Even twenty feet back the blast threw Sam backward to the gritty, hard ground, knocking the wind out of her so hard, she thought for an instant that her lungs must have collapsed.

But it was Bill collapsing. What was left of his lower torso and legs shuddered frantically for another dizzying second that seemed like forever, then fell in a gore-soaked, flaming mass into the flying dust.

6

When the world turned into one endless, rumbling explosion, Emily was leaning against a rock half her height and lowering her dizzy head. She had seen the flash in the sheriff's fist and knew the battle was over for him. Hot wind and sparks suddenly dashed at her as he became the sun, and she rolled back over the rock until she was behind it and protected.

Her skin stung, but she hopped back up as her eyes burned in the afterimage brilliance of a thousand flashcubes. Her ears were roaring, and she sucked in the taint of the powdery air. Then she saw Sam lying on the ground and covered with gleaming darkness. The hotel door had flown open and two dark figures stood silhouetted in the doorway. Emily ran toward Sam.

"Samantha!" She lifted the red, wet face, seeing that some of the blood was Sam's, though most was the sheriff's. He had splattered her, camouflaging her own wounds. Her button-down shirt was ripped open, though, exposing a wide gash over her ribs. "Goddammit! *Samantha!*"

The figures in the hotel doorway were approaching them now, and Emily saw six of them, three men followed by three long-skirted women. They laughed, coming toward the smoking pile of roast sheriff that covered the street.

Emily heard a horn honking . . . closer and closer.

"Sam!" howled Emily, beginning to drag her back toward the rocks. The horn blared with a thousand eerie echoes through the desert, and suddenly there were headlights growing huge. When they had become the size of apples, the truck spun with a grating squeal and kicked up clouds of dust between Emily and Sam and the remains of the sheriff.

"Shit-fire!" a man screeched. *"The fuckers ran us out of town and followed us!"*

Praying that the blinding dust would remain for at least a few more seconds, Emily uncapped the canteen she'd carried, spilling it over Sam's torn features. She brought the container to Sam's mouth, choking her with the spilling water. *"Drink it!"*

"Oh—" Sam spit, then swallowed and began to curl up. "Oh, no—"

The voices from the far side of the truck drifted near.

"Come on!" croaked Emily, hauling her up with one hand as she held the canteen before them protectively. The dark, gritty air was clearing to show the pickup and the three men and three women who had come to stand before it. Their red pupils spoke to Emily, and she crushed her lids against the lies. *"No!"*

Emily shouted. She inched to a cluster of the boulders, drawing their stares after her.

"You fucking shit-bitches followed me all the way from Dallas, didn't you?" snarled a sturdy vampire in a cowboy shirt. He cocked the wide-brimmed straw hat on his skull. "You came to fuck us up, didn't you?" His stained teeth shone in the final embers of Sheriff Bill. He pulled a half-naked blond woman after him. "But we're going to fuck *you,* bitch, instead. *We're going to fuck you and suck you so dry your skin will shrivel and float into the goddamn wind!*"

"No!"

He bent down and began to trot toward her, gnashing his horrible pointed teeth. Emily jumped with terror as a hand grabbed her from behind. She was pulled back, screaming, her face shoved into hot stone. Then she found herself meeting Jay Adwon's strained, dead-white face.

"Get down!" Adwon said, tossing a sizzling tube of dynamite weakly. It fell in front of the attacking cowboy's boots and he slipped on it and toppled to the ground in an impact that became an earthquake.

Emily turned from the blast, pulling Adwon closer. The blast spewed over them. The side of Adwon's face was burned black. A wriggling severed hand, charcoal-black and bloody, tried to crawl toward Emily. A shivering piece of the vampire's leg flopped, and a hundred other pieces of him still moved in a semblance of life. "Bastard!" she howled, pouring Holy Water over the hand in a steaming gush of dissolution.

"You're all fucking bastards!" she screamed, throwing a jolt of holy water at the ghouls creeping toward her. She looked back into the rocks, seeking one of the holes Bill had warned them of, and saw one in the shadows a few feet away. *"Come and get my blood, you asshole-licking bastards, or I'll fuck your dickshit town all the fucking way to the goddamn moon!"* She took careless strides back, hauling Adwon with her. There wasn't time to thank him.

"You are all so much *alike*." thundered a deep voice in an accent that was a cross between German and British—like the war films where British actors always played Nazis. "You seek to destroy us for killing, little bitch, but even in death, we bring *life*. We will give mankind the eternity it has always wanted without their ever bending a knee. I have lived generations and drunk deep from the well of life. I know your every sorrow. I know your soul and its secrets . . . *of the love you once spurned but long to die for!"*

Out of the clearing dust and smoke the tall man clad in white came forward, his face triumphant and grand. His high cheekbones shone with the luminescence of pale flesh, white as his lush hair. He held out his hands and, for a moment, looked like a beardless Jesus seeking the lost lambs.

"Come to me," he whispered softly. "Come to *us*. I feel your betrayed mother and father near us and crying out to you. We all cry out to you and implore you to be one with us, to suck our blood as we suck yours."

· Emily pulled Adwon back another step, to the edge of the dark mine's chasm. Dirt gave way behind her heel.

"Yes." The vampire glowed richly. "Stop and I will come to you *and finish the job that is only half done. You cannot harm us now! The lust for blood already fills you with blasphemy and desire!"*

The vampire's blue eyes enveloped her, prying into her thoughts. The others followed him.

"You have never belonged to anyone but yourself, never known the companionship of *another,* but you will be *ours*! Put down your weapons. Join our peace."

His bony hand stretched out to her confidently, but when his cold flesh brushed her cheek, Emily faltered under the heat of lust he passed to her. His face grew soft, changing, becoming the face of her own dead father.

"My sweet Emily," her father said. "Please give me another chance."

Her hated father!

Reviving, her revulsion overcame the supernatural bonds, and Emily's hands suddenly raised the canteen high and turned it up upon the false image, splashing Holy Water into his thick hair. She cackled hysterically with the sudden screech of pain that billowed through the bloody clouds of steam from his skull. The hair crinkled and burst into flame as the likeness of her father faded into the vampire's disbelieving shock. The hungry liquid drove down like acid, boring a ragged hole into the top of his head, liquefying his long-rotted brains with an overpowering stench of festering decay.

Emily grabbed his struggling fingers and stepped back, pulling him down with her into the dark cavern in the earth. As she fell, she saw two vampires jump onto Adwon. He held them tight, taking them down with him. Her fall stopped with unbelievable suddenness and the rush of a million dry rattles. She broke away from the smoking vampire and slammed into a soft, squishy bed of slithering movement.

Emily threw herself to the side as Adwon's body

crashed onto the white-haired vampire. The two female vampires were sucking his veins. Behind her and
before her stretched a dark tunnel. She shivered in its
cold, dank breeze.

"You get them, Señor Boss!" hollered a chuckling
Spanish voice from above.

Something sharp struck into Emily's legs and shoulders.

"Sh-shit!" she screamed. She reached for a match
in her pocket and cried out as her wrist was slit open.
With the opposite hand she struck the match desperately against her shoe and recoiled from the snake
hanging from her wrist. Its venom would paralyze her.

"Not *yet!*" She bit her bloody lip, trying to ignore
the new stabs as a dozen more teeth sank into the flesh
of her stomach, arms, legs, and face. Rattles vibrated
all around her as the nursery school full of angry
snakes drove their own vampire fangs deep.

The blackness of their poison hurtled through her.
"Warren!" she shrieked. "Dear *God! Help me!"*

God or Warren? some distantly leering memory of
herself queried sarcastically through the spreading
warmth of death.

Her hand dropped with the match clutched tightly
in her fingers. She thrust it down to her stomach, and
as she heard the sparkling sizzle of a fuse, she sighed.
She hoped she would be seeing both God and Warren
soon.

When the crumbling mine's walls lit up, she was
glad of the venom that had already stolen her senses
from her. She watched her body come apart in the
flash of white thunder that tore wide holes through
her eardrums. Her head tore soundlessly from her
neck. The Mexican vampire overhead turned to run

when he was struck by a hail of stones that ripped his body in two and drenched it red. The walls of the mine jumped into the sky and fell back down like a rain of stones from Heaven. . . .

7

The earthquake was overpowering. Sam felt the ground lurch, jumping and then sinking. Screams and shouts disappeared in an echoing crack that pelted a million tiny specks and pebbles into her aching face. Dust flew high all around her like a tornado of tiny glass.

As the surroundings settled, Sam wiped the tear-soaked dirt from her vision. "Emily?" She searched the gritty gray landscape as waves of dust continued to fall. Emily had poured Holy Water down her throat and revived her, and then the six vampires had surrounded Emily. Sam's vision had caught fire again, and as those bursts of light echoed through her, the earth had moved as if Judgment Day *had* come.

Sam scanned the rocks.

Nothing and no one.

Breathing hard, Sam pushed herself up awkwardly and stared at the long cut on her stomach where her shirt had torn and was soaked with stickiness. A few feet away, a clump of smoldering flesh was all that was left of Sheriff Bill.

Beyond him, the pickup truck was parked. The passenger door was open, the overhead light on. A pair of feet stuck out the passenger door.

"Mike?" she called hoarsely. *"Mike!"*

The feet shifted.

"Mike!" she screamed, limping forward, struggling for breath as she fell against the pickup's door.

"Ow!" screamed Mike.

Sam realized she had shut the door on his feet, and staggered back, then pulled it open. Steadying herself on the creaking door, she stared down at him lying across the torn seat. His face was ashen. He trembled weakly, saliva foaming on his lips, and she saw the blood caking his neck and wrists.

"Oh, my God." She stretched her hand out to his chest, feeling for a heartbeat.

A weak beat still worked inside him.

"Mike," she breathed hoarsely.

He jerked, banging his head against the steering wheel. "S-Samantha?"

Her hand cupped his whiskery chin and she squeezed gently.

"I think I'm out of time," he whispered. "But . . . I know that if I've got to die, I don't want to come back. Maybe I'm headed to Hell and there's no way around it, but I don't want to go like this!"

"I think Emily wasted them," Sam told him.

He just moaned.

Shuffle.

The sound filtered into Sam's awareness slowly.

Shuffle.

Straightening, Sam held tight to the side of the

pickup, feeling Mike's feet shiver against her jeans. She scanned the rubble, the darkness. Dust was still falling.

Then she saw something moving: blond hair hovered over a slender body in a torn V-blouse and miniskirt. She was moving quickly, coming toward the truck.

Toward her.

The blond hair was streaming behind the running figure as it closed in, faster and faster, and Sam saw the livid mouth that was wide open and full of sparkling teeth.

Sam dug her fingertips into the leg beside her. "Mike—I've got to protect you! I've got to get something to *protect* you!"

As he groaned again, she pushed herself away from the truck, trying to find some kind of weapon in the debris of stones, dirt, and ancient pieces of the mine's broken timbers.

Sharp, jagged timbers.

Sam dived for the nearest one, ignoring its splinters. It was big and rough and heavy like a railroad tie, but she pressed it to her body and got back to her crazy feet that wanted to step in two directions at once. Concentrating, she swung back around, panting with her burden. She tripped, and the heavy tie shot into the night, spinning round and round.

Sam struggled to regain her feet, wailing uselessly. The blond hooker bent inside the truck. As she straddled Mike's legs, his shoes flipped into her crotch in a demented, uncertain struggle. Her cackle bit into the night.

"You're *mine*!"

Sam pushed herself up on wobbling legs, and she

saw what had tripped her: the black priest's wooden cross. Sam bent toward it, the ground now seeming an impossible distance away. Her legs moved with a will of their own, like swaying block towers about to collapse. With an ungainly reach she stuck out her hand for it, her arm waving through the darkness for balance. She willed it closer, fingers brushing wood, then clutched it and dragged it up with her. She ran. "Mike!" she screeched.

He held the vampire's head up and away from his throat.

Sam gripped the cross tight and aimed it for the vampire's back. But Mike must have seen her. He released the whore and held his hands out past her, toward Sam.

Somehow, Sam understood, and she pushed the cross into his grasping fingers. She grabbed the whore's legs, hearing his groan as the deadly teeth connected to his throat.

Mike shrieked, his hands trembling, and with a quickness that must have contained every last surge of strength in his body, drove it down hard, smashing the ragged wood base into her spine.

"Nooooo!"

The bitch flailed and threw herself backward, the wood impaled through her torn, dripping blouse and flesh. She lunged away from Mike and struggled to catch the door handle as she went through the truck's opening and down. Her head struck Sam hard, knocking her back to the dirt.

Sam howled when her head thudded against the ground. She didn't think she could ever get up again. As uncoordinated lights flashed before her eyes, she pushed up to a sitting position.

The vampire's straining fingers were clutched around the door handle. She hung from it, her legs collapsing beneath her, the top of the cross a half inch from the ground. She snarled at Sam.

"Suck me now, damn you!" Mike yelled as he pulled himself from beneath the blood-soaked creature. He threw himself onto her, and her long nails sent sparks from the metal as her grip tore away. As Sam tried to get to her feet, the wood sank deeper under their combined weight, and Mike shoved the whore relentlessly downward, dropping his chest again and again onto her. There was a wet, splitting sound as the board broke up through the spasming whore's left breast, and then into Mike. His cry was a monstrous sound of agony and triumph as he forced her to the dirt, furiously driving himself downward, and as the wood thrust deep into him, the remaining torrent of his life rushed out. They both collapsed in the dust.

Sam sank to her knees as the bodies twitched together in their final dance, then stopped. Their blood ran and dripped with a pleasant pitter-pat as it mixed and pooled under them.

The sky was lightening, its black starriness fading into hints of orange and blue. She peered through raw eyes at the desolation the dawn revealed: the slope leading to the high surrounding rocks was split by a deep chasm. At its bottom was the dark hole of a tunnel. Emily's grave.

It was finished.

But the pain of her dusty throat overcame everything else, and Sam was filled with thirst rather than victory or remorse.

She coughed hard.

Not looking back at Mike or the dissolving form beneath him, Sam walked, very slowly, up the creaky steps of the hotel and onto the warped porch, licking her lips at the thought of tequila. The floor was covered in footsteps and dust, and it would remain that way without the vampires to sweep it up. She threaded her way toward the bar, thinking of the death she had faced and endured these past hours.

Thinking of her brother . . . of how she had to return to Dallas *alone*.

The ceiling fan creaked in a morning breeze, but turned no longer. Sam stopped at the bar, wiped her face, and leaned over to reach a glass and an open bottle of tequila.

"Pour me one too," a voice said as the door behind the bar whisked open without warning.

It was *Walt*.

"Hi, Sammy." He smiled with closed lips, not exposing the mysteries behind. He set another glass beside hers and wrapped his hand around the bottle. "Gets thirsty out here."

She took a step back.

"Nothing to worry about, Sammy," Walt said. "The sun's up. For some reason I don't feel hungry in the daytime. The light makes me feel like I'm just a walking *dead man.*" He chuckled merrily. "Besides, I had my fill last night. Sucked down at least a gallon of the red stuff when two illegals walked in here asking on the best place to go and how to hide out in this great land of America. They wanted one of us to go with them and show them the way, and if you'll just stick around till sundown, maybe we can *all* head back to Dallas, huh? In fact, I was hanging around the Big Bend park south of here the other night, watching TV through some happy camper's trailer window, and I heard that the Pentagon might even be interested in *me* visiting them. Seems that some kind of bizarre disease laid hold of Dallas, and they're just *dying* to get their hands on someone infected. . . . Maybe we can both get to Washington yet, huh?"

She backed another step.

"Oh, come on, Sammy. It's a long fucking walk out of here alone, and in the daytime that sun will fry you just as fast as it would me."

"Fuck you, Walt," she whispered. She dropped a hand to one of the sticks of dynamite poking from her pockets. Without the night's power, his eyes no longer compelled her. They showed her the truth of what he was.

What he had always been.

Her other hand dug for a match. "Fuck you, Walt." She struck the match against the bar, and her lips softened into a smile as she touched the flame to the dynamite fuse. It began to sputter. She held it for only an instant, then tossed it over the bar and behind him. *"Fuck you and go to Hell!"*

She ran for the door.

"Hey, Sammy—"

His words were cut off in a deafening boom, and the push of hot air slapped her like a speeding car, her legs working in a run even as she was lifted into the air and thrown out onto the porch. Her face scraped across the rough wood and then she was thrown off the porch side. She buried her face in the reddish dirt as glass and wood shot out above her. She seemed to hear the very rocks forming the hotel split. The pickup was pulverized in a furious spray of stone shrapnel that ricocheted at her. The structure thundered, expelling its form with cracks that made Sam's ears ring endlessly.

When Sam opened her eyes a half hour later, the barroom was a pile of broken, smoking lumber. The hotel's stone exterior was split wide, fire consuming its rotten walls. Strangely enough, at her feet Sam found a canteen—the canteen the sheriff had left for her a week before. It was cool and she bathed her face and scratchy mouth, and drank deep. When it was half empty, she closed the cap. Lying in the middle of the road, among the rubble, was the tarp full of dynamite Sheriff Bill had carried out to level Las Bocas and its catacombs of mines. Beyond it were the rocks that hid his lumbering Jeep.

Dallas.

She had to go back. She had to find that black priest. . . .

But not yet.

Forcing her aching body into motion, Sam headed for the dynamite, determined to finish Bill's final chore.

ACKNOWLEDGMENT

Special thanks to Steve for his knowledge and generosity in keeping my computer running.